SPELLCAST

(RAVEN CURSED BOOK 7)

MCKENZIE HUNTER

McKenzie Hunter

Spellcast

© 2023, McKenzie Hunter

McKenzieHunter@McKenzieHunter.com

ISBN: 978-1-946457-49-3

ACKNOWLEDGMENTS

As I wrap up Erin's final adventure, I would like to express my gratitude to the readers who have followed her journey. Your reviews, comments, and participation in the readers group mean a lot to me.

I am grateful for my amazing team who helps bring this story to life with their skills and dedication. A special thank you goes out to my alpha and beta readers: Elizabeth Bracker, Sherrie Clark, Robyn Mather, Stacey Mann, and Márcia Silva, as well as my editor and proofreaders.

A big thanks to my family and friends for their unwavering support and for checking in on me while I retreat into my writer's cave. Your encouragement means everything to me.

CHAPTER 1

I'd reversed vampirism. The seriousness of that hadn't fully sunk in even as I watched Dr. Sumner press his hand to his chest. From his solemn expression it seemed as if he remembered his heart slowing to an imperceptible thump until it had completely stopped, initiating his transformation into the undead. His glassy eyes settled on mine in confusion. Out of my periphery, I caught a glimpse of Mephisto's wary look of concern, his mouth twisted with shock. Taking in the gravity of what had just occurred, we remained motionless, the air thick with tension and uncertainty.

Wincing as he sat up, Dr. Sumner whispered, "I'm not a vampire." His statement was weighted by shocked relief. He pressed his hand to his chest again, confirming a heartbeat, and then he stilled as he took slow measured breaths and sighed. Wide-eyed and with his mouth slightly parted, he looked to me for assurance that his heart wouldn't just stop, and his breathing shut off and he'd be hit with the reality that he was in fact a vampire. A fate he'd expressed he never wanted.

In retaliation for me refusing to give him a family, Landon had attempted to force my hand by changing Dr.

Sumner into a vampire to guarantee that I wouldn't use the Obscuro Mors stake against him to end him and his bloodline. Taking a deep breath, I attempted to tamp down the rage threatening to overtake my emotions. My fists balled so tightly, my nails bit into the skin of my palms.

"No. You're not."

Mephisto's lips tightened at my terse response. His expression was inviting me to tell Dr. Sumner the full story. *Inviting* was generous. He urged me to tell it or he would.

"You…well." My mouth was a desert, making it difficult to brief him on the incident.

Retelling it served as a reminder of my painful and unsettling existence and the choices constantly taken from me. Familiar with the sense of helplessness it caused me, guilt settled hard in me with the realization that Dr. Sumner's safety had been weaponized against me twice and that he'd been stripped of his autonomy by both Landon and me. Landon did it out of spite; I did it out of a desperate act to save his life.

I had performed an untested spell on him and wasn't confident that I'd truly saved his life or if I'd just put him in a more compromised position.

Holding his gaze, I grew a new appreciation for his expressive peri blue eyes that displayed his myriad emotions: confusion, angst, fear, and despair. Warmth slithered over me, another reminder he was still warm-blooded, when he took my hand into his and linked our fingers. His touch appeared to seek more comfort and to have his fears assuaged. It held a level of possessiveness that didn't go unnoticed by Mephisto, who directed a scrutinizing narrowed eye at Dr. Sumner's hand.

"I fed from you?" It was a rhetorical question that twisted Dr. Sumner's lips into a grim scowl. His hold on my hand tightened. I vividly remembered me desperately weaving a spell to stop it and him writhing in pain.

From his expression, I suspected some of the details were coming back to him, too. His brows drew together, the rictus eased, and he inched closer. "You saved me?"

I nodded. "I'm also the reason you were put at risk."

He dismissed my acceptance of responsibility with a shake of his head. Unlinking our fingers, he brought my hand closer to him and cradled it against his chest. His eyes closed, and he sighed at the beat of his heart, the rise and fall of his chest, and the relief of being alive and human.

"If you hadn't done the spell, I would be a vampire?" His eyes snapped open. "When I fed from you, I was a vampire. At least for a little while, right?"

That was a great question that I didn't have an answer for.

"Technically you were in a transitional state," Mephisto provided, unable to rip his gaze from Dr. Sumner's hold on my hand. "Your heart stopped, and the vampire venom that would have changed you was injected into Erin through the bite Landon gave her. Once you were sated from feeding from her, you would have fallen into a death-like state and awakened as a true vampire. Erin reversed that process."

Dr. Sumner didn't seem to notice Mephisto speaking, his presence hadn't registered at all with him. His eyes were on me, intense, appraising, and yet soft, with traces of something menacing that I'd never seen before.

When Mephisto repeated his comment, Dr. Sumner acknowledged his presence.

He frowned. "No matter how transient, I fed from you as though I was a vampire."

"You've fed from Landon," I reminded him.

For a brief moment, he was no longer looking at me but through me. When he refocused on me his gaze felt captive. I snatched my eyes from his to look down at my hand held between his. It wasn't for comfort anymore. Definitely possessive.

"Release her hand, Jacob," Mephisto demanded, his steely

disposition and the removal of Dr. Sumner's professional designation leaving no room for misinterpretation. Dr. Sumner's eyes, shadowed with defiance, pulled from mine to Mephisto. He ignored the demand. Their eyes locked before Mephisto reluctantly pulled his focus from Dr. Sumner to the door. Dr. Sumner tracked Mephisto's movement as he walked to the entry to open it to the Huntsmen, who didn't have a chance to knock.

Mephisto's attention moved from Simeon, Kai, and Clayton back to Dr. Sumner's hand placement. His jaw clenched and his intense anger stifled the room. I tugged my hand away. Defusing a hostile exchange between my therapist and Mephisto wasn't something I needed or wanted and never would be placed on the list of things I'd have to deal with.

"If Landon had succeeded, I would have been his sired—his family. You stopped it. But I fed from you. Then you used magic to reverse it. Pain. Lots of it," Dr. Sumner said in a stream of thought as he kept his gaze fixed on Mephisto. The annoyance in it had moved to a glare since Mephisto's demand for him to release my hand.

It would have remained if I hadn't interrupted. "Dr. Sumner, why did you let Landon in? I told you to stay away from him." Vampires didn't need permission to enter a home, and of the few acts of societal propriety they complied with, entering a room without permission was one of them. Which led me to believe there was some type of consequence that they'd managed to keep hidden.

"I didn't," he said. "I answered and made it clear that I'd made a mistake approaching him the first time and that I wouldn't repeat it." After sustaining near-fatal injuries from Malific's attack, vampire blood had been the only thing that saved him. He'd quickly become fond of the lingering preternatural abilities it gave him. When they went away, he approached Landon about bartering his services in exchange for those abilities.

"The next thing I knew, he and his friends were in my home," he said. A vampire of Landon's age and skill would only need a brief moment of eye contact to compel. Again, I found myself battling the overwhelming anger that I couldn't suppress or hide. I wanted Mephisto to act on his vow to kill Landon. I wanted to do it myself.

"I need more information on what happened," Clayton stated.

Confident that Mephisto had already briefed them, I breezed over the information again, mindful of Dr. Sumner's response to the retelling.

"The transformation to vampire wasn't complete," Clayton whispered.

"It was complete enough. She reversed it," Kai provided.

I sat taller under the weight of their collective attention and interest. It felt intrusive.

They migrated to the corner, in what I assumed was an attempt to seem discreet. An action that failed miserably. Nothing about their presence could go unnoticed. Their mere existence consumed more space than their physical bodies. Unmuted magic filled the room, a subtle demonstration of how powerful the quad was. The four held similar looks: intense slitted eyes, tightly pressed lips, and knitted brows that clued me in to their silent discussion that probably included Dr. Sumner scooting closer and devouring the small space that I'd left between us. Noticing the change in their expressions to something indecipherable, I didn't need to speculate about the topic of the conversation. I already knew. Something was wrong with Dr. Sumner.

For them, this wasn't just a Mephisto and Erin problem. They worked as a unit. *They were a unit.* My problem was their problem now. It appeared that more discussion was taking place between them. Hating being excluded from the conversation, I shot a glare in their direction.

When the Huntsmen made a show of disregarding my response, I returned my attention to Dr. Sumner. "How do you feel?"

I knew the question wouldn't yield the answers I needed. *"Hey, Mr. Clingy, what the hell is wrong with you?"* seemed harsh and unnecessarily aggressive. *"Why do you seem wrong? You look the same, but something is off,"* would have been equally counterproductive and rude.

"Hungry," he admitted.

My throat clenched; I anticipated his focus to be on my neck. I sucked in a breath and held it. Would he want food or another source of nourishment?

Standing, he gave me a look, I assumed waiting for me to follow him. This was going to get old fast. Did the magic I used create something not quite human? He definitely wasn't a vampire. The Immortalis, creatures my mother had created, weren't clingy, just loyal to a scary fault. Was this his form of loyalty?

Dr. Sumner's movements were more fluid and graceful. He looked around his home as if seeing it for the first time, or through new eyes. When he moved toward the kitchen, he appeared uncomfortably aware of the increased distance between us. He stopped moving, waiting for me to catch up.

"You don't need her. Go." Mephisto's cold command startled Dr. Sumner into movement. Looking back at me from the kitchen, he became increasingly agitated.

Before heading to the kitchen, I made a detour to where the Huntsmen were standing.

"Stop," I hissed, shooting them each a chastising look as they simultaneously returned an inquiring one, feigning clueless to what they were being accused of. "Whatever conversation you're having, I should be part of it."

Mephisto retrieved the Obscuro Mors stake that he hadn't got to use on Landon, then sidled close to me.

"Tell me about the spell you cast," he whispered. I detailed the invocation that was part of the spells I used to make my creations, blending it with a reversal spell and an *adligatura* spell. Describing the process gave the impression that the weaving of the spells was more intricate and intentional than a creation from desperation and grief. *Go, Erin.*

Despite Dr. Sumner's clinginess that bordered on possessiveness—which I remained hopeful would go away or could be fixed—I felt a moment of unmitigated pride at what I'd accomplished. I had stopped him from becoming a vampire. I needed to believe that any side effects of the spell could be corrected. I clung to that belief even as Dr. Sumner placed considerable effort in keeping his eyes on the food he was preparing instead of on me.

Mephisto's brows furrowed while he processed my use of creative, reversal, and magic inhibiting spells and the *adligatura* spell to reverse vampirism. He was probably wondering how the *adligatura* spell was effective without the necessary accompanying runes. By all spell logic, the spell I created should have been a disaster.

Mephisto guided me farther away from Dr. Sumner's ears, and the others followed his lead. "We were trying to decide the best way to handle this situation," he said, glancing over at Dr. Sumner who was busying himself with preparing a burger and undoubtedly trying to hear our discussion.

Mephisto's eyes followed mine, assessing Dr. Sumner. His voice dropped even lower. "He can hear us."

Dr. Sumner's lithe glides of movements reminded me of vampires. They weren't as quick but exhibited a precision of movement not often seen in humans. Had he sensed the changes as well? Had his hearing and vision sharpened to those of a vampire? Was he lingering in a place between human and vampire? Would that be such a bad thing? Human with all the benefits of a supernatural and none of the disadvantages. Had I created a vampire-lite?

It was clear that none of them, especially Mephisto, wanted to discuss Dr. Sumner's condition in his presence. I agreed with them. Why make this strange situation harder for him? I knew our reasons for delaying the discussion were different. Even if Dr. Sumner was considered vampire-lite or another magical being, to them, he'd still be considered magically inferior, a person of limited magical abilities, or one of the many other disparaging ways they'd described witch, mage, and fae magic.

Dr. Sumner had finished cooking and prepared two plates. He shot the cadre of men an uninviting look when he placed the plates side by side on the table.

"This is for you," he said to me.

"Thanks. I need a moment to speak with Mephisto."

All the magic I'd used had drained me and I was famished. I needed to eat, and I could use the time to discover more about Dr. Sumner.

"I'll get a ride home," I told Mephisto. The others made it clear that it wasn't just a discussion between the two of us. They didn't hide their concern, nor the hostility they felt on Mephisto's behalf.

"No." Mephisto's word was clipped and pushed out through clenched teeth.

Easing closer to him, I rose to my toes. "You see the raven as a creature of death whereas others marvel at it for its ability to survive and thrive in a wide range of habitats." I repeated the very words he'd said to me when he switched from calling me demigoddess to raven. Because Malific had been known as a creature of death, I'd never wanted any association with it. His view of the raven gave me a new appreciation for the name.

"Please give me a chance to fix this." I dropped back to

standing and searched his eyes for understanding, but all I saw were concern and frustration. Mephisto, with his extensive knowledge and abilities, was faced with a dilemma he couldn't easily repair. The issue settled heavily in his expression and darkened his eyes.

It was more than a situation that required fixing. Dr. Jacob Sumner was my therapist, but more than that, he was my friend. My friend who was going through something that I'd caused, and I needed to do what I could to repair it and make sure he got through as unscathed as possible.

"I will leave the house, but I'll be outside if you need me," Mephisto said in a tone that didn't leave any room for debate. Giving the other three an imploring look to signal them to leave as well, I whispered "Go" when they didn't take the hint.

Rooted in their position, I knew they were responding to whatever thoughts or emotions were controlling Mephisto. Whether it was born from hostility or exasperation, something he expressed was fueling their tension, making the air oppressive.

I insisted again, gesturing firmly toward the door. After a few minutes of contemplation and Mephisto's grip on the stake increasing to the point I thought it would snap in half, they headed for the door. Mephisto shot a look in Dr. Sumner's direction and then leaned down. His fingers cupped the back of my head, pulling me into a passionate kiss, his tongue exploring my mouth and sweeping lightly over my lips before drawing away. He rested his lips against mine.

"Are you being petty?" I teased in a whisper.

"No, I'm concerned." He inched back, a feral grin spread across his face displaying an animalistic confidence, a hint of danger and amusement. "Mine," he breathed against my ear when he pressed another, lighter, kiss to my cheek.

I reared back and grimaced. "Don't be that person," I needled, hoping it would ease some of the concern that sharpened his eyes every time he looked in Dr. Sumner's direction. He saw him as a threat—something I'd never associate with Dr. Sumner. And I didn't like it.

"I'll be outside. Waiting," he said before leaving. Dr. Sumner kept a careful eye on him as he departed.

I took the seat near Dr. Sumner where he'd placed my food and took a bite—larger than intended.

"So, you are hungry," he acknowledged with a wide smile and a warmth and appreciation I'd never experienced with him before.

"I didn't realize I was this hungry." An understatement. Devouring the burger, I cast furtive looks in his direction only to find him staring at me every time. Not just looking. His gaze bored into me so intensely, it was uncomfortable. Bordering on creepy.

"Why are you staring at me?" I blurted. *Maybe Cory's right —I do lack couth.* But delicacy wasn't needed at this time. Directness was. Something was wrong. I'd brought him back wrong. I was faced with the inescapable truth that a person can't be snatched from the clutches of death and remain unchanged.

"Am I?"

"Yeah. Are you okay?"

"No," he admitted softly. "I feel odd." His face added context to his vague response and his unfamiliarity with being lost for words and unable to express his feelings.

He took several thoughtful bites from the burger, seemingly grappling with ways to express himself.

"I felt empty in the kitchen when you were speaking with Mephisto and"—he swallowed—"and it disappeared when you sat next to me." His brows inched together. "I didn't like being far from you." It hadn't escaped my notice that he'd inched his chair closer to me. There would have been a similar feeling if Landon had successfully changed Dr. Sumner. Newly turned vampires have a sirebond with their creator. The intense connection gives them the inescapable desire to please and obey them. It never severs, which is why a vampire is never completely their own person.

I'd never dated a young vampire or one who lived close to their creator, so I'd never witnessed the hold their creator had on them. But I'd heard the stories of that connection being exploited and abused.

Dr. Sumner wasn't an infant vampire. He was human. A human that I'd brought back from being changed to a vampire. Each moment it became more apparent that something wasn't right.

"It'll pass," I assured him with all the confidence of a person who'd done the spell a thousand times. I had no idea what would happen. "Other than a closeness to me, do you feel anything else?"

"Vacant," he admitted. "My body moves as it did but easier. I can hear everything. The wind isn't blowing that hard, but I can hear it against the window." He closed his eyes and opened them, his eyes scanning my face. "And the world is brighter and more intense. It's not the same as when Landon saved me. It's—" He searched for the words. "Different," he finally admitted.

I suspected it was the combination of vampire venom, elven, demigod magic, and the untested spell that raged through his body. The pride I felt earlier was slowly ebbing away. Bringing him back might have come at a cost—some of my magic. I hadn't considered that the very thing about me that Landon coveted so much could affect the spell.

"I need to check my magic," I told him. I was able to move objects, and after I Wynded out of his home, I returned to an overly anxious Dr. Sumner who didn't seem to have expected me to come back.

There wasn't any plant life in his home for me to use my creation spells. So I'd have to use something else. "May I look in your fridge?"

Brows knitted together in inquiry, he nodded. He was like a shadow next to me as I made my way it. Taking out tomatoes and strawberries, I returned to the table and made work of recreating the food. Dr. Sumner had abandoned the remainder of his food as I pricked my finger with the knife I'd borrowed from the kitchen. Rapt, he watched me perform the plant spell, replicating the food, springing forward something the same and yet different. Stems on the strawberries extended, bearing a peach and an apricot. The nightshade, instead of producing another tomato, made a green pepper.

"May I?" Dr. Sumner asked, pulling the peach from the vine. *Fates no, why were people determined to keep eating magically created food?* It was unsettling. I shrugged a response and he washed the fruit and started eating.

Satisfied that my magic hadn't been affected, I was curious about whether he possessed any.

"I need some paper, where can I find some?" I asked.

Directed to a drawer in the kitchen, I pulled out a notepad and pen and scribbled an invocation for an easy spell that would allow him to move objects.

"I want you to read this. Invoke this spell," I instructed after he'd finished the peach. Meeting his wide-eyed look with a half-smile, I added, "To save your life, I shared my magic with you. I'm trying to determine if you kept any." The Immortalis that Malific created possessed a great deal of magic. If Dr. Sumner couldn't do simple spells, I was positive he wouldn't be able to do the advanced ones.

He stared at the spell, discomfort and apprehension heavy in his expression. It was a simple levitation spell. I directed him to the fork on the table.

"Say the spell and focus on the fork," I said. In panicked anticipation, I watched him as he continued to review the spell. Had I undone vampirism only to have created something human-like? I was separated from humans and didn't have a place among the other magical beings. If he now had magic, what exactly would he be considered?

"Go ahead," I urged.

Nodding, he looked at the paper again, committing the spell to memory before reciting the spell and focusing on the fork. It wobbled and shimmied on the table but never moved to another location. Dr. Sumner became red-faced during his multiple attempts. When I placed a reassuring hand on his, he stopped.

"Let's try defensive magic." It was a step up from a levitating spell but demonstrated a different skill. Giving him the appropriate spell, I urged him to use it against me. After spending an exceptional amount of time coaxing him into doing the spell that could potentially harm me, he relented but was unsuccessful.

"Try it again," I said.

"No, I don't want to hurt you." Based on the ineffectiveness of the levitation and his first attempt, I was quite confident that even if he was successful, it wouldn't be strong enough to hurt me. He did. On the third attempt, I felt the shove into my chest. Not hard enough to be considered true defensive magic, but it was a nudge.

"I have magic," he concluded, looking at his hand and the new distance between us which was a result of me losing my footing when I was surprised by the magical nudge.

Technically he did. Ineffective magic. "I think it's a residual from the spell. In a few days, I believe it will go away, too."

"What gives you that belief?" he challenged. I heard the hope in his voice. Dr. Sumner wanted his normal back. Uncomfortable with his inexplicable draw to me, I hadn't considered how difficult it had to be for him, too. I'd snatched him from a human death, pulled him out of vampirism with dark and powerful magic, and was trying to convince him that things were just fine. I deserved the distrust that shone in his eyes.

"I don't know for sure," I confessed. My gaze dropped to the floor. "It was an impulsive thing I did, but I wanted to save you. I hope things will turn out fine, but if it's not… know that I'll do what it takes to make it right."

He cleared the distance between us, and when I looked up, his eyes were deeply focused on me. "Okay," he said, taking my hand in his. "I trust you."

It took several tugs before he released my hand.

"I have to leave, but I'll check on you tomorrow, okay?"

After several beats, he gave a slight nod of his head. "Tomorrow," he repeated with another nod as if he was accepting it as an oath.

If I didn't get in contact with him, I was certain he'd contact me.

CHAPTER 2

Mephisto drummed his fingers over the steering wheel as I gave him the information that I'd gathered about Dr. Sumner. He had been tense and hyper-focused on me ever since I'd left Dr. Sumner's.

"This isn't good, Erin," he acknowledged with a deep, exasperated sigh.

"It's likely I'm right and this oddity is just the result of residual magic and will resolve itself." Because concession wasn't an option, I wielded my words with the same unmerited confidence I'd shown with Dr. Sumner.

"Yes, magical anomalies have a history of just 'resolving itself'," he shot back.

"He's not a magical anomaly. He doesn't have magic—"

"He has magic. It's just not strong. The question isn't his ability to use it. Why does he have magic, Erin?"

His jaw clenched before sucking in an audible sharp breath. Thoughts that he chose not to share placed a frown on his face.

"The real question is whether the magic he's holding on to is his life source and enough for him to exist forever, or will he need to continue to pull from you? Did you actually undo vampirism or is your magic just delaying the inevitable? His behavior toward you reeks of a vampire siring," he growled out.

Studying him, I suppressed the smile. "Jealous," I teased, his speculation making me want to evade the topic.

Ignoring my objections and my persistent reminders that he was driving, Mephisto kept his intense eyes on me. "Jealousy is often rooted in low self-confidence and distrust. I've never suffered from that lack of confidence," he offered with an assured provocative grin. "I trust you and *us*." The arrogant deity wasn't immune from trite emotions like envy, despite his adamant objections. On multiple occasions his attitude toward Asher had been colored with signs of jealousy.

He scoffed at my expression that with certainty showed my thoughts.

"Asher never made me jealous, just annoyed."

"If that's the story you're going with, okay, whatever," I mumbled, directing my attention to the passing landscape. "If it is my magic keeping him alive and delaying vampirism, what happens next?" I would respect Dr. Sumner's wishes and not let him be changed. The alternative wrenched at my heart. I'd kept him from being turned, but if he died, my intervention was nothing more than delayed failure.

"If your magic is keeping him alive. It's strong. Hopefully, it will be enough to allow him to live a normal human existence."

"And in the worst case, I'll have to repeat the spell." I provided the part he seemed reluctant to say out loud.

He nodded. "But it might not have the same effect as the first time. Is it sustainable to have you as his life source?"

I blinked back tears of frustration. What type of life would it be for him, and me, if that were the situation? Our lives would never be normal, because he'd be forever linked to me— No, not just linked, *needing* me for his mere existence.

Mephisto took a long look at me, sighed, and clasped my hand. He brought it to his lips. Warmth teased my skin as he pressed a soft kiss to it.

"I hate that look. I understand why you did it. We just need to be prepared for what lies ahead. Then there's Landon. He only knows that you reversed vampirism. I don't believe he'll care to learn the specifics of the side effects. I'm quite confident that your abilities are being discussed with other vampires. They will see you as a threat."

I sighed. "We'll have to deal with the consequences of that."

He grunted. "I prefer to be proactive and deal with the situation in its nascence and do what is necessary to prevent the spread of this information any further than the vampire community. Perhaps silencing everyone who has that knowledge would be best for you." The threat of a brutal option laced his words. It took effort to have any sympathy for Landon, but I couldn't deny my hand in this. "What he did to you was cruel and unnecessary." Mephisto's eyes glanced to the rear-view mirror, looking at the stake on the back seat.

"*But* I played my role in this, too," I admitted. "I broke the deal I made with him and forced him to accept the Obscuro Mors as my chosen alternative instead of honoring his preferred repayment of the debt."

"And he was wrong for requiring an open-ended debt that benefitted from your desperation and pain. I understand the need for positioning oneself in a place of power, and siring vampires with you would have done that. If you were concerned about the type of vampire you would have created, then so am I. Don't ask me to find some understanding for Landon because I won't. He made you shed tears and he forced you into a situation where you had to make the choice: kill your friend or make him a vampire. That can't— No, it *won't* be overlooked or forgiven."

The finality of his statement and the urgency of Madison's ringtone made continuing the topic impossible. It was nearly one o'clock in the morning and she was calling me. Nothing about the situation suggested this was a spur of the moment, casual call.

"So, you're unmaking vampires now?" Madison said in a breezy, dry tone. Concern twined over her words, contradicting the faux nonchalance she attempted. Madison had never shown a heightened level of apprehension about my magical abilities before. But I didn't get that impression now. I was a juggernaut, and at some point, that would cause tension in the magical community. She'd be the one tasked with mitigating the damage to the supernaturals' public image as well as assuaging the fears of the denizens and humans.

"How much do you know?" I asked her, positive that the information provided was influenced by Clayton's perspective. Madison dating Clayton had placed a cog in the wheel of communication between Madison and me. Boundaries and rules needed to be established. I needed to be the first to disclose the information.

I frowned as she relayed the information in such alarming detail it was as if she had been there. Mephisto, the clear culprit of the retelling, looked totally unapologetic as we got out of the car at his home.

"What do I need to do?" Madison asked.

"Nothing. I think it will be okay."

"That seems highly unlikely," she grumbled.

After a long moment of silence, she whispered, "Mephisto cannot kill Landon."

Now I was the culprit of the long pregnant silence. The death of the new leader of the vampires would be met with a great deal of speculation and chatter. The other vampires would want answers and retribution, and since Elon and Dallas witnessed Mephisto's abilities and reaction, he would be the likely suspect.

"Did you hear her?" I asked, following him toward the house.

He nodded. It was clearly a response to hearing the directive and not his intention to comply with it.

"I'll talk to him. For the record, I agree. We just need to make sure that Landon keeps my abilities to himself."

"Yeah," Madison said with a sigh. She had just as much confidence in that feat as I did. None. Ending the call, I feared that our lack of confidence in the situation would ensure that Mephisto maintained his position and eventually acted on it.

"She's right," I said.

His noncommittal grunt held its initial dismissive intention.

I stopped in the middle of the hallway. When he turned to look at me, I said, "I'm just as angry with Landon as you are."

Moving closer to me, he grasped my hand. "I doubt it. You want to extend some form of understanding and courtesy to him. I have none to give."

"Because of me?"

"Yes. Have I once hidden the root of my anger? He broke you and I had to watch. And was unable to do anything about it other than watch you comply. Then I had to stand by while you performed a dangerous spell to right his wrong. We are living with the results of that."

"*And* we know that you won't be able to do what is necessary to correct it," Clayton's baritone voice quipped from in front of us. His voice was present before he came out from the direction of the living room. Mephisto didn't seem surprised by his sudden appearance.

"He cut off all communication. We were worried about him," Clayton offered in a fake concerned tone accompanied by a low, raspy, maudlin drawl, responding to my surprised inquiring look.

"At least make your performance believable," Mephisto snapped.

Clayton's annoyance was palpable. They were so used to freely communicating at any time, that loss of that ability bothered them on a level they were reluctant to admit. They showed irritation when the lines of communication were broken, but I always heard the flicker of concern and apprehension in their voices when they reprimanded someone for severing the com lines. Mephisto was the most frequent perpetrator of it.

"We were indeed concerned. Our Raven—" *When the hell did I become 'Our Raven'?* In the past, I'd been Mephisto's Raven, the Raven, and various combinations of the title. My presumption was that my issues were never just mine. Kai and Simeon were pulled into my situations by way of Mephisto, and Clayton was involved because of his alliance to Mephisto and his relationship with Madison.

"What is needed to correct the situation?" I countered, my heart pounding because I knew the answer.

Clay gathered the distance between us in seconds, a reminder of his disconcerting speed and his undeniable presence. He had oceanic powers, and despite his alluring charisma that he wielded like a shield, he was also all-consuming and intense. The dichotomy was the most troublesome thing about him.

"I often believe you don't recognize that you are Malific's daughter and capable of unique and problematic magic. Add your elven blood and it is a recipe for disaster."

"Quarter elf," I corrected.

"Ah, yes. That quarter allows you to restrict elven magic, recreate living things, and even restrict our magic."

"In a circle that you all can easily get out of. Not a real

restriction if you just step over the runes and suffer no consequences!"

It wasn't about the ease with which they could counter the spell but merely the fact I possessed that ability. That's what bothered them, and my ability to create fruits, flowers, and possibly creatures was probably the most bothersome.

Moving closer, I scrutinized his expression. "What are you saying?" I asked.

He glanced over at Mephisto and back to me. "You may have to destroy your own creation if he becomes an issue."

"He's not a creation or anything to be dealt with," I refuted, although I didn't have the level of confidence I held earlier. And that reality and Clayton voicing a concern I had suppressed made me wince. "Clay, we'll discuss this tomorrow, okay?"

Clayton's lips pulled into a tight line, and his agreement was reluctant. He started out the door when I called after him. Pulling from Mephisto's grip, I turned to whisper, "I need to talk to him."

Mephisto's gaze darted between the two of us, and after a few moments of speculative silence, he headed upstairs.

I jutted my finger in the direction he'd originally came from and followed Clayton to the living room.

"Have you said any of this to Madison?" I asked.

"Not yet."

I had no doubts he'd tell her as soon as it was a reasonable hour to do so.

Washing my hands over my face, undoubtedly smearing whatever makeup had managed to survive the night, I then ran my fingers nervously through my disheveled hair. A reminder of how my night started and ended.

"We have to establish some boundaries and rules," I asserted with a fatigued sigh.

"Boundaries and rules?" His brows knitted together as a smirk tugged at one corner of his lips. "I'm intrigued."

"When it comes to Madison and me, there have to be rules as to what you get to share. I have to be the first one to tell her anything that relates to me. You have privilege to a lot of information because of Mephisto. You cannot exploit that."

His smirk moved into a smile. An incredulous smile, then a boom of laughter.

"I'm sorry but that is a boundary I'm setting," I pressed. I knew I was being a little fast and loose with the definition of boundary.

"I reject that rule and plan to step over that boundary at every turn. Are we done?" he shot back without giving the request a moment of consideration.

"No. This is a problem."

"For you. Believe me, I don't enjoy being the first to give Madison any information about you. But far too often you withhold information from her. Or allow her to find out through other means, causing her unnecessary worry and undue stress and forcing her to scramble and intervene to subvert PR disasters, or save you from being imprisoned or your abilities from being discovered. I don't believe this is done to be cruel or to hurt her in any manner. Quite the opposite. It's not about intent, it's impact. You do a lot of things that impact her life significantly."

He ran his fingers through his locs and gathered a handful. They fell in sync with his heavy sigh. "I've known her for less time than you have, and I realize she doesn't need you to protect her. But she seems to function best when she's fully informed. Even if there is nothing she can do to help."

"I would have told her about Landon and Dr. Sumner."

"I'm sure you would have. It is quite unfortunate that you were too busy tending to your..." He frowned. It wasn't Dr. Sumner anymore. Not the one we all knew. "To the former Dr. Sumner."

"Don't call him that!"

He shrugged. "I told her. I did what you couldn't. And I'll continue to do so with all situations, Erin. You need to understand that." Not giving me a chance to respond, he moved past me in that weird imperceptible way they did and was out of the house before I could manage a rebuttal.

I was left thinking of Clayton's parting words and his assertion that I may have to destroy my creation. And Mephisto's counterargument that the peculiar magic situation with Dr. Sumner wouldn't just resolve itself.

CHAPTER 3

By the time I'd made it to the bedroom, my concern had morphed into anger and frustration, an unreasonable amount of it directed at Clayton and his departing words.

"Clay's charisma and wit does all the heavy lifting in masking that he can be an asshole sometimes," I complained.

Mephisto stopped in the middle of removing his blood-stained shirt, his lips curled into something that had nestled between a smirk and a smile. "That was hidden from you?"

"I got muddled by his charm and his effortless wit and humor." I kept my comments about his distracting good looks to myself.

"It's just you who was *muddled* by it. I'm quite aware of Clayton's ways."

"You've had hundreds of years with him," I shot back.

Mephisto moved closer to me, sharp humor darkening his eyes as he wrapped his arms around me. "True. But he's not hidden it. Perhaps it was something you turned your eyes from." From the weight of his words, I knew it wasn't just Clayton we were discussing. Hooking his finger under my chin, he lifted it and planted a kiss on my lips.

"I've always appreciated Clay's candor and tenacity. In fact, it was helpful on many occasions when you were involved." His eyes dropped from mine. In the past, he reluctantly accepted that he tended to be vulnerable when it came to me. A source of his uneasiness now. The others acknowledged it, but it was Clayton who did the most to intervene to ensure it wasn't a detriment to them. Gliding his hands to my back, Mephisto unzipped my dress and gave it a little tug, helping it to the floor.

As if he'd sensed my apology forming, he pressed his fingers to my lips and curled in closer. "If I am to have a weakness, I want it to be you," he whispered. His hands slid down my arms until they came to my hands. He clasped them in his. "I suspect you have your own vulnerabilities when it comes to me. Madison appears to have the same sentiments about me as you do with Clay. She had no issues voicing them when she arrested me. And had choice description and words for Clay when he attempted to intervene. She managed to see past his charisma, wit…and good looks," he teased. I might have kept that tidbit to myself, but Mephisto was aware of all aspects of his friend. "She definitely didn't find anything witty or charming about him that day. I'll admit, he had them on full display then."

His humor lacked mirth, dulled by the grudge he held from that situation. *Pettiness doesn't diminish with years of living, I see.*

He wasn't the only one arrested during that time—Asher received similar treatment, as indicated by Cory's retelling of the situation when Elizabeth had sent me to the demon world. Busy trying to find me, Madison hadn't responded well to Asher and Mephisto's toxic intervention and fighting. She gave them a time out. One that they continued to begrudge and remind me of at every chance.

I dug my foot in, stopping his lead to the shower. "You are

going to have to let that go," I teased. He'd admitted to forgiving Madison, but a dark cast lingered when he discussed her and always moved to the scowl on his face when the topic was mentioned.

"I have," he lied.

In one swoop of movement, he'd gathered me in his arms and deposited me in the shower, which we were both in need of. Not just from the long day, but blood from his fight with the vampires stained his hand. His shirt had suffered the most and was speckled with crimson on the front.

He watched me with intense eyes as the water fell over us, our failing attempt to *just* shower after we'd washed our hair. I lathered the light citrus body wash into the body net, gliding it over my body. Mephisto quickly gave up any pretenses of showering and looked intently at me, his eyes darkening as he pressed me against the cool tile, a direct contrast to the steam in the shower and the heat from his body pressed against mine.

His gaze bored into me as the magnetic pull between us heightened. His magic didn't feel like an imperceptible tug at my need. It felt sentient, tactile, rolling over me in a languid, seductive graze. Dancing over my skin, prickles of warmth flitted over me. My nipples hardened until they were so sensitive the slightest touch of his tongue against the hollow of my neck made me shudder with pleasure. He grinned at my response, a low entreating moan as I arched into him.

His fingers stroked over one nipple, a taunting tug at his lips as he watched my response. Base need taking over, I threaded my fingers through his hair and pulled him in for a deep soft kiss. The sensual exploration of his mouth quickly escalated to hot and hungry.

Mephisto's fingers curled into my hips, nails biting at my skin, sending shivers down my spine, igniting a fire. His hard cock pressed against me. I ran my hands down his back, exploring his contrasting soft skin and the hard delineation and grooves of muscles.

My migration went down the defined crest of his chest and abs. The soothing sound of running water created a cocoon around us. I took his cock in my hands, stroking it as water made trails over his body, falling and pooling in the deep concaves of muscle.

Mephisto's finger hooked under my chin, drawing my attention to his lust-darkened eyes. My sensual stroke earned me a slight shudder and pant. His eyes wild with need, he pressed me into the tile. Cupping my breast, his tongue laved over my nipples. He captured the pebbled skin in his teeth. Bit down. I shrieked as a jolt of pleasure and pain rushed through me. One hand hoisted me into him. I curled my legs around him, securing my body to him. He turned off the water with the other hand. Mephisto devoured me with desperate hungry kisses and bites to my bottom lip as he navigated to the bedroom.

A combination of primal hunger and rough tenderness. The towel he managed to grab on the way out of the bathroom snaked over our skin in such a rushed manner, I was barely aware of the interruption of soft fluffy cotton rubbing over my skin before he placed me on the bed. Mephisto cupped my breasts again, kneading them in his hands, tasting and nipping at the hard peaks.

"Fuck, I want you," he panted out in a rough growl. He'd passed a simple want; there was unequivocal need. His eyes were dark and searing as he ground his turgid cock against me. Then he repositioned, and with decisive expert strokes moved his thumb over my clit, igniting an intoxicating wave of pleasure throughout my body. Need seized me when his fingers slid inside me, stroking and teasing.

My whimpers were desperate and pleading. His dark raspy chuckle filled the room as I writhed and ground my hips, each stroke of his skilled fingers taking me to new heights of pleasure and igniting a fire that only he could quell. Synchronizing with his thrusts, I rode them, seeking an orgasm that he denied me when he removed his hands.

"No," I begged.

He responded to my desperation with a teasing smirk.

"Have I displeased my demigoddess?" His hunger was palpable. It lingered in his lust-filled gaze that probed my every movement. I despised his ability to deny it.

I was prepared to lob some very hostile four-letter threats and other colorful words at him, but that wish disappeared when his lips covered mine. The roguish god's tongue pushed farther in a rough, possessive kiss. I moaned into his mouth as his hand grazed over my skin, exploring the curves and sensitive spots on my body with an erotic reverence.

Relaxing into his touch, I longed for more.

"I'll remember this," I said through short, sharp breaths as I attempted to regain some of the composure that his touch had taken from me.

"That's my Erin. The woman who prides herself in playing dirty." A ravenous glint sparked in his eyes and lingered over the word *dirty*. A definite departure from what I meant.

I shrieked my surprise when he lifted my legs and pulled me down toward him. Our gazes met, his dark eyes never leaving mine as he nestled his face between my thighs. His lips and tongue created an unbearable hunger as they explored the most intimate parts of my body. As the pleasure intensified, I moved my hips to meet his thrusts and laves. My arousal became intense and overwhelming with Mephisto's expert mouth and tongue. I clawed at the sheets and wailed my pleasure, surrendering into an uncontrolled orgasm, while Mephisto delightfully continued to stimulate the sensitive areas.

My response ignited something carnal and dark in him.

Positioning himself over me, he devoured me in another dominating proprietary kiss. If there were any questions of what I meant to him, they were answered in that moment.

He rolled me onto my stomach, his hardness gliding over the wetness. A deep growl reverberated in his chest. His strokes were deliberate, slow, and measured as I accommodated his size. Once he was fully seated in me, he pulled us to our knees. One of his hands moved over my sensitive erogenous bud, while the other caressed my breast. I gasped for breath while his lips and teeth grazed over my neck and shoulders as he drove into me.

A blissful mix of pleasure and pain surged through me as I surrendered to another climax. I made an ardent effort to stay upright but quickly needed to reposition to my hands and knees. Mephisto's nails grazed over my back, sending shudders through me and a low moan as his thrusts came harder, seeking his own pleasure.

The air thickened and our moans resounded in the room along with the erratic, climax-seeking movements. With each frenzied pleasure-driven movement, I felt my body teetering on the edge once more heading toward an explosive orgasm. I lost track of time as the intensity built, my senses overwhelmed by the many times I'd come.

I cried out an unrestrained moan of satisfaction when another one crashed through me like a wild storm, my moan mingling and eventually getting lost in Mephisto's deep guttural growl as the rhythm of his movements became faster, more urgent, driving us toward the peak. His raw, primal energy whirled between us before his cataclysmic release.

"Fuck," he managed to finally growl, his voice rough and thick.

We collapsed onto the bed, still connected, my back pressed against his chest. Pulling me closer, he made claims over my name calling me his raven and demigoddess.

Rearing away, I rolled to face him. "Which one? You can't have both. Raven or demigoddess?" I complained.

"Why can't I have both? When they both embody you," he whispered, kissing me lightly on my forehead. I recalled his words: 'You see the raven as a creature of death whereas others marvel at it for its ability to survive and thrive in a wide range of habitats. Ravens are one of the few birds that exist in the Veil. You constantly show yourself to be the epitome of that, my demigoddess.'

It brought me comfort in a way that being addressed as the signifier of death never could. Slowly, my fingers trailed from his chest, migrating over the hard grooves, the cords of muscles and then traced the iliac crest that I was becoming increasingly fond of.

"This is my favorite part of your body."

He grinned, his brow cocked. "I don't think that's true at all," he said, watching my eyes continue their venture to his erection.

Jerking my attention from it, I looked him intently in the eyes. "I like being both the raven and the demigoddess to you," I admitted. "I love that you see the many facets of me."

"That's what I love about you. There is so much more to you. I look forward to loving and exploring each layer."

"So, M—"

He frowned at the use of a name he only seemed to allow from Clayton.

"Mephisto," I purred in correction. "Which one did you satisfy earlier? The raven or the demigoddess? And don't you owe one?" I teased, my finger caressing his silky skin, enjoying the slow, ragged breaths that it stirred.

"I'm ready when you are, princess."

I rolled over and straddled him. Kissing him, I whispered, "Princess? That seems like a demotion."

His roaring laughter pierced the quiet as I traveled down his body planting kisses and laves of my tongue.

"You're right, demigoddess," he said in a low sultry rumble that felt like an erotic caress.

"Ah, so it's the raven who needs to be satisfied next," I said, taking him into my mouth as he sank his fingers into my hair and groaned his satisfaction.

31

CHAPTER 4

I'd slept better than expected, getting a much-needed reprieve from my thoughts which would have spiraled into the endless possibilities of how the situation with Landon and Dr. Sumner could play out. Mephisto had distracted me with a night of torrid activity and the reminder that he was fully a god and had the stamina of one. I was made exhaustingly aware of my human side. The phantom touches of his magic that he used throughout the night to enhance the pleasure, along with the scent of his soap and shampoo, lingered. Our clothes and towels discarded from the day before were gone. So was Mephisto.

I hadn't heard him moving, which wasn't saying much, but I thought I'd feel him getting out of bed. Nothing.

After I showered, washed my hair, and placed it in a bun that was as loose and chaotic as the situation felt, I rummaged through the overnight bag on the dresser that I'd ignored earlier. It was nothing like the bag I kept in the trunk of my car. The soft cognac leather bag could handle a rugged day, but it wouldn't be as pristine as this was. But like my bag, it had the basics: underwear, v-neck t-shirts in blue, black, and a moss green. Several pairs of leggings, a pair of jeans, two sports bras and two lacy sheer bras. Really, Mephisto? An extra toothbrush and a phone charger. Mephisto had suggested I leave clothing and essentials at his home, but whenever I dressed, the clothing managed to end up back at my home. I assumed this was to add to it.

I slid on the moss green t-shirt over the lacy black bra, pulled on the jeans, and was heading out the door when my phone chimed, notifying me of a text message. Grabbing my phone off the nightstand, I saw that I had more than one text message. There were three from Dr. Sumner along with five missed calls. A message from Cory letting me know we needed to talk. Delivering the message "you know what about" in all caps. I wondered who'd told him about the Dr. Sumner situation. Madison, I guessed. There was a text from her inquiring about Mephisto's response to the protection order she'd placed on Landon's life.

Landon. I needed to talk to a vampire. In any other case, he'd be the one I'd ask, since Grayson, my ex who I'd turned over the Supernatural Task Force, was unlikely to accept a visit from me in the Perils, where he'd been sentenced to a time long enough that he'd definitely hate me for being the person who apprehended him. My other vampire exes and casual relationships didn't end on bad terms but had been built on a foundation of lust and sex. We never developed a connection healthy enough to form trust, and I wouldn't feel comfortable disclosing to them why I needed intimate details of vampire siring. Besides, they all had an association to Landon, and I didn't want to give him any insights or access to me.

I sent a text to Madison and Cory asking them to meet me at my apartment later. Hopefully I'd have an established plan and Mephisto's promise that he wouldn't kill Landon. The former seemed more probable.

Making my way down the stairs, the sweet smells of unidentifiable spices had me changing course from Mephisto's office, where I thought I'd find him, to the kitchen. If he wasn't there at least I'd have food. My stomach growled in anticipation.

"Erin," Benton called from behind me. I changed course again and followed him into his office where Mephisto was seated on the sofa, his head resting back as he looked at the ceiling. His exceptional ability to hide his emotions made reading him and the situation difficult, but Benton didn't possess such skills and wore his concern heavily etched in his scowl.

"Have you heard from your sired?" he inquired. Mephisto's head snapped in his direction, pinning him with a stony glare. "Are we pretending that's not what he is?"

"I can't sire anyone, I'm not a vampire."

"No, you aren't, but you are the daughter of an Archdeity, which gives you the ability to create other beings and things. Is that not what vampires do?"

Benton's curt and wintry disposition made me wonder if he'd been pulled from the Veil to assist with this situation. Like Kai, did he prefer it there? Perhaps he felt his skills should be put to better use than helping Mephisto's girlfriend out of a unique situation.

"It is. I was just trying to save his life." Keeping my voice level was difficult and the emotions broke through. It softened the coolness in his eyes.

"I know. Your magic is such an anomaly that erring on the side of caution should be chosen practice in all incidences." Worry cast deep brackets into his frown.

"I should have allowed him to be changed into a vampire?"

"Yes. At least we'd know what he was and how to deal with that," Benton asserted without a moment of hesitation.

Shocked by his answer and his directness, I looked at Mephisto. Despite the lack of emotion shown, I gathered he agreed with Benton.

Benton crossed the room to his desk and started looking through the papers and opened books and began a series of questions regarding the day I brought Dr. Sumner back. They were questions Mephisto had missed. "How fast was his heartbeat once it started?" "Was he tired after he used his magic?" "Was there an eye color change?" "Did you offer him blood?"

"Why would I offer him that?"

"Perhaps his magic isn't at full capabilities because he's fueling as a human and not a vampire. Or the hybrid that he may be." Benton tossed the papers he was holding onto the table, closed his eyes, and massaged his temples.

Mephisto studied Benton for a long moment. With his eyes fixed on him, Mephisto said, "You have to be hungry, Erin." Then he turned to me, a wayward grin on his lips and a tease in his words reminding me of last night's activities. "Let's get something to eat." In just seconds, he was next to me, his hand against my back, guiding me out of the room. I noticed the cautious concerned look he gave Benton as we left.

In the kitchen, I took a seat across from Mephisto. Isley brought us a cup of coffee and placed more coffee in the center of the table before I reached for the cream and sugar. "Taste it first," he advised.

I took a sip and made a low throaty sound of appreciation.

Mephisto's lips tugged into a smirk, and one brow rose. "That's a familiar sound. I thought it was only reserved for me."

My lips parted, and surprise flashed over Isley's face. He rushed to place the fresh biscotti, culprit of the sweet smells from earlier, on the table.

"You embarrassed him," I said, once Isley was out of earshot.

"I assure you I haven't. Based on the color on your cheeks, he's not the one feeling a little coy."

"When your best friend is a person like Cory, your threshold for embarrassment gets really high. I'm just showing second-hand embarrassment for you because of your jealousy of a cup of coffee."

His eyes fixed on my lips as I started devouring my second biscotti. "I am envious of the pastry, too," he teased.

"If it makes you both feel better, I'm embarrassed enough for everyone," Clay said as he entered the kitchen, followed by Simeon and Kai. Cory's friendship hadn't prepared me for *this* level of embarrassment. My cheeks were on fire. I quickly attempted to adopt a cool look of indifference as I took in the group's attire of dark jeans, and v-neck t-shirts molded to forms that were designed for battle. They looked lithe, quick, and durable. Even the otherworldly way they moved could never be contributed to human or basic supernaturals. Despite decades of attempting to blend in, there was something off about them that would always place them in the 'other' category.

Clayton had on his favored black, Simeon in a jade green that complemented his champagne-color hair. Kai's cerulean-colored shirt reminded me of his wings. His demeanor was unexpectedly light. Kai had worn the heaviness of being confined to my world in his rigid posture and forced composure as if he was impatiently waiting for the time when he could totally be himself. He belonged in the sky. I thought the dragon shifter brothers did too, but they preferred their human form where they could exist by stealing and attributing it to being "their way" because dragons hoarded. I'd pointed out that dragons hoarded trinkets and things that weren't of great value, whereas the brothers preferred to hoard designer clothing, expensive electronics, jewels, and illegal or black-market magical objects. Magical objects they didn't mind surrendering for the right price. So no, it wasn't their dragon need to hoard; they were just thieves.

Kai found solace in the sky. It was where he excelled in battle and felt most at ease. Behind the Veil, he could truly be himself, unbound by the limitations of land. His newfound freedom was evident in his bright expression and eyes that had lost their troubled heaviness. Now they held a look of bashful disapproval of the current conversation.

"We can't find him," Simeon disclosed, his attention outside. I knew he was looking for the okapi that he'd gifted Mephisto. I remained convinced his search was for selfish reasons. If he had to interact with bipedal mammals, he wanted the option to visit his animal friends when it was complete. Animals were obviously his companion preference.

I blinked at the abrupt response, realizing I'd been dropped into the middle of another of their silent conversations and was not being given clips of information from it.

"I'm here. Shouldn't I be involved in all aspects of the conversation?" I asked, looking at each of them.

"It is a habit we must learn to break when you are around. We'll be more mindful," Mephisto offered. The others' agreement held a level of sincerity that made me realize just like their glamours, this mode of conversation had been their survival and was now instinctual.

"Mephisto contacted us early this morning asking us to look for Landon again. We looked yesterday without success. It's the same today. He hasn't returned to his home, his safe home, or any of his usual places."

Although it wasn't surprising, I disliked that I hadn't had that information.

"What about Dallas and Elon?" Mephisto asked.

"They're gone, too," Clayton said.

Mephisto leaned back in his chair, taking a thoughtful sip from his cup.

Isley had stepped back into the area to confirm if steak and eggs were okay for breakfast. The pastry hadn't put a dent in my hunger. The three I ate just seemed to make me hungrier.

"Call Landon," Mephisto told me.

Landon wore his hubris and entitlement like a designer perfume, but I wasn't convinced that his arrogance would extend to these heights. I called him. It went directly to voicemail. Then I attempted to videocall. Nothing.

The image of Dr. Sumner on the sofa, his life drained from him, flashed in my mind. "What if he returns to finish the job with Dr. Sumner?"

I couldn't believe I hadn't considered that.

"He's fine, he said he's tired a lot. But he looked well. I had your friend put a ward at his home. It would be better if it was a witch's ward than ours," Clay provided. With effort, he'd managed to say witch and not his preferred *lesser*. That may explain why I hadn't gotten a response from Cory.

"Thank you."

"It wasn't my idea, it was Madison's." He frowned. "Jacob was able to use the spell to disable the ward if necessary. Madison and Cory tested it."

That was new and different. Was his magic getting stronger or was he getting a better handle of it?

Kai bit his bottom lip and then turned his attention to Clayton. "He didn't look well. Something is off. He isn't human." He directed the last part to me. Said with conviction, like he was trying to convince the last holdout.

It was getting harder to deny that something was wrong. Their concern and accusation were pinned on me. Even Simeon pulled his attention from the animal out back to me.

"If he went through a partial vampire transition—" Kai started.

I cut him off. "He didn't." My denial caused him to scrutinize me more.

"My understanding of the situation is different," he provided. This was one of the rare occasions that I was happy not to have been part of the secret discussions.

Isley placing a plate filled with steak, potatoes, and scrambled eggs and a bowl of fruit in front of me interrupted the tension-filled silence. I'd devoured half of my eggs before realizing Mephisto hadn't been given anything.

"You're not eating breakfast?" I asked him.

"Brunch," he corrected. His eyes sparked with amusement that momentarily replaced the worry lines etched on his forehead. "I ate earlier. I've been up for several hours." A devilish smirk lifted the corners of his lips.

"Will you bring her ketchup?" Mephisto requested from Isley before he could leave.

"Ket-ketchup," Isley fumbled out. He managed to keep judgment from his expression. Clayton shook his head.

"You're biased because you don't like ketchup." I frowned, recalling Mephisto saying "he doesn't get it."

Simeon had exceeded his people time and had started fidgeting. After a series of nods between the four, Simeon headed for the back to play, chat, debate, gossip, who knew what with the okapi.

Clayton and Kai headed out of the kitchen.

"You're meeting with Madison later, right?" Clayton asked. "Will you discuss possible complications of an interrupted vampire transition? She may have more information or options to correct the situation."

"Nah, I've decided to make you my administrative assistant and allow you to relay messages for me. Make sure when you do, use my lovely tone," I teased, grinning at him as he watched, with abject horror, me take the ketchup from Isley and pour some over my steak.

Eventually he pulled his attention from my culinary crime to me. "Is it lovely, or has Mephisto convinced you of that? I think it suits the taste of the person it's meant for." He gave me a wide, genial smile, and before I came up with a good response, he was gone.

Mephisto occupied himself with his phone, leaving the undiscussed matter a taut overwhelming cord between us.

I'd just started on the bowl of fruit after devouring my food, keenly focused on the blueberries but failing to ignore Mephisto's intense gaze on me. When I couldn't stand it any longer, I lifted my eyes to meet his.

"When it comes to Dr. Sumner, you don't seem to be as pragmatic. Is there a reason?" he asked in a crisp, even tone, his lips tugged into a brittle grim line.

"I don't suffer from the inability to be pragmatic when dealing with him. It's guilt," I admitted, shoving the plate away. The lingering taste of berries felt like sawdust. I took a drink of the water Isley had brought with the meal.

"When Dr. Sumner took me on as a client, his intentions were to improve his knowledge and visibility within the magical community. Admittedly, he was using me for that. But he provided a great deal to me as well. He became an emotional safe haven for me. In his wildest thoughts, he couldn't have imagined Malific would critically injure him and subsequently cause Landon to use him as a bargaining tool. I did that to him."

Mephisto leaned into the table, a comforting warmth inching into his eyes and words. "Dr. Sumner isn't innocent in this. He tried to make a bargain with Landon, which only led to him being on Landon's radar. Did you keep pulling him into your world, or did you advise him to stay away? I find it unlikely that you didn't."

I had, so many times. Our client/therapist relationship was so blurred and had morphed into an inappropriate friendship. "We took a lot of wrong turns and ended up here," I said with a mirthless hollow chuckle. It didn't ease the tension. "He's my friend—I screwed up my friend's life. I'm scared my spell may not have worked, and I just staved off the inevitable, that he's a vampire, something he never wanted. Even worse, he's a vampire with magical abilities. And what if he's a peculiar hybrid and has different nutritional requirements that can't be met? I doubt that's anything he'd want, either. I know something is wrong with him, and it's going to put his life in jeopardy and put him in the crosshairs of the vampires."

"Erin, don't take on that burden. It's not yours to carry. This will be fixed."

"Even if it's with his death?"

"Unfortunately, that might be the final option."

That's what bothered me the most.

Backing out of the driveway in one of Mephisto's borrowed cars, I came to an abrupt stop at the presence of Kai's impressive cerulean and black wings that obscured my line of sight. In the sky, they were overpowering, but now they blocked the view of the sun. Snapping them out of sight, the mere sight of his extended wings appeared to bring him comfort.

"Let's talk," he suggested. When I agreed he opened the car door and invited me to walk with him. I preferred that to sitting in the car with few distractions.

Kai's deliberately slow, measured steps made it easy to keep pace with him. "Don't make us protect Mephisto from himself," he finally said after minutes of silent walking.

"What?" I stopped, turning my full attention on him.

"He'll choose whichever option will leave you feeling the least amount of pain. We've always been confident in Mephisto's ability to do the right thing. *Collectively* the right thing. A magic-wielding vampire cannot exist in this world. And make no mistake, that is what Sumner is. He doesn't have fangs to sustain his necessary diet, he has a heartbeat, so he's not immortal, and he needs oxygen to live. Do what is necessary and make him a true vampire. The true transition will hopefully remove his magic."

"He doesn't want to be a vampire."

"That decision was made when he didn't have to choose between life and death. That is the decision now. Because if he exists as he is, the world will be looking for his maker. Your life as you know it won't be the same. And that's best-case scenario. You know there are those who don't tolerate abnormalities. That's why everyone is hiding what you are, right?"

I swallowed down my answer with a heavy sigh and simply nodded.

He looked away. "I'm not sure he'd even survive in the Veil, which I considered an option. So, let him be changed."

"If that doesn't work, I'm left with an immortal being who has magic. My magic."

He frowned, sorrow filling his eyes. "Raven, that won't be a situation you have to deal with. I'm sorry."

I hissed at the empty space where he'd left me when he disappeared through the shimmering wall that appeared behind him. Everything pissed me off. Their easy access to the Veil, the walk back to the car, and the fact this wasn't an easy solution no matter how I looked at it.

Things weren't that simple. Even if I agreed with letting Dr. Sumner fully change, I didn't have a vampire I could ask. Now I was dealing with the second time one of the Huntsmen had alluded to them handling the situation.

I knew how that would end for Dr. Sumner.

CHAPTER 5

At my apartment, Cory and Madison's questioning felt more like an interrogation than a debriefing of the past day and a half. Things were made worse because I couldn't guarantee that Mephisto wouldn't act on his anger toward Landon. Instead, we focused on the things that were in our control, even if minimally.

"Landon isn't responding to my requests. I've sent agents to his home."

Both Cory and I looked at Madison. Once again, she had stepped outside her job description for me. "I'm responsible for upholding our laws," she reminded us.

"So, you're arresting him? How is that going to help?" Cory asked.

"Not arrest yet."

That's where things got complicated with magical wielders. Factions typically handled their own. The Supernatural Task Force involvement meant that the situation was a community risk or a public relations nightmare that would crumble the fragile relationship between the humans and supernatural force. Groups against the co-existence of humans and supernaturals lay in wait, ready to pop up at any opportunity to show the dangers of the supernaturals' existence.

She sighed. "He's the one who's supposed to reinforce the rules of the vampires." She cursed under her breath and dropped onto the sofa. It was rare that she looked exasperated and overwhelmed by her job, but it was obvious she was. "There are a lot of things that can be said about Landon, but he's never had a problem with rogue vampires changing people." Compulsion was another story. It was illegal, although old vampires were so proficient at it, its use was hard to prove. Vampires' allure made compulsion unnecessary for food, sex, and whatever other activities they wanted humans for.

Cory's attention and gentle worried eyes had fallen completely on a dispirited Madison.

"Erin, you have to stop." Cory's sharp plea jerked Madison's gaze to him. "Stop it. All of it. This exploration of your magic was fun and entertaining, initially, and I was on board for it all. I rooted for you to be this powerful being that would demand people stop messing with you and allow you to lead a quiet life. Now you're just making yourself a target. Eventually one of the shots will land. The elves hate you, the witches don't trust you, and you have a fragile alliance with the fae. They know what you're capable of. I think it's a 'keep your enemies closer' situation."

When Madison chewed on her bottom lip, I knew Cory may not be completely right, but he was close.

"They know you removed the elves' magic, and our close relation to them gives you a power over them that makes them feel cautious of you," she said.

"I explained to them that they'd never have to worry about it because of you," I refuted.

She nodded. "It gave me value to them, but they also

understand that I could be a catalyst that could provoke you against them as well."

The warning in her voice reminded me that fear doesn't encourage loyalty but distrust, and the potential for betrayal, retaliation, and desperate actions to prevent the feeling of fear.

My magic was unique, something nobody else had seen before, and there would be people who'd want to exploit it. Or get rid of it.

I stared back at my friend, who looked pained at the prospect of me dying. I couldn't be upset at his outburst, but I couldn't apologize for exploring my magic, even if it was out of desperation to protect and save someone else. Now I was being forced to deal with the consequences of that exploration.

My phone vibrated and I snatched it up quickly with a naïve hope that it was Landon, and tried not to let my disappointment show in my tone.

"Sumner, what's up?"

"I can't get out my house," his panic-filled voice told me.

"What do you mean, you can't get out of your house?"

"The ward. I can't bring it down."

Cory's mouth parted before twisting into a confused scowl. "He disabled it twice while we were there. I made sure he could, as well as erect it."

That meant he didn't have access to magic anymore. Pessimism made me tamp down my excitement. It could mean something worse. I jumped to my feet and headed for the door, with Madison and Cory right behind me while I suppressed the smile threatening to form.

He didn't have magic. If I got to his home and he moved as he did before and didn't have his weird Erin obsession, it would be worth it, and I wouldn't care about the enemies I'd made. Landon would have to be dealt with, and at this point,

I wasn't above saying "keep your mouth shut and leave me alone or I'm going to let Mephisto have at you." I wasn't above threatening to undo his vampirism, too. I had no evidence that I could, but he didn't know that.

CHAPTER 6

"Shit!" Cory's growl rivaled any shifter's at the sight of Dr. Sumner's opened front door, splintered near the lock where it had been forcibly opened. The ward had been disabled and there was no sign of Dr. Sumner.

We panned out, searching through the house. There were limited signs of struggle, just a small piece of glass where something had been broken. It looked as if the place had been tidied to remove all evidence of his abduction.

Cory clenched his fists. He scanned the room again, frowning, and shook his head. He looked to me and then Madison, neither one of us able to move, assessing the room and dealing with the reality that Dr. Sumner had been taken.

"The ward was disabled, so someone with magic was involved," I said quietly. "I don't think this is a witch's doing."

"I don't either," Cory said, taking his phone from his pocket. When the person answered, he said, "I need a favor. I need your nose. Can you come to Sumner's house?"

He'd called Alex. His involvement meant that the shifters would get involved. Asher would be involved. At this point, I didn't care. I needed answers. Scanning over the room, I couldn't help but feel I already had some. Landon, along with the help of a witch, had taken Dr. Sumner. Now I needed solutions. I contemplated calling Mephisto but decided to wait because I wasn't confident that getting him involved would increase Sumner's likelihood of survival. It definitely would ensure that Mephisto explicitly rejected Madison's protection order.

Fifteen minutes after Cory's call, Alex entered dressed in his typical style: crisp slim fit shirt, dark blue pin-striped slacks, what I suspected were Italian shoes, and perfectly coifed hair. Every time I saw him, I couldn't determine if he had just come from home or the office since he dressed the same for both.

Alex scanned over everything as he moved through the house, lifting items, smelling and assessing and returning them to their exact original location. He and Cory were perfect for each other.

His eyes screwed closed and he inhaled. When he opened them, he stood taller, the muscles of his neck bunched as if he was trying to ward off the various scents inundating his senses. Shifters learn to suppress their distinctive eyes, which were a combination of human awareness and predatory alertness. It was the same reason vampires went through the motions of inhaling and exhaling to seem less obtrusive and different. That didn't work any better than it did for shifters. Glints of gold let you know they straddled both worlds, but it was more than just their eyes. It was the way they moved, their presence, and their acute awareness of the world as seen through the eyes of a predator.

Alex was struggling to keep his wolf at bay.

He went through the room again, then moved to Cory, inhaled, a bewildered sneer forming, before stepping back and breathing in the room again. He migrated to me and then Madison, giving us the same treatment.

"Magic. Maybe a witch—I can smell hints of that form of magic." He wasn't as confident as I'd like. "And the vampire scent isn't familiar to me. Their magic reeks in here." Thanks to me, shifters were now immune to magic in both human and shifter form. Once again, I was faced with the reality that I could be considered a menace. In an effort to help my friends and undo so many wrongs, I was changing the world and magical abilities.

"More than one vampire?" I asked.

He nodded. "Possibly more than one witch." He moved throughout the room again, coming closer to Cory. Closing his eyes, he inhaled, did the same to me and Madison. His face strained with the effort of figuring out the nuances and scents of our magic. "But definitely vampires." He bit his lips and scanned the room again. "Or a person who has magic." Confused frustration moved into his frown.

Distancing himself from us, he took another whiff of the air. "It's not Landon's scent," he said.

I was glad I hadn't wrongly accused Landon to Mephisto.

He shook his head. "Nor anyone who is typically around them. We make it our business to be familiar with their scents and some of the more"—he looked at Cory and gave him a weak smile—"compromised witches."

His polite way of saying the ones who'd do unscrupulous things for the right payout.

The most unscrupulous of them all came to mind. "Do you know Wendy of the Lunar Marked Coven?"

"Formerly of the Lunar Marked Coven," he corrected. Of course, he knew that she'd been disavowed by her coven for her attempt to blackmail the fae and her link to the abduction of the queen of the fae. Although she'd been exonerated, her repeated use of dark magic had been exposed and her coven didn't want anything to do with her.

Alex shook his head. "I'm familiar with her. She's on the list of ones to watch. It's not her. I've never come in contact with whomever this magic belongs to." A troubled look inched into his eyes. "Or the vampires. Maybe they're new."

"Or someone none of us are familiar with." Landon was ruthless when he needed to be, but also pragmatic. Could he have sent someone else, to make him an unlikely suspect? My gut was telling me that wasn't likely.

"His smart displays are missing. There was one here?" Alex pointed to a spot where, upon further inspection, was a light splatter of dust that we'd missed. "I suspect whoever took him has made it a practice of efficiently abducting people. This isn't Landon's typical MO," he said before looking at his watch and moving close to Cory. "I have to leave. I was in the middle of an important work project that needs to be completed in the next two hours," he told Cory, with a quick kiss on his cheek.

"You should have told me—"

"You needed me, I could hear it in your voice. So, I came," he interrupted. Alex's finger traced over a wave in Cory's hair.

"I'll see you tonight," Cory told him, but he didn't sound confident. It would probably be a long night of looking for Dr. Sumner. But I'd make sure he made it to his date with Alex.

Such little information to go on made the search for Dr. Sumner and the culprits impossible. Periodically I called Dr. Sumner's phone, which initially rang but thereafter went to voicemail. His office was locked, and I considered breaking in. Madison discouraged it.

"No one knows that he's...*different*," she'd managed after several beats searching for the right word. "Someone will call him in missing soon. It will be handled by the police, not STF. It would be a bad look if you're linked to breaking into his office, even if you explained it was to look for him. You might be forced to disclose more than we should."

It wasn't the police that was the problem. It was a particular police officer: River.

Desperation left me checking all possibilities, which included Wendy, who didn't appreciate our unannounced visit.

"What?" she demanded, opening the door just enough to show her face and shoot us daggers. Hostility from her assigning fault to me for the trouble she suffered.

Sure, blame me and not the fact she tried to blackmail the fae, her constant practice of summoning demons made her the perfect scapegoat for Elizabeth and Fabian to use to punish me for declining their offer to join them, and not to mention her attempt to blackmail the vampires that led her and several of her coven members to nearly die at the hands of Dallas. Yeah, but it's my fault they kicked her ass to the curb.

Madison took the lead, showing her badge and telling her she had a few questions.

Wendy's eyes dragged the length of my body, her frown of disdain deepening before she gave Cory the same scrutinizing look. Then it jerked to Madison.

"I know this isn't official Supernatural Task Force business or they wouldn't be with you. But I'll cooperate as long as you remember this." Her eyes narrowed on Madison. "Will you remember this?"

This woman never missed an opportunity to exploit a situation for personal gain. Madison stowed away her badge. "As long as it's not illegal or compromises the integrity of STF," Madison replied firmly.

Wendy scoffed. "Just treat the favor as if you're dealing with something Erin is involved in and look the other way."

The unscrupulous witch reared back when she cast a look in my direction.

"Erin," Madison eased out in the same manner one would a riled dangerous animal or a person who needs to be talked down from committing unspeakable damage. I was feeling midway between both. Her words prodded at the guilt that I already felt for the concessions and actions Madison had made on my behalf. But the implication that it was of devious and corrupt behavior pissed me off.

"We aren't the same!"

"I just make deals with demons. You piss them off so much they abduct you to their realm. Maybe because they don't think you should be here, elf and demigod. From what I've seen you're a catastrophic combination. I've been keeping up with the chatter about you. Nothing that can be confirmed, just gossip and speculation, but I believe a lot of it to be true." After sneering at me, she redirected her attention to Madison, then moved aside to let us in but didn't invite us any farther than the landing. "What do you want?" Wendy's lips pinched together, and she nodded for Madison to proceed with the questions.

"Has anyone attempted to hire you?" Madison asked.

"Hire me for what?"

"Hire you for anything."

"I need you to be more specific, shifter or vampire?" she asked.

"Vampire." Madison said after a few moments of consideration. She knew, like I did, that we needed to give Wendy minimal information. I wouldn't put it past her to attempt to sell whatever information she gleaned from our conversation.

"No. Even if they had, I'm not allowed to perform magic. The condition of me returning to my coven is a year without magic." She exposed her wrist to us, displaying markings, the sigils surrounding an oval shape similar to an eye without a pupil.

Seeing my lack of awareness, Madison said, "It's a lituus. It will notify her coven when she uses magic."

Iridium would have prevented Wendy using magic, but

this wasn't about restricting her magic, just her ability to control using it.

"I haven't been approached and if I was, I couldn't help." Wendy slumped into herself. It would be a long year for her. Her spell ingenuity, strength, and ability to bring the coven a great deal of money was the only reason they were giving her this chance. They didn't mind some of her questionable ways of getting money for the coven, but she'd gone too far and brought in the fae and put them on STF's radar. That was her biggest crime.

"Contact me if anyone approaches you or if you learn of any witches approached by vampires. Any vampire," Madison urged.

"What have you done to piss off the vampires?" Wendy asked me.

"Thank you for your time," Madison responded, nudging me toward the door, aware that my patience with Wendy was just a worn strand on the brink of snapping.

CHAPTER 7

Navigating through the streets to my home, I tried not to make much of Madison's pinched scowl. This was nothing short of a clusterfuck among clusters. Dr. Sumner was well known in the field; his work with the supernatural had made him a professional darling among those interested. If his abduction was linked to a dangerous spell, it was going to be devastating not just for general relations but also another conflict between the police department and the STF over who'd handle it. I needed to find Dr. Sumner and keep him escaping the fate of vampirism.

And I couldn't dismiss the fact that Alex said it was a magical person but seemed to settle on witch. *Magical person* had my mind reeling with all the possibilities.

Distracted by my thoughts, I was slow to recognize the precision movements of a G-wagon slipping in front of me and slowing. The black MDX next to me prevented me changing lanes. The car behind me stayed far enough back to respond if I made any quick stops but close enough that slowing down wouldn't put enough distance between the cars for me to maneuver around them. A quick assessment of the cars' sturdier build and puncture-proof tires, and I figured they were bulletproof. I had no intention of using bullets against SUVs, but forcing them out my way wasn't an option, either.

"What the hell is going on?" Cory asked, looking around.

Recognizing the familiar Z4 that Landon's niece Robyn drove made me less concerned about our safety and fully aware of what was going on.

"I think I'm being escorted to a meeting," I said. A polite way of describing them aggressively corralling me to a location.

"Great, we've been pulled into a scene from *Sons of Anarchy.*"

"I don't know what that is."

"Do not play with me right now, Erin!" Cory spat with teasing agitation, but his eyes had flattened with apprehension. Madison's calm did nothing to help my warring emotions of anger, frustration, and slivers of fear that I couldn't rid myself of. Robyn, the pampered human, wasn't the issue; it was the occupants of the other SUVs that concerned me. Most likely vampires, and if they had any idea about the discourse between Landon and me, disgruntled, wrathful vampires.

After they navigated me to a side road, they quickly directed me into a subdivision heavily populated by vampires. This wasn't a safe space. Before I could get out of the car, Robyn had hopped out of hers and was at my door. Her flowing, lithe movement on the stage had transferred to her gait. She didn't possess the same stage confidence when she tapped the gun against the window cuing me to get out.

"Get out," she demanded when I didn't comply. I reached for the door handle and so did Cory and Madison. "No, just her," she directed.

A frustrated, overly confident Robyn didn't bother me. But the addition of a gun that she didn't seem comfortable brandishing did.

Slowly, I got out, keeping a close eye on the gun trained on me and the vampires from the SUVs who now surrounded me. I made sure to track Dallas at every moment. Of the familiar vampires that surrounded me, he was the most dangerous. Before I discovered that he was Landon's inconspicuous assassin, he was just the pretty man with the deceptively alluring personality.

"Where is Landon?" Robyn demanded, her voice as tremulous as her hand. It made me more nervous that I was going to be a victim of a bullet discharged accidentally rather than fangs in my neck.

"We can talk, but lower the gun," I insisted.

Her face flushed. "You are not in a position to make demands," she snapped, jerking the gun with each word. We were all going to end up with bullets in us if I didn't get a handle on the situation.

"You're right."

That relaxed her some, and with an unobtrusive flick of my hand, I shoved her back with magic, startling her. Just two steps, clearing the short distance between us, and I landed a quick strike on her nose. She screeched in shock and pain. While she was occupied tending to her nose, I was able to snatch the gun from her grasp. Jerking her in front of me, I kept her secured to my chest and the gun pointed at her.

It was a solid hit, but I doubted her nose was broken, just hurt like hell. I felt bad for the whimpering and heaving woman delicately touching her nose and ignoring that she was being used as a shield and now had a gun trained on her. Landon hadn't prepared her for this world. That much was apparent from her choice of clothing: a champagne-color silk shirt that draped over her slim frame and a pair of tailored, high-waisted black trousers. At least they were snug enough to allow for easy movement. Couldn't say that for the strappy heels. They could possibly be used as a weapon, but she didn't strike me as the type that would think to do it.

"It's not pleasant having a gun pointed at you, is it?" I said against her ear.

She exhaled a shaky breath.

"Where is Uncle Landon?" Her inquiry held a desperate anger that caught toward the end in her effort to restrain tears. It chased away my anger. I felt like a bully, using magic and now holding her at gunpoint.

"Do you think you're faster than a bullet at this range?" I said to Dallas, who had readjusted his stance and was ready to strike with viper-like precision and speed. He defied even the speed of most vampires. "Do not move."

The small dangerous smile he shot in my direction ensured that I needed to keep Robyn close despite her trembling body and tears that splattered onto my arm.

Girl, what were you thinking? You are not prepared for this.

My annoyance faded into indignation at this novice who'd managed to get a gun and enough vampires to ambush me.

I leaned in closer. "Calm down. Tell them to stand down so we can talk."

"I will not. If you're responsible for Uncle Landon being missing, or worse, I don't care what you do to me. I want them to kill you."

Damn, and she's dramatic. This was a recipe for a complete and utter disaster.

"If you truly believe I've harmed Landon, then you should be more afraid than you are right now. If I was capable of abducting him and causing him harm, do you think I'd have any qualms about getting rid of his troublesome niece who seems intent on creating problems for me?"

My response fueled more defiance. Robyn curled her fingers into the arm that had her secured against me and dug her nails into the skin. Biting back the hiss, I shook my head at Cory and Madison. They remained motionless, their faces devoid of any emotion, watching. I figured they were looking for a signal to intervene.

I really wanted to defuse the situation. Landon missing and Dr. Sumner abducted wasn't a coincidence. I'd rather we work together than spend my time fighting vampires and thwarting future ambush attacks and poorly executed revenge plots.

"Then do it. Whatever she does to me, you deliver a punishment tenfold," she insisted with a fiery growl through clenched teeth as her focus shifted to Dallas. Her demand, made with the confidence of her belief she commanded the vampires in Landon's absence, added to my surprise that they'd followed her instructions in the first place. It was probably in reverence to Landon. In the event that he was found, he'd look upon her treatment with favor.

"Don't let the witch or her sister off, either." Taken aback by the fierce anger in her voice, I glanced at Madison and Cory, who remained expressionless. This destructive thirst for revenge was borne from Robyn's fear. Her breathing was ragged and her fingers were clammy against my arm.

Pity coursed through me. She was attempting to be brave and full of revenge when she was just fearful and sad over her uncle's disappearance.

"Robyn," I soothed, "don't make this worse than it needs to be."

"How much worse can it be? He's been missing since his incident with you." Her voice dropped. "I know what you're capable of doing. Did you make him human and then kill him?"

Either Elon or Dallas gave her that information. I turned my focus on Dallas, searching for some answers, but his face revealed nothing.

"Dallas, kill her," she ordered. Her voice cracked on the last syllable, revealing fear and sorrow that only those who loved Landon could feel. She knew Dallas's actions would set off a series of events leading to her death.

Damn. I leaned down and whispered in her ear, pressed the gun to her temple. "Goodbye, Robyn."

She let out a blood-curdling scream. I wasn't sure if she fainted, but I had all her weight on me. I let her slide to the ground and gave a wide berth to let Dallas get to her. Keeping the gun trained on them, I nodded at the car and Cory and Madison got out. Madison scanned the area, taking in the six vampires and Robyn on the ground, her head lolling sideways as her eyes fluttered.

After a few moments, Robyn blinked up to full alertness. Her pallid face quickly became flushed with embarrassment. Turning an ire-filled glare first on me, she then looked at Dallas who'd removed a handkerchief from his pocket and was about to clean the stains from her streaked face. She took it from him, giving him a pleading look as if asking him not to console her like a child in distress.

This situation had deteriorated fast, and I didn't want to make it worse. "You're not ready to die for this. Nor am I. I'm asking you to live and help me find your uncle. I had nothing to do with his disappearance, and I want to find him, too." I'd have to give her busy work or I'd spend more time saving her ass or assuaging her bruised ego. I had time for neither.

I eased closer but kept the gun at the ready. "I won't insult your intelligence and say I'm blameless in the strife between me and Landon. But I'm not the reason he's missing, and I need to find him because..." It dawned on me that they could be responsible for Dr. Sumner's disappearance. But Alex said they were unknown scents, and Elon and Dallas were major players among the vampires. But it could have been someone recently turned, another one of Landon's surprises, assassins, or fixers. "Did you have anything to do with my friend going missing?" I asked Robyn, playing along with the illusion that she was in charge, although the question was directed to

Dallas who was more than likely handling things. Or the absent Elon, putting things in motion in the background.

"No, we've been following you. We want Landon back, so you have our support. They are equal priorities. You don't want to find your friend and *not* Landon, because if that happened, all your efforts would've been in vain," Dallas said, pulling back his teeth to reveal his fangs.

I snapped my head in Cory's direction and shook my head, unable to stop the forming mass of magic he was ready to attack with for the threat. A person could only take so many without retaliating, and I suspected Cory took the threat against Dr. Sumner as personal as one against him. It was rational, since it was highly unlikely they'd stop with just Dr. Sumner.

Dallas's dagger-sharp gaze bored into Cory and his defiant expression. Dallas's slow roving smile made me wary.

"Don't react, he's just nervous," Dallas instructed the vampires with predaceous amusement. Turning his attention from Cory to me, his cold smile melted into a warm amiable one that had fooled me once and wouldn't again. "Now it's your turn to tell yours to stand down. It would be good if he did."

No one missed the warning in his tone. We were just one misconstrued movement from chaotic violence.

Before I could respond or ask Cory to, he squelched the magic, his reluctance to do so heavy in his frown.

Dallas stood, pulling Robyn with him and keeping a careful hand around her waist. I knew it was firm enough to prevent me snatching her away and using her as leverage.

"I need to check some things. I'll let you know what I find. And I hope you'll extend the same courtesy to me," I said.

They nodded in agreement.

"When did you last see Landon?" I asked.

The warmth drained from Dallas's smile and required a

lot of effort to return. "At Dr. Sumner's home, when I had a knife plunged into my chest." His lips slid back to show his weapon of choice.

That's on you. Wrong place, wrong time. But I kept my snide response to myself. "You don't know if he met anyone or had an appointment?"

He shook his head, maintaining his deceptive warm mien. "Elon doesn't know, either. Our last sighting was that night. You're the last call he made from his cellphone."

"You have his phone?"

"No," he admitted.

Of course, they had their resources as well. I wondered what else they'd discovered that led them to suspect me. It didn't matter, and bringing it up would have the opposite effect, casting the suspicion that I was mining for information to cover my tracks. I eased toward the car.

"You have my number," I reminded Robyn. She'd obtained it when she discovered Landon was searching for people to sire for his family. Since Landon had made it known that I'd be involved in the selection process, she'd contacted me and petitioned to be included.

She nodded and I quickly got in the car, along with Madison and Cory. Once we were several miles away, I stopped the car, rested my head on the steering wheel, and heaved a deep sigh. "Landon and Dr. Sumner are missing, traces of strange vampires and witches were found in his home, and I have no idea who is involved. This is a nightmare."

"If we don't find Landon, I think they're prepared for mutual destruction just to make a point," Cory said.

"That's what I suspected," Madison said, shoving her fingers in her hair that was thicker curls since she'd stopped relaxing it and grown it out. The style made her look younger, but the worry creases in her face and dimmed eyes showed experience beyond her years. As the guilt of that began to trickle over me, I pushed it away. This was the consequence of so many other actions as well.

Cory opened his mouth several times but snapped it closed before he blurted it. "You're certain the Huntsmen didn't have anything to do with Landon's disappearance?"

"They're not above doing it, but they would have told us." That was one of the few things I was certain of. They dabbled in the gray and had no qualms about owning the behavior. It was the byproduct of knowing not many could do anything about it. Same arrogance that the powerful often shared.

"I can't use STF to look for Dr. Sumner," Madison said. The unspoken implication of him now falling under STF jurisdiction was loud in her silence. "There's no way the vampires will want Landon to be officially classified as missing. Erin, we have to find them both. And quickly."

"Find Landon, and I'm nearly positive we'll find Dr. Sumner."

CHAPTER 8

Mephisto's foreboding silence, severe jaw clenches, and barely contained thirst for violence made the name of the sitting area I'd previously dubbed the war room, apropos as I retold the events of the morning.

His voice strained with frustration and anger as he asked follow-up questions.

"I've lost my patience with the vampires." His words resounded with an eerie finality that felt unsettling as he sat back in his chair, fingers interlocked in front of him. "Why didn't you contact me the moment you saw them?"

"I considered it," I admitted. "But if I handled the situation, it would be less likely to end in violence."

I had taken small liberties with my answers. Calling Mephisto was a fleeting consideration. I knew that once he and the Huntsman got involved, the vampires would be on high alert and quickly escalate the situation to a violent confrontation. The Huntsmen were masters at maintaining their polished facades, and it served them well. But when faced with acts of aggression, the facade dropped quickly to reveal the truth behind their masks. It would be inevitable that the vampires would retaliate in kind.

"You made an assumption that could have had deadly consequences," he pointed out.

I nodded, aware that was a possibility no matter how slim a chance I estimated it to be.

"They were merely acting on behalf of a worried family member. I wanted to deescalate the situation in case they could be of use in finding Dr. Sumner," I admitted softly.

"Do we really believe that a group so easily swayed by their emotions and willing to follow a novice's lead could be any help?"

"She's Landon's niece," I reminded him. "They were honoring her connection to Landon, not blindly following her."

Judging by his dismissive grunt, that information held no significance.

"Erin," he said softly, "never put yourself at risk for such a meager payout."

I exhaled a slow breath. "It's not meager. I can't afford to make more enemies, and if defusing things provides the potential of gaining a situational ally, I will always choose that option," I asserted. "I have had more success than failure with that tactic, haven't I?"

After several moments he reluctantly conceded with a nod. "I don't think your decisions are always strategically motivated but made from the fear of becoming Malific. Do not allow those trepidations to become your weakness or albatross," he advised gently.

I accepted the advice with a faint smile, aware that Malific's involvement in lives and events was a blight that irreparably changed lives and led to macabre events that could not be so easily shrugged off. I wished it were that simple. She represented a morbid history, and as her daughter, I did by association.

The next morning, I awoke in Mephisto's bedroom to an empty bed and silence. No matter how much time I spent with him, I'd never get used to his silent stealth and the lethality that it showed. The oppressive tranquility of the room begged for sound to keep the thoughts away, because Mephisto and I had stayed up late trying to devise courses of actions to deal with the vampires and find Dr. Sumner. Eventually the evening devolved into me desperately performing location spells using me as a source and Mephisto offering consolatory smiles of support.

My continued denial of being Dr. Sumner's sire didn't mean we weren't connected. But it was by magic, not a sire bond, which spurred optimism that I could locate him through our magical connection. Mephisto's solemn smile turned pensive before he finally said. "Erin, stop." He encouraged me to eat, and after dinner, I showered and prepared for bed. I refused to sleep until he promised not to retaliate for the forced meeting. His reluctant concession hadn't convinced me that he wouldn't address the vampires about the situation. Mephisto managed a yes, but through teeth clenched so hard he could have made diamonds from coal.

I'd stopped with the magic, but my mind was a whirl of thoughts and plots. I couldn't even enjoy my 'I told you so moment' regarding Dr. Sumner's loss of magic because Mephisto's thoughts were revealed in his expression. That made Sumner even more defenseless.

Tugging the duvet closer to my chest, I sank deeper into it, giving me the false sense that I could burrow myself into a cocoon of safety and normality. Cory's words haunted me: *Can you stop?*

I should have stopped long before this. I should have left my exploration of magic as is and used safe magic. Protective, defensive, and offensive magic only.

After wallowing too long in guilt, I pulled myself out of the well of what-ifs because they served no purpose. I couldn't pretend that things were going to be business as usual with my ability to reverse vampirism lingering. I had to figure out a way to keep us safe. But that was easier said than done.

I swung my feet over the side of the bed and stood up, heading toward the door, determined to take control of the situation, when three abrupt knocks at the door stopped me mid trek.

Benton's shrewd scowl deepened at the appearance of my bed head and the sheets wrapped around my body to hide my nudity.

"You haven't answered your text messages and your phone is going to voicemail. Mephisto is waiting for you in security," he informed me.

Security? I took several slow breaths to ease the rising panic. He stopped me from closing the door. "They've waited this long, I'm sure they can wait for you to get dressed. Perhaps fix that," he said, waving a hand in the direction of my hair.

I flashed a wide smile. "Mephisto and I are good together. But me and you"—I extended my finger between us—"are truly the best couple."

He sneered, shaking his head and muttering something I couldn't make out. The edge of derision in his tone made it certain it wasn't nice or flattering.

I took a quick shower, tossed on a t-shirt and jeans, and headed for the security room where the Huntsmen were looking at several screens that gave different views of the property. My attention went to the view of the gate to the house. There was a car awaiting entry. Two vampires stood beside the vehicle, their eyes fixed in the direction of the cameras. The woman's short, coal-black hair was brushed back away from her skin. Vampirism hadn't stolen the soft brush of apricot over her ash-brown skin. Midnight eyes continued to look at the perimeter camera. *Vampires blinked.*

Why the hell isn't she blinking. The chartreuse long-sleeve dress made of light silk fabric and a scoop neck gave her ethereal silhouette a contrast to her angular features. Her expression gave nothing away, although I had an idea why they were here.

Platinum bangs fell over the brow of the parchment-pale man who accompanied her. Despite his washed-out appearance, his presence commanded attention. Wearing a forest-green slim fit button-down shirt with rolled-up sleeves, paired with dark olive slacks, he was dressed more casually. But his stern, determined look implied there wasn't anything casual about him.

Could they be the vampires with the unfamiliar scent from Dr. Sumner's home?

"How long have they been waiting?" I asked.

"About thirty minutes. They want to speak with you. Apparently, my home is the secondary stop when you can't be found at yours." Mephisto shared my frustration of people freely visiting my home as if I hadn't maintained an office.

Turning on the microphone and the video so they could see me, I asked, "What do you want?"

"Erin Jensen." The male vampire said my name with too much familiarity and with a tinge of an accent I struggled to place. Cajun? Creole? I struggled with deciphering between them, but it was definitely a dialect from farther south.

"You could have just called me from the comfort of your home in Louisiana, if you just wanted to talk." I took a stab at the location to further identify the accent. People and super-naturals moved, and these vampires could be new residents I hadn't met, although my gut was telling me that wasn't the case.

A smile lifted the corners of his lips, but there wasn't anything pleasant about it and the smile never made its way to his eyes. "I like to look a person in their eyes when we speak."

"Video chat?" I suggested. Pulling back his lips in what should have been a mirror of my expression showed nothing but malicious intent. He couldn't disguise it for the few minutes it took to negotiate an audience with me.

"But I'm here now," he pushed out through a tight smile, gritted teeth, and narrowed eyes. Mephisto stayed out of view of the camera, but I could see him noticeably tense. The reassuring look I cast in his direction did nothing to ease it.

"Who are you?"

Indignation flared and faded. "Xavier. Xavier Landry." The unabashed arrogance indicated that he believed I should know him.

The worst of any sect wasn't just discussed in school; it was wise to commit names and faces to memory whenever you learned the information, especially with vampires. It wasn't unheard of that vampires considered gone and forgotten had just learned the art of lying low and changing names until the hunt ended or their misdeeds and infamy quieted. Humans knew the names and faces of people who committed the most heinous crimes in the past and present. Due to vampires living longer than any other supernatural beings, they were given the privilege of reinventing their image. Unless their behavior threatened the tenuous relationship we had with humans and social standing, it was rarely handled. Xavier's name wasn't familiar but everything about his mien boasted he'd lived under the radar.

"Sorry you've come all this way, but I don't—"

"Please," his companion entreated, moving him aside. Her low melodious voice held a similar accent. If there was any hostility or malcontent intended, she was better skilled at hiding it. "We heard of what you're able to do and I am desperate for your help, which is why we consulted with your friend Jacob to determine the best way to talk to you." Emotions clung to her tremulous voice.

When she beckoned someone from the car, I switched my

view to another camera to see a young woman who looked to be in her late teens or very early twenties step from the car. Dark wide sorrowful eyes overtook her heart-shaped face. A round nose offset her sharp cheekbones that seemed out of place on her. Tightly coiled dark curls were piled on her head, and like the woman with her, the young vampire's umber skin maintained a warm coloring over her nose and cheeks. Underlying keenness in her appearance and swift grace verified she was a vampire. I wasn't sure if she looked that way from a recent feeding or if that was her normal look.

"I want to be human again," she whispered in a small voice. "Your friend is well taken care of, but we have not been completely honest. We consulted with him as a means to talk to you. But I wanted to make sure he was wholly human. He is."

Consulted. What a lovely way to say abducted and coerced into giving information about me.

I cursed the vampires in every language I could think of and came up with some creative four, six, and eight letter ones as well. But her appearance and optimism chipped away at my anger and reticence. Before me were vampires, possibly dangerous vampires, who wished me harm, but I saw a desperate vampire, probably under the age of eighteen, which was the legal age to give consent to be changed. What if she was younger than she appeared? Even if she was the age of consent and regretted the decision and I could reverse that for her, should I?

Seeing my resolve diminish, Mephisto shook his head.

I mouthed, "Let me hear them out."

His lips pressed into a disapproving line, and he allowed every emotion he was feeling to course over his face. It served as a reminder of how much he muted himself here, outside the Veil. It also piqued my desire to see him fully. Raw, unfettered, brutal Mephisto.

"One moment," I told the young vampire, whose face in the camera obscured the other two who had moved off to the background.

I wasn't sure when it happened. Clayton, Simeon, and Kai had stepped out of the room, and Mephisto had guided me to the wall. My back was pressed against it, one arm stretched above me, and his face inches from me. The fingers of his other hand cupped my chin, raising it to eyes steeled with conviction.

"What are you doing?" he growled.

"I need to talk to her. I want to hear her story and get Dr. Sumner back."

Assessing me for a long time, he sighed. "You have no plans of entertaining her request to be changed back?"

My lips pressed tightly together; I allowed the growing tension between us to supply the answer.

"Erin, you don't know how reversing vampirism will affect you, your magic, or the people involved. Sumner's magic has gone, but is it temporarily? I understand taking that risk for Jacob"—hearing Dr. Sumner referred to by only his first name was still weird—"but a stranger? You're making decisions on limited information and putting your safety at risk."

"Let me at least hear her out. I doubt she'll give me back Dr. Sumner without me doing at least that."

Mephisto's look of reprimand said more than any words could. He didn't trust them. I didn't distrust them, and I was approaching the situation with a high level of apprehension and skepticism, but I didn't want to be closed off to opportunities of how my magic could help in a way diametric to that of my mother and the elves.

"If nothing else we'll get Dr. Sumner back, find out if they are involved with Landon's disappearance and if they have any ill intent toward me. They learned of my abilities and their first act is to bring the young vampire here? It's been days since the discovery. If their intention was to hurt me, wouldn't they have made an attempt on my life instead of taking Dr. Sumner?"

His objection didn't waver as his face moved closer to me, eyes in deep concentration as he traced the lines of my face, his lips beveling into a rigid frown. It made me recall the many times he admitted I was his weakness. Making the guilt feel worse.

"I will be careful," I promised.

"You can't make promises on their actions," he countered.

"So, we turn them away and never learn their intention? It seems so short sighted."

"Treat them as a potential threat with everything. I plan to do the same. Their decision to come here may have deadly consequences."

Guilt quickly sparked into panic. "You plan to kill every vampire you believe will be a threat to me?"

His eyes possessed fierce determination and a harsh truth. "This is not a time to give the benefit of the doubt to anyone. When you extended it to Landon, Jacob became the consequence. If we had handled it the way I suggested, things would have been different. You want to attribute virtues to me that I do not possess. I have always been a pragmatist and I will remain so while dealing with this situation. I am not a monster, but I am prepared to be one if necessary. It was unfair of me to show you a softer or gentler side without making sure you were explicitly aware of the other side."

"Was I present during this performance of the softer, gentler Mephisto who didn't show pragmatism at every turn and disguised the lurking monster?" I asked. His dark chuckle filled the space. I couldn't tell if he was insulted or amused. "I know what you're capable of. It didn't deter me before and it won't now. I'm asking that you recognize that you're not in the Veil and respond accordingly," I countered.

I was aware that in the Veil, he dealt with the worst of the worst with unfettered violence, strategy, and magic, and what I'd seen was just a fraction of his capabilities. The short time he spent there must have rekindled it. I didn't want to think about navigating our relationship dealing with various versions of Mephisto.

"What is your true nam—?"

Before I could fully finish my request, he leaned down and whispered it to me, dropping the glamour to reveal his true face, as well. Then it was up again with the ease of taking a breath. "Erin, you will get all of me. The true me. Parts you will love and other parts I ask that you accept and at the very least, understand."

I nodded. "I do. But I request that you do the same. I'm not naïve and I am just as pragmatic. It just doesn't mirror yours. I acknowledge that sometimes I'm fighting against baggage, but I'm not shy about wallowing in the gray if I need to. Let's talk to them. Please."

He gave me a reluctant half nod and moved aside, giving me space to return to the cameras. The vampires were still standing, their positions unchanged. They didn't seem to possess the urge to assimilate and appear anything close to human. They stood with statue-like stillness, not pretending to breathe, and never softened their eyes that were dark pools of abyss. Although some might have found their behavior uncomfortable, I was comforted by it. It was a blatant reminder that I wasn't dealing with humans. They'd abandoned all aspects of it and had no desire to show any hints of it. I wouldn't forget.

While we spoke, Kai, Simeon, and Clayton returned to the security room and gave Mephisto a slight nod.

"My office is safe for conversation with them. Invite them in," he said.

"We can talk, come in," I told them, opening the gate for them.

By the time I'd made it to the entrance, Benton had

opened the door to the vampires. The youngest vampire was in front. As I moved toward them, I was quickly met with a wall of four bodies. The back of Clayton's free-flowing locs blocked my view. Kai's black t-shirt obstructed my view to the right and Simon's beige tunic to the left, and Mephisto had sidled close enough that I'd have to side-step him to get through.

I huffed a low demand to move that no one responded to.

"Go ahead, speak," Clayton urged, his tone devoid of the light warmth it often held. Instead, it was blistering with an air of lethal intent.

"If hostility is what you offer, then perhaps we need to plan another time to speak with Ms. Jensen. We'll keep Dr. Sumner safe until then," Xavier snapped.

When I tried to navigate around Mephisto, he wrapped his hand around my waist, pulling me closer to him and rendering me immobile. Using magic against someone when they didn't use it on you first is an act of aggression, and probably worse if it's the person you're dating. But I gave him a warning to show I wasn't above it. With vampires' hearing, I couldn't speak, but everything I needed to get across made its way into my sneer. Mephisto smirked and kept his hold on me.

"I just want your help, the hostility doesn't bother me," said the small voice from the desperate young vampire. Feeling Mephisto's eyes on me, I looked up at him. Whatever he saw caused him to release me. At his movement, the wall of bodies separated, and I was face to face with the trio. If being flanked by the hostile quad bothered the vampires while I led them to Mephisto's office, they didn't show it. Their faces were constant blank slates that allowed their gaze to breeze over the three men who'd fanned out to opposite corners of the room.

And I thought shifters were dramatic. *Y'all doing too much.*

The vampires did a quick sweep of the room and gave me

a scrutinizing look, making me wonder if they knew that the room had been spelled to prevent them Wynding. The disadvantage of the spell meant none of us could, either. I planned on this being a civil engagement without the use of magic. Hope for the best but prepare for the worst.

"I'm Lilith," the young vampire offered. "Annalise, and you've been introduced to Xavier."

"Landry?" I asked, attempting to confirm whether they'd all been sired by the same vampire. It was common practice to adopt a sire's name with the change.

"Yes, but he's not who sired me." Her voice wavered. I was drawn to her anguished eyes and unshed tears. "Technically I'm a Bianchi, one of the last."

Xavier had given his last name with an air of importance, but there was shame in her admission.

"As in Calder Bianchi?" I asked.

She nodded. Calder Bianchi was one of the most notorious vampires, known for rash binges creating vampires and leaving them to fend for themselves. Leaving them rabid, impulsive, and unable to manage their new abilities and thirsts. Based on everything I'd read about him, having him as a mentor wasn't of any benefit since he hadn't mastered his own adolescent sensibilities despite being over half a century old. He was famous for his preternatural abilities and his charm, which allowed him to obtain rare, sought after magical objects. He caused fights between witch covens and mage consortiums. He'd destroyed entire vampire families for the most minor slights. And compelled humans with reckless abandonment. His behaviors eventually led to his infamy and downfall. Some believed his behavior inched supernaturals to revealing their existence. Like Landon, he was one of the few vampires who could compel other vamps and supernaturals, putting him in a position of being both admired and feared—a precarious place to be.

Lilith moving closer to me triggered Mephisto's hands to

clench into tight balls at his sides, while Clayton treated me to a side-look of disapproval. Kai offered a cool warning and Simeon a sharp look of caution.

"Can you tell me about your change?" I asked.

Her smile was weak, barely lifting her lips. "You've seen pictures of him and you're aware of how charming he was. I never expected someone like him to have any interest in me. He approached me while I was reading in the library." That memory lifted her mood. Standing taller, she held my gaze as she continued. "He invited me out. It was such an exciting night of dining, partying, and enjoying life in a way I never thought was possible for a woman like me. That night, when he asked me if I wanted more out of life, I couldn't help but say yes. Of course, I wanted more, who wouldn't? I had no idea what I was agreeing to—or perhaps I did, but in the moment, I didn't care." Her eyes dropped to the floor. "The next morning, I awoke a vampire. Alone and confused—"

"Xavier took you into his family?" I asked.

She nodded, looking fondly at the pair of vampires. Their cool expressions of indifference fell, and they returned her look.

"They are my family, but I don't want to be like this. I never wanted this, and if you have the ability to undo it, I beg that you do. Please."

Taking in her words, I studied her then directed my attention to the other vampires. After a moment of deliberation and poor attempts at ignoring Mephisto's hard gaze, I asked, "How long have you been a vampire?"

The doe-eyed vampire lifted her gaze from the floor to meet mine. "Twenty years as a vampire."

"What's your vampire birthday?"

She provided it with a tremulous voice and whispered, "I was turned two days after my eighteenth birthday."

Nodding, my expression softened at her hopeful look.

"Does that matter? Does the age of the vampire determine if you can undo it?"

"I don't know. I've only reversed it once and he wasn't completely changed. I'm not sure what the results would be for a true vampire of your age. Are you willing to be my first?"

Unable to contain his objections, Mephisto murmured my name. I nodded and locked eyes with him, hoping to give him the assurance he needed. It wasn't enough. "If I can help," I added, "I need to help her. Please allow me to do this."

With brows inched together, he studied me for a long moment, then eventually nodded his concession.

"When he approached you," I asked Lilith, "did you know he was a vampire?"

"No. I just found myself charmed by him. I suspected he wasn't human. And his offer came with questionable consequences, but it didn't seem important. The foolishness of youth." She sighed. "I was a bored young woman living a mundane life. I live daily with the regret of a decision made from boredom." She offered a bleak smile.

Her expression moved between blankness and immense sorrow as she inched even closer to me with a pleading expression.

"What's your zodiac sign? Human zodiac sign?" I asked, causing confusion to sweep over her face.

"Sagittarius." The words had just slipped from her lips, and that quick admission without thought gave me the information I needed. Unfortunately, we came to the same conclusion at the same time. Teeth bared, she lunged at me. With barely any time to react, I hit her with a surge of magic that slammed her into the back wall where I kept her pinned once she'd come to her feet.

Violent shudders at futile attempts to Wynd were an indicator she was older than she'd attempted to lead me to think. It often depended on who sired them and their abilities, but young vampires rarely had the ability to Wynd. The older the vampire, the easier they were able to travel in that manner. She'd lied about who sired her. I didn't know how much of the rest was utter bullshit.

I stared at her. "It's easy to lie about a birthday, but we automatically respond to our signs because it's what we know." Even if you didn't believe in the Zodiac having any bearing on your life and could not care less, people knew their sign. "It was early October when Calder was captured by an angry witch, whose coven he had attacked for funsies, I guess. That's not such a little-known fact. No one heard from him after that, putting his true death around that time. He's never been one to lie low. He wore his infamy as a badge. Either he miraculously resurfaced after his true death, or you are lying through your fangs. We both know it's the latter. But I do appreciate a good performance. Perfection." I gave her a chef's kiss. "The tremulous pained voice. The you *want more out of life* that definitely tugged at my heart. How could I not want to help after that? You kept your story vague to ensure you could be consistent with any follow-up questions. At least you're aware which tactics to use to prevent being caught in a lie. But I guess you're not quite skilled at it." My eyes roved over the trio of vampires. "I'm sure whenever a situation needs to be manipulated, they just trot you out with your big eyes, docile appearance, amicable demeanor, and faux sincerity."

Her mask of gentility dropped, pulling her lips back into baring her teeth. If she wasn't restrained, she'd be using them against me.

"Whether it's changing an existing vampire or stopping a change, you don't interfere in our business. You have no right!" She growled out her words, her voice carrying a sharp edge of ice that sliced through the air. Not a vestige of the veneration and meekness remained. She was a striking contradiction to her appearance.

"He was my friend and he didn't want to be a vampire. So, it was well within my rights to make sure he wasn't."

"You took from us!" she accused, her voice a sharp rasp that dripped with anger and resentment.

"And you took from me. Where is Dr. Sumner?"

"From you," she scoffed. "He is not yours to take. When Landon started the process, he became ours. The moment you did that, he should have ripped your throat out!" She was seething more than Xavier, which made me think she may have been the architect of this plan. Maybe even the head.

"There goes the sweet cloying tone. Even that was fake." I scoffed at the vampires who had been wrangled to the ground by Clayton and Simeon before they could intervene.

"He was far more curious about your magic and cautious of your life than he should have been." Anger swelled in Lilith's expression as her eyes grew arctic cold. If she were in Landon's place, there was absolutely no doubt I'd be dead.

"Is Landon dead?" I asked.

"If my orders were followed, then yes."

Xavier's and Annalise's eyes snapped in her direction before they removed the aghast shock from their faces. *Looked like someone didn't follow protocol.*

She was a wild card. Dr. Sumner wasn't safe.

Moving closer, Mephisto sidled in next to me and leaned in, humor in his tone. "Please allow me to do this?" He mocked my earlier request in a whisper. "As if I have the ability to *let* you do anything. I can barely get compromises from you."

"Hey," I said, "you're making it seem like I'm out here just rogue and throwing caution to the wind."

"I wouldn't say caution to the wind. I am aware that no one is in the position to *let* you do anything. I'm just pointing out the obvious." Mephisto's eyes breezed over the deceptive vampire. "Did you know the entire time she was lying?"

"No. But something was off. Too much effort put into

looking harmless." Dallas's deception had affected me harder than I expected. He wasn't trying. Just an innocuous, handsome vampire who appeared to accept his existence as one but not love it the way the others did.

Lilith's eyes flickered in anger, but the way they settled into a calm made me nervous. The change wasn't missed by Mephisto, either. While we kept the vampires secured, Kai returned with Benton and zirconium metal cuffs with sigils on them. Zirconium weakened vampires, providing an advantage if you had the ability to place them on them. That was a harder feat. I couldn't decipher the sigils on the locks.

Xavier hadn't given up his fight to be released. "Let go of me," he demanded. Desperation edged into his command that for a few moments overshadowed his curiosity about Mephisto and the Huntsmen. His intense glare reflected his thoughts as he attempted to figure out the men who had so quickly and easily rendered a vampire immobile.

He'd probably assumed they were shifters until Clay enclosed the manacles around his wrist and whispered a spell. The locks glowed and the vampire's fight drained from him before he collapsed. Annalise and Lilith received the same treatment.

"They'll stay asleep until awakened," Benton informed me. He'd joined in the furtive looks being exchanged by the men. I appeared to be the only one clueless.

"He's in the group chat, too!?" My complaint sounded whinier than intended, but I hated feeling as if I was missing vital communication. "As long as I'm with you all, I forbid this type of communication."

I willingly admit that my objections were quickly devolving into the grumblings of a petulant child, and I didn't care. My mandate was met with a collective of smirks that turned into smug defiance. A palpable air of arrogance rippled through the room of men who were not accustomed to obeying the demands of others.

"I'm involved and should know what's going on," I said.

"We're trying to determine what to do with them," Mephisto told me. "You realize that Lilith had every intention of killing you?"

I nodded. I'd gotten my answer. They weren't here to talk. Used deception to gain entrance with the sole purpose of killing me. Obviously, I'd been in Madison's bureaucratic Supernatural Task Force world too long, because my first thoughts weren't about my protection but about how my response to these vampires could cause instability in the supernatural world. If it was handled by the Huntsmen, it would eventually threaten their anonymity.

"Your safety is more of a concern than maintaining my anonymity," Mephisto said in response to me expressing my worries.

"We have diverging concerns," I admitted softly, looking at each one of them. "I don't know your plans, whether you'll stay here or return to the Veil." The idea of Mephisto doing that sent a pang through me. "Or split your lives between the two worlds. The revelation of gods living among them won't be handled lightly by humans or other supernaturals. Those who've dealt with you only have their speculations of what you may be, but no hard evidence. Revealing yourself will cause a lot of apprehension. Your magic immunity, inability to be killed—"

"I can be killed," he reminded me.

"With Omni swords." It wasn't just the swords but the spells engraved on them that allowed the Huntsmen to be killed. The Veil had as many supernaturals as we did, including elves at one time. But thanks to my mother, the elves were wiped out in an act of vengeance at feeling slighted by their refusal to join her.

"Your magic is stronger than anyone else's. Their fear of you will lead to a reactionary response. Promise me, you won't reject being cautious of this for me."

"No. Do not limit me with requests like that," he said remorsefully through a gritted smile. He looked at the sleeping vampires.

"I need to question them and find out where Dr. Sumner is, and I need to inform Robyn." I frowned at that, giving up any pretense that she was really in charge. "Dallas and Elon." That left a foul taste in my mouth.

"They also need to be questioned to determine how far the knowledge of your abilities has reached and if this was just the first of a line of attempts on your life." His voice was laden with heated contempt and the promise of violence.

"Just question them for now. Madison needs to be involved as well."

He shook his head. "I question them, and they pay for trying to kill you. These attacks by the vampires can no longer be tolerated," he said, advancing on Xavier.

When I took hold of his arm, he looked down at it before drawing his eyes up to my face. He frowned at my expression. Concern. It shadowed all the emotions I was feeling.

"Don't hold me to moralities of this world that would ensure my demise in mine," he entreated in a whisper before removing my hand from his arm.

CHAPTER 9

Mephisto dragged the vampires to the wall and set them next to each other against it. Mephisto, Kai, Simeon, and Clay all had their swords and knives in a sheath at their thighs.

Simeon frowned. "It is not a good sign that this is no longer a local issue," he said to me. "We need to find out everything they know about you. Killing you because of Dr. Sumner may be one of the many reasons they want you dead."

"Many reasons?" I whispered, looking over at the sleeping vampires.

"Elves aren't extinct. That can be jarring information. Just as there is a small community here, do you believe there aren't others around the world? It may be nothing more than a small grouping of three or four, but if they are as talented as Fabian and Elizabeth, that could be trouble for many," Clayton provided.

"It is possible that the elves have allied with the vampires. This could be more complicated than anticipated," Kai said.

"Could Alex have mistaken elven magic for witch magic?" Kai asked me. His question was asked in a manner that led me to believe I'd missed a discussion they'd had among themselves. That was becoming increasingly annoying.

"Why do you believe elves are involved? Nothing indicates that," I pressed.

"The ward was removed by magic. It was a simple ward that anyone could have removed. They showed up without knowing anything about Mephisto, just that you were here. They didn't bring someone who possess magic with them. Seems like a poor strategic move. It would make sense for them to bring the people who removed the ward, unless they want that person to remain unknown. Who would have the most motivation to do that?"

"Just like the shifters all over the world awoke one morning to a new existence of being immune to magic in all forms, there are elves who awoke to being magicless for several days only for it to be returned without reason. How many know it's because of you? I doubt the elves here would have kept it to themselves. They'd want the others to know how dangerous you can be. So, if it were me, I'd want to stay under your radar and be the enemy you don't know," Clayton considered.

"You said that Alex felt magic but didn't feel confident that it was a witch. 'A person with magic' is what he indicated. Correct?" Benton inquired.

I nodded.

"How proficient are they? This is a new skill, and distinguishing between the various types of magic is very difficult," he offered.

My frown deepened as my eyes trailed from the men to the vampires. It was doubtful that Landon told them what I'd done without telling them what I was.

"We won't know until we ask them." I nudged my head in the direction of the vampires.

"Then let's ask them," Mephisto said, but I got the impression he wasn't convinced we'd get answers. He left the room and returned with the Obscuro Mors stake in hand.

He whispered a spell, the bindings on the vampires glowed, and they awoke. Shaking off the magically induced sleep, they shot contemptuous looks at the manacles before shifting their attention to us. Lilith's and Anna's eyes breezed over everyone in the room. Xavier homed in on Mephisto, then he glanced at the Obscuro Mors, then his steely glare returned to Mephisto, where it stayed. Clearly, he viewed him as the greatest threat in the room, and Mephisto did nothing to disabuse him of that belief.

Mephisto inched closer to Xavier. The cold cruelty of his nature as a god responsible for maintaining order among the most powerful flooded into the dark pools of his eyes. Beast. Discarding the magic used to mask their magic, the vampires' heightened curiosity flashed in their faces.

Xavier looked with calculated curiosity, Anna with abhorrence and speculation. The youngest vampire was dismissive. I couldn't determine if it was rooted in naiveté or arrogance about her own abilities.

The air was suffocatingly thick with tension, and The Huntsmen closed around the vampires with slow, predatory movements that exuded a domineering aura of unforgiving violence and sadistic cruelty. I knew they needed that for their position in the Veil, but the knowledge didn't make it any less concerning. It hit me with the sudden urge to close the Veil, keep them here, with the hope that they'd abandon the level of brutality they needed to exist in that world. I wanted them to be the men they presented here. But in doing so, would I be essentially forcing them to change, or would it be a conformity they would willingly accept? Perhaps, Clay, Simeon and Mephisto could. But not Kai.

From across the room Benton watched the vampires cautiously.

Xavier was the first to come to his feet, a pompous smirk

hitched to the corners of his lips. The other two followed. He looked down at the manacles and then to Mephisto.

"When you must restrict another's power, you only show your weakness," he hissed in a venomous whisper that cut through the air like a serrated blade.

"I assure you, it is not weakness that I am showing, it is restraint. If you believe for one moment that I couldn't end your existence before you could form a thought on how to best me, then you are more foolish than I initially believed." The dark shadow of Mephisto's looming threat washed over his face. Xavier's arrogant façade dropped for a few moments before he reasserted it. He approached Mephisto, positioning himself inches from him. His eyes narrowed.

"What are you?" Xavier asked, pulling his eyes from Mephisto and giving a sweeping look in the direction of the others. No longer masking their otherworldliness, their miens and energy were nothing the vampires would ever see in the fae, mages, or shifters. Even the less seen supernaturals didn't possess such presence.

"You want to kill Erin. Why?" Mephisto's lethal tone asked, ignoring Xavier's inquiry. Despite standing directly in front of Xavier, Mephisto directed the question to Lilith, the soft-faced, decorous woman who presented with none of those qualities now. A chill ran through me at the icy stare that had landed on me. With the camouflage gone and the deception abandoned, she smugly presented her true self. I was reminded that lamb-like vampires typically were the true monsters. Often assassins disguised themselves as the beautifully innocent, charmers, and subtly unassuming.

"You interfered with vampire business. The mere fact you dared do so makes you worthy of death."

"I was saving my friend," I asserted.

She scoffed, furling back her lips to reveal her fangs. All hints of humanity were gone from this woman. I held her gaze with effort because I refused to cower, but it was an inhumane abyss of darkness that effortlessly revealed the cruelty she wouldn't mind inflicting if given the chance.

I wouldn't display fear to this toddler.

"She has no plans of ever doing that again. It was done to save someone she cared about. Landon should have made a different choice. He should be the target of your blame," Mephisto responded.

"It is directed at the right target. The hybrid creature who reneged on her agreement to give him family. We were anticipating those new vampires." Xavier's expression flashed the same blaze of excitement and curious expectation Landon had when I'd revealed what I was.

"Then you understand why I couldn't fulfill the obligation," I said.

His shrewd look turned from me to the Huntsmen. Studying them for several moments he made a harumph sound. "Elf-god hybrid," he whispered to himself, repeating how I'd described myself to Landon. "Gods or elves or are you all hybrids as well?" he asked no one in particular, although he'd made the assumption that we were all the same. In the room with them, if I showed any ethereal uniqueness, it was outshone by the Huntsmen.

They remained silent and expressionless, heightening the vampires' whetted curiosity.

"Whatever benefits of the special vampire you would have created doesn't exceed the detriment someone like you existing can cause." The assertion came from Annalise, the one I had marked as being the most reasonable of the three.

"I have no intention of undoing vampirism," I said softly, approaching them with apprehension. Their manacles suppressed some of their preternatural abilities, but it wasn't entirely gone.

"You exist. That is the problem. Can your word be accepted when people can be forced, coerced, or bribed into compliance?" Lilith's frown and sharp eyes depicted a person who had lived far longer than her appearance would indicate. "Landon shouldn't have left without being able to guarantee that the problem had been handled. He deserved our response to his failure."

The last part unnerved me. Their response. He controlled the north, so I assumed these were major players in the south, but I hadn't kept up with the politics and key people there. Now I wished that I had. I maintained my composure.

"True. I have no intention of doing it again. Stay away from my friends and loved ones, and my ability to undo vampirism will never be a concern of yours."

Xavier's expression had softened, but I wasn't sure if it was a ploy. "And you would make an oath to that?"

"Since Landon is the ruling vampire here, the oath should be with him," I asserted, feeling Mephisto's weighted narrowed eyes on me. He probably wished I was included in their magical group chat now. "Give me Dr. Sumner and Landon back and we can pretend you didn't try to kill me. But I expect the same oath from you. No more attempts on my life or my friends or my loved ones. Can you do that?"

Lilith's earlier comments about Landon gnawed, and I hated the guilt that shrouded me like a heavy blanket. Shrugging it off was damn near impossible.

"Landon is probably dead by now," Lilith shot back. "And if we don't return, your friend will be next. You don't have the advantage you believe you have."

My eyes dropped to the Obscuro Mors in Mephisto's hands, drawing their eyes to it. A flicker of fear flashed over their faces for only a moment. I wasn't sure who it would affect because the Obscuro Mors ended the bloodline of the staked vampire, and they hadn't given me the indication that they were from the same line. Despite my veiled threat, I wasn't prepared to eliminate an entire bloodline for the misbehavior of three individuals. Judging from Mephisto's expression, we shared the same viewpoint.

Mephisto made a quick sharp invocation. The sigils on the manacles glowed to ember and the vampires collapsed to the ground without warning. Within seconds, Mephisto was next to me and his fingers linked with mine, leading me out of his office, through the house, and into the room I'd once dubbed the war room.

In an attempt to ignore his imposing presence, I looked out the large bay window at the enchanting landscape that was enhanced by the soft melon cast of the sun.

Mephisto stood in the center of the room, his gaze distant and his expression a mixture of concern and frustration. His gaze followed mine to the scenic view of brightly colored blooms and vibrant mature trees. It served its purpose as a distraction from the teeming tension and guarded silence that brewed between us. Once I felt his gaze on me, I turned to face him. Despite the surprising warmth and coziness of the room, our silence didn't mirror it.

"What are you doing, Erin?"

"I want Dr. Sumner returned to his home."

"That's understandable, but why are you negotiating for Landon? Let them handle him the way they see fit."

"Because I won't make an oath to them, just Landon."

"An oath that will be short lived. Do you believe the plans I have for him are different than theirs?"

His candor felt like a physical blow knocking the breath out of me. It took a few minutes to rebound. "He's the devil I know. He dies, another vampire controls the city. What if that one's worse? Or what if it becomes the trio in your office?"

"It won't be them. I have no intention of allowing them to leave."

"Your game plan is to wipe out the vampires?" I shoved my fingers through my hair, feeling the heat of my frustration radiate off my skin. Predator. Beast. Same people, different titles from Malific. All the descriptors used when talking about the Huntsmen revived themselves vividly in my mind.

I couldn't help but take his silence as an implicit yes. "I *will* hold you to the same rules of this world. Because this is where we are. We aren't wiping out the vampires."

"When did I suggest that?" he asked, clearing the distance between us, the rasp of his voice low. His lips pressed to mine, his response feeling like a conquest. Not a conquest, a seduction, that I was fully attuned to. Pulling away, his dark eyes held me captured in their intensity. "I'm only campaigning for your safety, and if it must be gained through initial acts of violence then so be it. You wanted to live without apologizing for who you are, but I feel that you are too accommodating and entreating for people to accept who you are."

"That's not it. My job called for me to straddle the line between gray and grayer." Many times, Mephisto was behind me toeing that line. "I am comfortable there, but I am aware of how people viewed me as a person who was the embodiment of death with a simple kiss. I took magic and left behind a shell of a person. Now I have my own magic—powerful magic. I defaulted on a debt I incurred. We can't ignore that. That decision had consequences that I didn't like, so I used my powerful magic to fix it and—"

I held up my hand when Mephisto attempted to rebut. "I really appreciate you took my side on this matter. I know you'll do that always, while ignoring my role in causing the retaliation. I own up to what I've done to incite Landon's act. And Landon will pay for what he did to Dr. Sumner, and those assholes in your office, too. But it shouldn't be a death sentence for Landon, nor should we kill off the vampires for the mistake of four. I'll commit to the oath with conditions." I took a deep breath. "Landon must agree to one that will restrict him from forcing my hand to sire more vampires and protect the ones I love. I shouldn't have accepted an open debt, nor reneged on it. But I can't create vampires with him. I've done too much to change this world already. I'll deal with Landon because he is the devil I know and can handle."

"If he's dead, that will no longer be an option," Mephisto pointed out.

"Hopefully he's not."

The command had been given by Lilith; the other two wanted him alive. It made sense to do so because he was the source of information about me, the one I dealt with. His death would make the Northern vampires more accommo- dating. It just wasn't worth it. I hoped whoever was holding him saw Lilith as the arrogant, impulsive, and volatile vamp she'd exhibited with me and disobeyed her command.

The thunderous sound of plaster and drywall being demolished pulled me from my thoughts.

Debris, dust, and particles of plaster made the area hazy, but I could see the swarm of bodies spilling into the house, moving with the swiftness that vampires were known for. The magic Mephisto released hit two of the approaching vamps, sending them out through the gaping hole in the wall left by whatever explosive device they used to remove it.

The other vampires moved with a single-sight mission. I knew what it was. Rushing back to the room where we'd secured the three vampires, I found Lilith cradled in the arms of a tall female vampire. Her eyes landed on me, recognition in them along with the prolific debate. I was a target. Tossing an offensive ball of magic in her direction, it hit the wall as she disappeared with Lilith.

Someone grabbed me from behind. I slammed my head back into their nose, tossed them over my shoulder. My foot stomped down hard on the floor, missing the vampire. He swiped my feet with his hand, sending me crashing to the ground.

Kneeling over me, he bared his fangs before moving toward my neck. My cupped hand pushed into his chin to prevent access. The fight to keep him from biting me made it hard to use any defensive magic that wouldn't affect me, too, which I knew was intentional. I needed to use contact magic—the *Venenum* spell, the one I used on Fabian that pulled away life. Would it initiate a true death for a vampire? I was about to find out. The spell required a dab of my blood. I ran one of my fingers over his razor-sharp fangs. Whispering the spell, I saw the vampire shudder. His persistence to bite me waned some, but it was still a challenge to ward off his attack. Then he was back at full strength. It hadn't worked. I was exerting more pressure on his chin to either raise his neck or get a finger close to his eyes when he was snatched up.

Mephisto's movements were blurs of movement and left a lifeless vampire whose head was twisted at an odd angle, his mouth gaping open and face distorted in shock as he lay at my feet. That wouldn't kill a vampire, but the wood I grabbed from the splinters that littered the room would. I drove it into the vampire's chest, completing the job.

Mephisto moved to me, touching my arm. His gentle touch didn't possess the level of unfettered anger and violence thirst that dwelled in his face. "Are you okay?"

I nodded, finding it difficult to maintain his gaze. Hostility, violence, power-lust, and raw fury were looks I'd seen hundreds of times and thought I'd developed an immunity to them. Mephisto was more. Powerful magic thrummed from him as if it was shoved into packaging far too small and needed an escape. He'd worn the refined mask of geniality and now he'd discarded it entirely.

"Find a safe spot to hide, please," he urged before he whipped around, plucking the lunging vampire mid-air as though its over-six-foot-tall build was a waif. The air filled with the nauseating sounds of bones cracking, wails of pain, and thuds of bodies slamming to the ground. Scanning my surroundings, I took inventory of the chaos. Simeon and

Clayton were on opposite sides of the room, fighting off cadres of vampires whose sole focus was to get to me.

Feeling naïve that I ever thought this could be handled amicably, I yanked the stake out the vampire who was now at the end stage of a vampire's death. No amount of feeding would save him. I headed for the room where Mephisto stored his magical objects, which seemed like it would be the most secure room in the house. On the way out, I glanced at the destroyed wall. The twenty or so vampires that had come through it could have easily destroyed the door instead of the wall. This was their declaration of hostility and unspeakable violence they'd planned to inflict to get to me.

Heading for the room, I was met with another thunderous sound and watched in horror as the wall to my right collapsed. Dropping the stake, vision obscured by the cloud of dust and particles, I turned toward the group spilling through it and expelled the strongest magic I could summon. A cacophony of crashing noises and grunts filled the room as the blast of magic smacked into them. Quickly snatching up the stake before they could recover, I drove it into the one closest to me. Snatching it out of his heart and spinning from him, the body coming to stand was met with my elbow smashing hard into his nose. I wasn't sure if it broke, but it was enough to make the vamp blurry eyed and distort their vision. Some of the dust cleared to give me a view of Kai and his look of keen determination. His eyes swept over me. "You okay?"

I nodded.

"Go," he urged. Any feelings to stay and assist went away when he flashed a dark smirk that seemed a little too excited as he snatched two vampires by their shirts. Stepping out through the destroyed wall, he expanded his wings and then he was soaring to the skies with the vampires. Where I was sure he'd drop them before ending their vampire existence.

I hauled myself to the room, scanning my finger on the

entry pad, preparing to lock myself away, when I heard Xavier's familiar voice.

"I'll take you to your friend," he announced softly. The venom from earlier had completely depleted from his voice.

"Or you can bring him to me," I countered.

Huffing a sigh, he said, "I don't want you dead. But we need to explore your magic. Perhaps we can make a mutually beneficial arrangement."

Mutually beneficial? Yeah, more like if we see you as a threat, we'll let you decide how you die.

He lifted his hand up in surrender, and I watched him carefully as he removed his phone from his pocket and started to approach.

"Don't come near me," I commanded, trying to ignore the soundtrack of violence around us. But the sound of crashing bodies, demolished walls, and unfettered violence was hard to disregard.

Oddly, they sent my thoughts to Benton and his safety. I hadn't seen him. I didn't know what his fighting skills were, and as a Druid, he was a wealth of knowledge without magic. None of the Huntsmen would let him get hurt, so I refocused on Xavier who kneeled to slide his phone to me. Snatching it up, I kept a careful eye on him before glancing at the screen of a live feed that gave me a frontal view of Dr. Sumner in a posh-looking room. He was seated on an off-white sofa, rich brown wood with intricate detailing accenting the curved arms of the sofa. An expensive-looking coffee table was on a patterned rug. I took in the warm taupe walls complemented by what I assumed were original pieces of art. Sculptures on pedestals were on the far end of the view.

Dr. Sumner looked miserable, his eyes dropping to the plate of food on the table in front of him. His eyes kept drifting to the right where I suspected whoever was guarding him was stationed.

The room wasn't familiar to me, and I searched for

anything that would be identifying, which was the art. But I couldn't make out the artist's name on the bottom of the canvases.

My attention went back to Dr. Sumner's pensive expression as if I could determine the location from there. At least he was comfortable. That gave me a modicum of relief.

"See, he's fine." But I heard the unvoiced *for now* in Xavier's tone.

I took another look at the room, but before I could figure out a way to send the livestream to my phone, Xavier snatched it from me and returned to the distance we had before. Most of the room had been committed to my memory and I'd be able to identify it.

"If he's hurt—"

"Hold your threats. As I said, he is safe. My only desire is to explore the extent of your abilities. He's a means to that."

"Lilith's attempt to murder me is making that hard to believe."

His heavy sigh wasn't directed at me but at Lilith, something I felt sure he'd done on numerous occasions. "Although I do not agree with her reaction—"

"Attempted murder," I corrected.

He glared. "Her response to your insertion into our affairs was warranted. But it was our intention to keep you alive. Lilith panicked when her ruse was discovered."

Ruse. Such an innocuous word to describe that level of deception. "And was her response to Landon warranted?"

The genial mask fell, replaced by a storm cloud of anger and frustration moving over his face. How much had his patience thinned from dealing with the impulsive and violent Lilith?

"See, you can't trust her! How can I trust you when your trio has someone so unpredictable in it? You are going to bring Dr. Sumner to me."

Xavier's dark ominous chuckle overtook the space

between us. "I don't believe I led you to believe that was even a choice. In my attempt to be polite, I must have misled you into believing you had a say in that. You have the choice to come willingly, improving your chances that you and your friend will be released, or you will come by force."

The moment he made the threat, I was calling on magic, ready to level him and anyone in the area. Nothing. It took everything in me not to toggle my hands as if it was on the flicks.

I made another attempt, Xavier's miscreant smile turning to a roar of laughter.

"Is something wrong, Erin?"

I didn't have magic.

What the fuck was going on?

CHAPTER 10

Xavier's taunting smile was short-lived, turning at Mephisto's approach. Before he could react, he was met with Mephisto's fist slamming into his jaw. It sent him back, but not with the same force that his strikes had with the other vampires. Mephisto moved like a skilled fighter but not in the same lithe, graceful, swift movement I was accustomed too. Xavier's return punch caused Mephisto to shuffle back several feet, his eyes widening in shock at the unexpected land.

Mephisto's jaw clenched, driving in the point that we were magicless. When Simeon attempted to use his, his expression changed to shocked fear. Switching strategies, he grabbed the vampire next to him and knocked him into the wall, his knife penetrating the wall instead of the vampire who maneuvered from his grip. Simeon's mouth parted and he blinked several times, hazarding a look in my direction. The only thing I could offer was a shrug.

Before the vampire could counter Simeon's attack he was yanked up by a figure and thrashed into the wall several times before the attacker was handed a stake that he promptly used on the vampire.

I blinked several times. Landon. His face was flushed from a recent feeding. He looked feral. His eyes breezed over me and landed on a battling Mephisto and Xavier. He barreled toward them, and I charged to stop him from attacking Mephisto. He side-stepped me and with a whir of movement, crashed into the fighting duo, fighting Mephisto to get to Xavier.

I was going to have to pencil this in as another unexpected event of the year. However, it was the least of my issues. I needed to figure out why we didn't have magic. The only answer I could think of that would remove my magic and the Huntsmen' was the *adligatura*. Which meant there was an elf on the premises.

I ran out of the room in the opposite direction of the fighting, down another hallway, until I came to one of the blasted openings, running until I got sight of the sigils used for the spell. Clayton had beaten me there and stood a few feet away, scanning the area. Assuming the *adligatura* would be closer, I moved back several feet from where he stood. Making it as wide as possible would be ideal, but that was time consuming, and they would have to exert a great deal of magic to keep it erected.

Just a short distance away, I got a glimpse of a beech-wood-toned woman with brunette hair pulled into a loose top knot and wearing a teal sweater and dark blue slacks, before the body slipped behind a tree. I wanted badly to see her ears, but she could have glamoured them the way most elves did when in public.

The beautiful, lush trees that offered an abundance of privacy now created an annoying obstacle to discovering the sigils. The thick grass created another one. Because I didn't have magic while in the sigiled area, I needed to be on the opposite side of it to disable it. Like Clay, my god magic didn't leave me restricted from moving past it. I just needed to find its borders.

"It's here." Kai's presence surprised us when he called out from the other side of it, pointing to it. His face was flushed, his lips forming a small O as he took slow, measured breaths. Being stripped of his magic had really affected him and he was willing his balled fist to relax.

"Are you—" I asked, meeting him on the opposite side of the *adligatura*.

"Please disarm it," he said, cutting off my inquiry of his current state to a question I really didn't need answered. The desperation in his voice not only spoke of his but what the others inside were probably feeling as well. Quickly, I disarmed it, and the moment the spell fell from my lips, I was rushing toward the tree where I'd seen the woman, but the space was empty.

"It was an elf," I said to Clayton once he was beside me looking at the same vacant space.

"Of course it was. I understand why you took the elves' magic away, but in doing so, you may have become a target of retaliation. I don't think attacks from them will stop. Your death would be considered as a means of survival. Despite your reasoning for divesting them of their magic, that action made you the villain in many people's stories. Talk to your people and find out who it was. Try to mend things between them, or you will be forced to do what your mother started if you ever want peace."

What my mother started was the attempted annihilation of the elves for their mere slight of refusing to join her in her pursuit of complete power. Despite our reasoning being completely different, I'd never complete what she started.

We ran back to the house to find Mephisto and Simeon surrounded in the center of the room. Some of the vampires hadn't survived. Blood, debris, and ripped clothing littered the room and Mephisto stood in a defensive stance, glaring at Landon, Dallas, Elon, and an unfamiliar vampire. The trio of vampires accompanying Landon didn't look as if they had participated in the violence but were ready to incite their own.

Within moments of taking in the scene, Kai and Clayton were standing next to Mephisto and Simeon before I realized they were protecting a body. Xavier. I scanned for Benton, who was off to the side, leaning against the wall, hair mussed, blood on his clothes, and cuts and bruises on his face and hands. He was alive, although I wasn't sure if it was from the efforts of the Huntsmen or his ability to protect himself. I couldn't imagine he'd survived this long aligned with them without being able to protect himself to some degree.

"Leave, while I'm feeling generous enough to allow you to," Mephisto bit out in a strident demand. "Your circumstances with Xavier and the others do not absolve you of your actions against Erin. I've made this request twice. If you don't leave, I'll assume that your actions are just your farewell letter to the world."

He took a step forward. I whispered his name, but the person who answered me wasn't the Mephisto I wanted. This person was filled with violence and ill-intent and couldn't be reasoned with.

I didn't see the promise of compromise in Landon, either. "Your arrogance will make your death even more pleasing."

Xavier lay on the floor, battered and injured from a stake wound that had missed his heart by just inches. He was in desperate need of feeding to efficiently heal. The longer he went without feeding, the less likely the donor would survive.

"Stop," I breathed out, exhaustion heavy in my tone. My patience had been strung so tight it was seconds from snapping and me kicking everyone in their man berries, as I was positive testosterone was the source of their reluctance to stand down. "Everyone just fucking stop! You managed to survive an attempt on your life, so did I," I hissed at Landon. "And you're the reason we both suffered this. I just want it to stop, and leaving Xavier here to be questioned is a means to that. You'll stand down if you have any hope of me ever forgiving you for what you did to Dr. Sumner and inciting this attempt on my life."

Landon's lips drew back into a sneer. "I do not need or desire your forgiveness. My life was placed in jeopardy because you didn't die. I had the audacity to value your life. I will not make that mistake again."

I was just quick enough to position myself in front of Mephisto, hands on his chest. His eyes trailed from my face to my hands. A request to remove them.

"Did Annalise escape?" I asked Mephisto, pulling his attention back to me. I'd seen Lilith escape.

He nodded.

"Landon, did they mention a relationship or an alliance with any elves?"

I maintained eye contact with Mephisto, whose stern cold eyes began to warm as practicality and reason slowly eased into them.

"I don't know if they have an alliance, but when I told them of my deal with you, they didn't seem as intrigued by your elf half as they were the god lineage. They've sired with more witches, mage, even fae, but nothing has changed our abilities. You don't understand the power we'd have with your magic. I was not aware that elves still existed, but like I said, they didn't seem enthusiastic about that aspect of you."

"Because immortality and Wynding is just so trivial," I snapped, turning my glare on him.

"When you've lived as long as I have, it is. But I do have to thank you for being the reason I was almost buried in a coffin, to be driven to madness by hunger. Can you imagine that death? If you can, then you will understand why I do not care to obey Mephisto's commands."

"Neither Xavier nor Annalise knew that orders were given to kill you. It was Lilith. Your beef is with her, not them. If you want revenge for the abduction, then wait until we have the information I need. You can't get revenge if you're dead." I dropped my hands from Mephisto. "*But* if there is any chance for us to establish a non-adversarial relationship, you will need to put your revenge on hold until I have answers. Can you do that?"

It was Dallas who spoke. "We've exhausted every resource we have, spent thousands of dollars, and acquired a debt with Asher to find Landon."

Moments ticked by, leaving me time to think. This was no longer a local issue, dealing only with Landon who I thought I could handle although that was becoming increasingly difficult. I'd managed to be at war with vampires I knew very little about, including their alliances. I continued to hope that Landon had enough animosity about the punishment he received to be of use to us.

Weaving its way through my planning and strategizing was the existential crisis of me second-guessing my decision to save Dr. Sumner. If I knew this would be the aftermath, would I have been ruled so blindly by my heart and emotions?

"I don't need us to reconcile the relationship we had," Landon said. "I had every right to respond to your refusal to give me a family as I did. But I am curious about your human's outcome, or if he is still human. And if I refrain from my revenge, then you understand that I may call on you to use those gifts for me."

Why in the hell would he ever want me to reverse vampirism? I had no idea the workings of his mind, but I knew there would be some form of weaponization of my agreement.

"No. There will be no more debts to you. The only thing I can promise is I won't exact revenge for what you did to Dr. Sumner and to me. You are the reason I've had to deal with

Lilith, Xavier, and Annalise and the destruction they've caused."

Landon looked over the house and the aftermath of the vampires' visit. After moments of consideration, he nodded. "I remain curious about the extent of your abilities. Will you agree to share it?"

I nodded. It wasn't exactly the free and clear proposal I wanted. "I'll share the information, but if you ever make any attempt to force my hand at using it, I will consider this agreement void."

Landon didn't seem as concerned about my retaliation as he did Mephisto's. And in the moment, I didn't blame him. Mephisto had dropped all pretense of humanity and looked like a shadow of wrath that didn't belong among simple beings. I didn't care for this version of Mephisto. He seemed so far removed from humanity.

Landon nodded and turned to leave, but I stopped him.

"Xavier showed me a video of where they're keeping Dr. Sumner." I described the room and they all seemed to come to the same recognition at the same time.

"Ramos's home. It served as his personal foodbank," Landon provided. Vampire speak for where Ramos held people from whom he fed regularly. Vampires operated in shades of gray when obtaining food. They weren't supposed to compel anyone to provide blood, but I remained convinced that the thrall humans had for them was linked to their ability to compel. It could not be proven. And vampires had favorites who, in exchange for being their personal blood bank, were given compensation in many forms.

"It has been empty since his death. I wasn't aware they knew of it or had access." Landon considered the new information. "Perhaps he shared," he suggested softly although he remained weighted by speculation.

Perhaps the trio had a closer relationship with Ramos than Landon knew. They had access to his house. He asked for paper and pen, which Benton retrieved, giving me an opportunity to do a more thorough assessment of him. His movements were better than I expected.

Dallas scribbled the address on the paper, and they wasted no time leaving. I was happy to see them go but wondered how long their restraint would last. They didn't seem reluctant to start a war between the vampire families.

CHAPTER 11

Driving, I prayed to the fates that the vampires' first act after leaving Mephisto's home was to regroup and heal and not to relocate Dr. Sumner. Many were injured, but the person I wished was injured enough to require downtime was Lilith.

Leaving so quickly, we didn't have time to properly question Xavier, but having him gave us room to negotiate Dr. Sumner's release if necessary. Simeon stayed behind with Benton and a hungry and cuffed Xavier. He'd need to feed, but it was better to keep him in a weaker state. As they put the cuff on Xavier, Clayton's uncertainty was unsettling, the results of the *adligatura* still raw. He and Kai wore the distress of being magicless worse than Simeon and Mephisto. We gathered our weapons and left for the address.

Pulling up to Ramos's cream-color brick, colonial-style home with the contrasting black shutters and contrasting roof, I remembered Ramos: uniquely exquisite yet withdrawn. He'd lived so long that he became a distinctively odd creature who'd grown bored with his existence and those who surrounded him. It led to him asking Landon to end a life that he considered too insipid to continue.

The landscape and flowers around the house reflected the

traditional décor of the room I'd seen Dr. Sumner in. I became suspicious when there wasn't any opposition or a ward in place to prevent us entering the unlocked home, so I wasn't surprised to find it empty. They hadn't bothered to straighten up. The food I'd seen earlier remained untouched and still on the table. Searching through the house, we found evidence of their presence and a few insignificant personal items left behind.

Standing in the middle of the living room, I racked my brain and searched for clues to a possible secondary location. After everything that had transpired with Landon, they were unlikely to go to one of the vampire homes. I didn't think they would use a hotel where they wouldn't have a strategic advantage. Where could they go that would give them that?

It came to me in a flood of awareness and nausea.

"I want to check another place," I told Mephisto. This time I directed him to a location I hoped I'd never visit. The vampires' dungeon. Despite using my knowledge of it to scare off a potential sire candidate who had piqued Landon's interest, I had never been there. I'd heard the tales, which had been dismissed as hyperbolic, but I knew that if a vampire created a problem that threatened the livelihood, convenience of living, or freedom of the others, it was handled promptly and severely, leading to a visit to the dungeon. It was doubtful it was an actual dungeon, but I wasn't oblivious to the level of barbarism that likely took place in it.

We passed stretches of land, scenic views of thriving farms and dense clusters of vibrant trees, until we took a right onto a desolate single-lane road leading to the dungeon. The road was poorly paved, and the trees were stunted and failing to thrive. Continuing down the road, we saw abandoned ranch homes that I was sure at one time boasted vibrant fields.

They were now overtaken by weeds and wildflowers. The entire area was probably owned by the vampires, with only one home receiving their attention; the remaining area would serve to deter people from traveling farther. This road was traveled for a purpose.

The silence in the SUV was deafening.

A chill ran down my spine when we finally arrived at our destination. Taking a deep breath, I mustered my resolve as we pulled up to the wrought-iron gate that surrounded the two-story farmhouse about eight miles from Ramos's home.

If I wasn't aware of what the fence was barring, I'd have an appreciation for its austere beauty. The onyx hue, devoid of any warmth, seemed to absorb the light around it, giving it a uniquely solemn appearance. Delicately crafted swirls and curves decorated the iron bars. The irony of the delicate beauty protecting such a foreboding place wasn't lost on me.

Once up the winding driveway we saw three cars and a SUV. A quick mental calculation confirmed that we were drastically outnumbered.

Before getting out of the SUV, we rechecked our weapons and I checked how easily I could remove the stakes from the holster I had them secured in.

I slowed my approach to the beautiful, tranquil white home with charming white clapboard siding. Large windows were accentuated by dark blue shutters. Dark cedar shingles created a striking contrast against the crisp white paint, and adding to the innocuous charm were spindle rails. Deception at its finest. I sneered at the swing on the porch.

Advancing quietly, I hesitated at the door, which was ajar. We wouldn't have the disadvantage of announcing our presence when we broke down the door, but something didn't seem right. The door was open. No matter the level of arrogance and confidence anyone had, they wouldn't leave the door open.

"I'm going to cloak myself," I told them. "I promise to

come back as soon as I see anyone or if I feel any amount of danger," I added to Mephisto.

Casting the spell, I moved throughout the house, surprised by how silent it was. But my level of discomfort increased. Something was wrong. And I couldn't quite put my finger on it. Kneeling to examine the piles of dust in various sections of the room, it was as I suspected: They were the same remnants left behind when vampires were staked and did not have the opportunity to feed. The newer the vampire, the less likely they were to survive a staking. But the older ones could. I suspected the visiting vampires were old enough to survive a simple stake assault if they were fed. If they were desperate enough, they could have used Dr. Sumner. After coming across the fifth dead vampire, I stopped my search and returned to the door, dropping the cloaking spell.

"Something's wrong," I said before recounting my findings. They followed close behind as we continued throughout the house to the stairs leading to the dungeon. Lanterns lit the path downstairs that went deeper than I expected. The temperature dropped the closer we got to the landing, sending a chill through me.

The dungeon, a large single room, was a stark contrast to the minimally furnished upstairs. It was utilitarian and lacked any form of warmth, but it was nothing compared to this portentous room. Exceeding the worst of what I'd expected.

A few sconces provided very little light in the large, windowless room. Hearing movement, I scanned for a switch that would provide more light and immediately regretted it. Heavy chains were secured to the wall. And a torturous-looking steel chair with arm and leg restraints was bolted to the floor.

"Looks like it has a zirconium overlay on it," Mephisto pointed out, heightening my disgust.

A cart a few feet away held a selection of knives, pliers, and other implements of torture. It held my attention long enough for bile to rise in my throat. I knew the threat of unspeakable brutality was to discourage bad behavior, but just seeing this room could successfully deter a misbehaving vampire.

Fortunately, Dr. Sumner was tucked away in the far end of the room, bound to a wooden chair, his mouth covered with duct tape. My eyes moved from his to the three piles near him.

I slowly removed the tape while Mephisto unbound him.

"She killed them all," he rushed out in a low rasped voice. His face folded into a hard grimace.

"Who?" I asked, expecting him to say Lilith. Perhaps she'd erupted in a tirade of anger, punishing them for not killing Landon.

"Me," a soft voice said from behind us. We whipped around, moving closer to the voice to find the elf from earlier standing at the bottom of the stairs.

She waved, a pleasant smile tugging at her lips as if she hadn't just admitted to killing a house full of vampires. She tossed a bottle of water toward Dr. Sumner who caught it.

"You've been through a lot today. That is unfortunate. You don't have to worry about them anymore."

Ignoring us, her eyes narrowed to give him a thorough assessment. Wearing the same clothes from earlier, her dark hair was now in a looser twist. Her round face was offset by a sharp chin, hollow cheeks, and haunting amber eyes. Expressionless, her aura was intense despite her diminutive frame and average height.

"Why did you kill them?" I asked.

"He's wholly human now. You just needed to do a *minesa* spell. You are familiar with it because of Fabian, right?" The mention of Fabian rekindled the memory of him deceiving me to use a pin prick to take my blood and using it later against Asial, a demon I had been forced into a contract with. To satisfy my contract, Fabian made the demon corporeal, then performed the *minesa* spell to age him to death.

"You were already bound to him when you reversed his vampirism. I just modified the spell to complete his full return to human." Her gaze darted in Dr. Sumner's direction. "He didn't trust me at first. Squirmed and resisted. But all is well now."

Sliding the look of abhorrence from his face, Dr. Sumner sifted through several until he settled on the gentle regard he'd used on me often in sessions. It was disarming.

"I apologize, it's not often that I witness a group of vampires escorted to a new existence with a spell."

Clever way to say murdered with a spell.

She smiled at him, seemingly appreciative of him softening her act.

"Why did you kill the vampires?" I repeated my question, without the pretty euphemisms Dr. Sumner used.

"You're not going to thank me for helping your friend?" she asked with an admonishing smile. Her enigmatic eyes quickly became as warm as the sun, but the effort she put into it was off-putting. Even with the faux gentleness of her new mien she observed me like a specimen under a microscope.

When I didn't respond, all emotions faded from her face, and her intense haunting eyes returned to picking up any minute movements I made.

The stilted silence became more uncomfortable with each passing second. Realizing she had no intention of moving on until I responded to her command, I offered, "Thank you for saving my friend." It didn't sound genuine to my ears, but she accepted it with a pleasant smile and nod.

I couldn't be fully relieved by Dr. Sumner's recovery because it was ushering in a slew of new problems. The murder of a bunch of visiting vampires who were killed with a spell was at the top of the list.

She followed my eyes to her hands, where gold etched sigils from the onyx stone in her hand carried over her skin, crawling up her fingers and ending a few inches above her wrist. Ignoring the inquiry in my look, she returned her eyes to mine.

"The vampires claimed to be interested in the extent of your magic, but I heard them admitting that their findings or any oaths you gave to never use those abilities didn't matter. They decided you could no longer live because you would always be an existential threat to them. And you could prevent them creating vampires as they pleased. *I* was curious as to whether you could change an older vampire." She frowned. "I still am, but I think it's a curiosity that should not be satisfied." It felt like she was chiding herself for considering it.

My impression of her was wavering between her being a magical genius or an avenging unstable philanthropist.

"They lied and were going to kill you." She directed her attention back to me. She brushed away hairs that had fallen from her updo and covered her ears. "They did not honor their agreement to me. By doing so, they voided their right to safety. I didn't want you dead."

Maybe it was my imagination and lingering pessimism, but I suspected there was an unspoken "yet."

I trod very carefully with my next question, softening my voice and inching closer to her. With a quiet invocation and a slight move of her finger, the markings needed for the *adligatura* spell revealed themselves. I figured walking over it would seem like a hostile act and an unnecessary demonstration of my power, so I stayed behind it.

"Were you close with Fabian?" I asked.

She nodded. "Close enough, but I don't care that he's dead. Nor do I care that Elizabeth is, either. I acquired an acceptable amount of knowledge from them, among other things. I wouldn't give them the last Black Crest grimoire. They viewed me as a liability anyway. I'd be treated as they treated all liabilities for the good of the collective. I suspect since I wouldn't bend to their will, I'd die at their hands." She frowned at the word "collective," seeming to hold the same feelings I did at the cultish language. There was something cynical about the way Fabian always used it.

She had the last Black Crest grimoire. A book of spells that allowed magic wielders to mimic elven magic.

"It's a good book and shouldn't be destroyed." She sighed. "Perhaps our magical abilities should be shared. Too often great power is used to subjugate others. It's not right." She inched closer to the runes on the floor. "Just like that abuse you exhibited when you took our magic." Her icy look stabbed into me. She turned away to look at the stairs. "You shouldn't have done that."

Before I could answer, two vampires barreled down the stairs, their murderous gaze locked on her. The vampire in front barely got out his disparaging "bitch." With quick rote movements of her hands and a whisper of words, they met the same fate as the others.

Damn.

She'd held the *adligatura* spell while performing another spell. This woman was dangerous, and I had no intention of being on the receiving end of any of it. This elf was a threat that needed to be apprehended. I moved quickly toward her. The runes illuminated gold and pushed me back, the same way it kept Cory and Madison enclosed when I practiced the spell on them. Mephisto moved toward it and the spell responded to him in the same manner.

Kai and Clayton were also unsuccessful in their attempt to breach the *adligatura*. Shock was visible on their faces, along with anger. They looked like predators facing another predator, determined to declare they'd come out the clear winner. Me clearing my throat appeared to bring them back to themselves, and they made extreme efforts to remove all signs of their intent. The space was overtaken by the soft sounds of them taking slow, measured breaths. I couldn't offer them any comforting words, platitudes, or assistance because I was fighting my own anger and frustration.

The lack of knowledge did more damage than anything because the elf before me was the unknown of all unknowns, starting with the object in her hand that illuminated along with the sigils on them each time we neared the border of the *adligatura*.

"This must be hard for you." She directed the question to the trio but kept moving until she was directly facing Mephisto.

He met her question with a rigid expression. When he didn't answer she gave the others equal time to do so. "Why didn't you stay away?"

It was another question that went unanswered.

She returned to stand in front of me, dividing her attention between me and Dr. Sumner. "I understand you two," she said softly, her eyes darkening when they moved between me and Mephisto. "Elizabeth was a talented practitioner and wise about many things but equally unwise about a number of other things. Her belief that the Veil should be closed with all its occupants secured within is a belief that we shared." She inched a little closer, making sure not to touch the sigils. In her state of confusion, she looked younger and a little more unhinged.

"Who was Elizabeth to you?" I asked.

"Mentor, initially. I'd piqued both Fabian's and Elizabeth's interest in the way you did. I was jealous at how much attention they directed to you. They were always bringing you up. You had a deity-like presence, and they seemed to fear and adore you. I didn't like that," she admitted softly. "I was the one they saw so much potential in until they realized I couldn't be manipulated into doing their bidding. Like the vampires, they didn't honor their word, and power was too important to them. Their deaths were inevitable, but I have not decided how to feel that it was you who delivered such a fate." She started pacing, mumbling to herself, "Should she live or die for it?"

I revisited my thoughts as to whether the elf was a magical genius or an unstable avenging philanthropist.

Before I could answer the question, Dr. Sumner said, "She may have had Elizabeth's attention but not her affection. She was Erin's aunt."

We were all surprised when he walked over the barrier without any problem. He kept his distance from her, watching her with the same curiosity and apprehension she'd given him. Her head canted to the side, eyes slowly narrowing to scrutinize him. Her interest was piqued. She waited in silence for him to continue.

"Did she show you any affection? Clearly, she liked you enough to be your mentor, but did she care about you? Did you want her to care about you?"

The elven woman frowned, pain flickering over her expression before she was able to suppress it. My attention stayed divided between her and the object in her hand, which was clearly the source of her increased magical ability. I searched my memory to place the object but came up empty. I could see similar searching in the Huntsmen's expressions. Kai couldn't tamp down his expression, which looked violent and just seconds from explosive. They shared a mutual concern, but with their magic restricted, their means of communication had likely been disrupted as well.

"She did. It was a love/hate relationship. Intrigued by my abilities, she wished to push them to the limits. But she feared me at times. Fabian saw me as a talent that would help them achieve their goals. I didn't like their goals." She turned in my direction, but her eyes skated over me to look at the men. Her frown deepened. "Perhaps Elizabeth and I didn't get along because we shared the same duty to be 'the justice and the balance needed in a world where magic exists'."

I grimaced at her repeating one of Elizabeth's favorite tenets.

"He liked that we were the strongest on this side of the Veil and that it would guarantee our safety. But we will never be safe if *they* can freely move between our world and the Veil."

She moved closer to Dr. Sumner, studying him with renewed interest. "Jacob, with everything that magic has taken from you—how do you feel about that?"

Dr. Sumner's jaw clenched, feeling the same weight of doom in her question that I had. He gave her the disarming smile that made it apparent why he was such a popular professor at his college; it didn't appear that she was immune to it, either.

"I feel at a disadvantage here. You know me but I don't know you. May I have a name?"

She hesitated as if giving it would give him power over her, but our magic never hinted at possessing the same vulnerabilities fae had with people knowing their true name. Or did we? I had never explored it. My mother gave me my name, so I had no knowledge if I'd had another. I hated that because elves were considered extinct, so much information was withheld because it was no longer relevant. I knew of palladium because I made it my business to know ways to disable an opponent with access to magic when I didn't have any. I was still under the belief that there was some crossover with magic inhibitors. Although iridium might not stop fae from being able to use their magic the way lead did, they seemed to handle it with care and didn't like to hold it too long. There was a reason for that.

"Damia," she finally said.

With a warm smile, he repeated the name. Dr. Sumner

took more time considering her question, which she appeared to appreciate. "Magic has helped me more than it has hurt me. Your magic helped me." He turned to look at me. "Erin used her magic for good, to save me from magic that was meant for malice. And your magic protected my friend, and I'm thankful that you chose to use it for good as well." His statement was accompanied by a reverent nod.

Her brow rose, urging him to elaborate.

"The vampires would have killed Erin if it wasn't for you. That spell could be perceived as bad, but it had favorable results as far as I'm concerned."

"They had no right to make that decision. I have not decided if she should live. Erin has immense power and she is reckless. Elizabeth ended Malific's life, which was the best choice for all. Did she carry out full justice by leaving behind the one person of our kind who would try to stop me when I close the Veil?"

It was insulting that she spoke of me as if I wasn't there and how flippant she was being over whether I'd live or not.

"What?" Clayton demanded.

"I plan to close the Veil. Elizabeth and Fabian were right about it being important not to let the creatures of it have access here. No good can come of it. We weren't meant to coexist." She waved her hand in our direction then looked at us with pure disdain. "This is wrong. It's all wrong. Even when you aren't actively attacking us, your existence manages to cause us harm. That was proven already. Our magic was stolen from us because of you."

"We didn't do that to you!" Mephisto snapped.

"No, but it was done to create a pathway for you to return. See, you have the ability to hurt us even when you aren't an active participant."

Dr. Sumner took advantage of the moment of distraction to take the object from her. The overly observant doctor hadn't missed the attention I'd placed on it. She made no effort to keep hold of the stone. In fact, it looked as if she released it to him. The moment it touched his skin, his body seized, his eyes rolled back, and he collapsed to the floor. Color drained from his face.

I rushed the circle and it slammed me back. On my hands and knees, I crawled to where he'd fallen, looking for signs of life that weren't there. His chest didn't move. His head lolled to the side. His face was the pale shade of a person deprived of oxygen for too long. Even his lips started to take on a bluish color.

Moving slowly toward him, Damia knelt next to him, appraising him for several beats, one hand cradling his face. I couldn't understand why she looked at him as if he was something she'd never seen. Finally, her lips twisted to the side. Moving her hand from his face to his chest, swirls of white mist swirled over him. It felt like eternity as it moved and slithered over him. Then his body moved in disjointed jerks like a marionette and when she was done, he sat up. His face was blank, and he looked around the room with very little recognition. He closed his eyes and when he opened them again, he blinked several times.

"Erin," he whispered.

I exhaled the breath I'd been holding since Damia knelt next to him.

"Magic saved your life again," she whispered. Disappointment flooded her eyes as she looked at him. "I see that you can't be trusted, either, or is it just when it comes to her?"

Not giving him time to answer, she just disappeared, along with the sigils from the *adligatura* spell and the remains of the vampires.

"Jacob," I said, rushing to him and putting my hand over his where it lay over his heart.

"Two lives down, do I have seven more?" His voice was tight at his attempt at a joke, but he was clearly terrified.

"You weren't dead," Mephisto assured him. My head

snapped in his direction. Had he seen the same thing I had? He'd looked dead. Several hours dead and she just brought him back to life.

"It was similar to the state you'd put people into when you borrowed their magic," Mephisto explained. "She wasn't entirely truthful when she said that he's wholly human. He may not have magic or be a vampire, but he's linked to magic to live. The real question is, will we all respond that way if we attempt to take that object from her? I'm willing to bet she won't try to save us."

I agreed. But I couldn't help but wonder why she'd saved Dr. Sumner. Then the answer came to me.

Leverage.

CHAPTER 12

Mephisto took his pent-up anger out on the gas pedal, barreling the car through the streets, his face stone, his anger stifling.

"Fucking Malific," he ground out in disdain. His head shook and lips furled when he exhaled. "Fucking elves." Noticing me tense, he rested a reassuring hand on my leg, taking his eyes off the road, which I really wished he wouldn't since he was inching close to a hundred miles per hour and the only two people who seemed concerned were me and Dr. Sumner.

"I always admired that the elves were a people of peace despite their great power. Malific's terror robbed them of that. I don't want to blame them for their response to her violence, but Damia worries me."

"I was worried when she held the *adligatura* spell and killed a vampire with a strike of her finger. I'm terrified after seeing her kill"—I stopped and rephrased—"divest Dr. Sumner of his magic and return it so effortlessly. She's following in Elizabeth's footsteps and wants to kill me."

No one made any effort to dissuade me of that or offer reassurances.

"I hate that I can't fully read her," I admitted. "If I had a better understanding of her then I could better predict her actions. Why would she announce that she planned to close the Veil? Why not just close it without telling us?"

"She's a string of contradictions," Dr. Sumner offered, his eyes fixed on the speedometer. I squeezed Mephisto's arm. He looked at Dr. Sumner in the rearview mirror and slowed the car down. Dr. Sumner unclenched his fingers. He started looking out the window and after a long minute he said softly, "I don't think she wants you dead."

"What makes you think that?"

"If she did, why would she kill the vampires who wanted to kill you?"

"Because she wants to do it herself," Kai provided. It had taken that amount of time for him to calm from his loss of magic. And the moment we were out of the dungeon he'd spread his wings wide and taken to the air for a few minutes. When he returned to land, he was still reeling with anger.

"I need to figure out the name of the stone she held," Mephisto said.

"What happens to you all if she closes the Veil? She clearly doesn't want you here and if you refused to leave, can she do something to you?" Dr. Sumner inquired, voicing a concern I was sure we all shared.

Damia had exceptional magic—or rather the stone she held did. If she could keep them in the *adligatura* and kill vampires with a spell with a few movements of her hand, what other capabilities did she possess?

I was sure we were all still thinking about Damia and her abilities as we pulled up to Dr. Sumner's home. I was reluctant to let him return home by himself, but after a series of debates and an overly confident Dr. Sumner assuring me that he would be fine, I reluctantly conceded. I don't know if he was as confident as he attempted to sound, but he was likely in a rush to get away from us and everything we represented. A vampire's death, resurrection, given new life twice, and witness to a massacre at the hands of magic. I didn't blame him for wanting to put as much distance as possible between us.

"Your door," I said before he could get out.

"I'll have it repaired today and if it can't be done, I'll find a safe place to stay."

"If you leave, text me your new location."

"I'll be safe," he quickly responded and dashed out of the door. No lingering looks, needing to be close to me, or anxiety at the thought of not seeing me soon. Damia's magic had fully completed the process. I was simultaneously appreciative of her talents and fearful of her abilities. And more pessimistic of my capability of reasoning with her.

"Be careful," I whispered to his back.

Mephisto placed a hand on my thigh, which was meant to be reassuring, but he was stiff with struggling to suppress his anger and vulnerability from having his magic restricted.

"Are you okay?" I asked.

"I'm fine," he lied.

I asked the others and they responded similarly, but their voices had a detached nature. Probably dealing with an emotion they'd never felt before: a sense of helplessness, even if it was just for a short period of time.

None of us were fine and wouldn't be until we resolved our Damia problem.

Once back at Mephisto's home, we were presented with a reminder of the earlier events, which included the demolished gate.

"Why didn't the police come?" I asked. "Or security?" It was good that they hadn't, but I still wondered why nobody showed up with all the commotion.

"It's a closed monitoring system. I'm the only one who needs to know who my visitors are. My house can't be monitored by outsiders."

Protecting him and the anonymity of the shady people he interacted with. I was surprised to see a contracting truck, ladders, and a crew of men already working to repair the damage.

"It must be nice," I teased, nudging my head in the direction of the people working on the house.

He grumbled a sound, looked down at his phone, and shook his head. It must be nice and very expensive to get someone to come out to do same-day repairs. And what did their silence cost?

Benton was waiting at the entrance and beckoned us to follow him to the basement where we had trained before. Xavier rested against the wall looking tired, desperate, and hungry.

"I gave him enough to maintain consciousness and to keep him from going wild from blood lust," Benton supplied.

He didn't have to provide the rest of his strategy of keeping him weak enough that he couldn't overpower him. The bespelled zirconium braces were placed on him. It weakened vampires but didn't leave them entirely debilitated.

"Tell me about Damia," I demanded of Xavier once standing directly in front of him.

Xavier just glared at me, resting his head against the wall in a show of defiance.

"I'm hungry," he said.

Simeon and Kai crossed their arms over their chests, unwilling to provide food. Clayton looked reluctant, as well. I was about to offer my wrist when Mephisto lowered to the floor and extended his arm. Xavier scrambled closer to him, grabbed Mephisto's arm, and sank his teeth in. Drawing greedily from him, he only pulled away a few times to exhale a delighted sigh. Mephisto had to coax him into stopping. He returned to his position against the wall, an insolent twist in his lip.

I repeated my request about Damia.

A slow smile inched at the corners of his lips. "You've met her," he drawled. Although he attempted to exhibit bravado, something was off. It was like the shocked look he showed when Lilith announced she'd ordered that Landon be murdered. The look of a man presented with a wildcard.

"How long have you been working with her?" Mephisto asked.

"Not long. She found us and we listened to what she had to say because she guaranteed that she could make it possible to apprehend you quickly. Lilith was immediately intrigued by her because of the relative ease with which she found us. It's not as if we made a show of our presence in your city. And yet she was waiting for us at Ramos's home. It wasn't our planned first stop."

I'm sure it wasn't nearly as difficult as he'd like us to believe. He didn't seem like he was discreet about his presence, and neither were his cohorts.

He laughed, a deep melodic roar that resounded off the walls. "Seeing the look on your faces when you couldn't use your magic was worth allying with the peculiar woman."

"You should have declined, because she killed your vampires," I told him, which collapsed the smile from his face.

His mouth opened but he couldn't find the words. He snapped it closed and licked his lips. "What?"

"She wasn't fond of their decision to renege on your agreement to keep me alive. Her reaction to that displeasure was their death."

Fury erupted. He drew back his lips and lobbed threat after threat, becoming angrier with each barbaric description he gave of the harm he planned to exact on Damia.

"She killed them with a spell. I was there for one of them, and the vampires died in the same manner a new vampire would have if staked."

His frown deepened but the emotion disappeared from his eyes. Lost and confused.

"She's no longer your ally. Damia is as much your enemy as she is mine," I said.

He rested his head against the wall. Watching hopelessness take over his expression tugged at something in me that wanted to feel sorry for him. But remembering that just hours ago he was cosigning to my abduction and possible murder kept my compassion from fully forming.

"Tell me everything you know about her," Mephisto demanded.

"There isn't much to tell," he said. "She found us at Ramos's home and introduced herself and told us she was aware of the reason for our visit. Since our interests were mutually aligned, she wanted to help us apprehend you. But only if she was allowed to question you as well. Damia wasn't happy that you had taken her magic. She seemed more disheartened by the reason it was done." His eyes shifted to Mephisto, then me before languidly gliding over the others. "She rambled on about you protecting the monsters that shouldn't be here," he provided with a rueful smile. "I'm assuming you're the monsters that shouldn't be here?"

Their faces were devoid of expression as Xavier studied them. His earlier interest in them reasserted itself but wasn't as intense, dampened by his losses.

"Did she keep something in her hand with her during any of your interactions?" Clayton asked. "Or had any strange markings on her?"

"No," he said without any consideration or thought. He

scoffed, his eyes glazing over. I suspected he never imagined he'd be on the receiving end of the skillful elf.

"What are your intentions for her when you find her?" Xavier asked. He dismissed me and looked at the Huntsmen as if they shared camaraderie and blood lust.

"I don't know. She needs to be contained," Mephisto provided.

Or reasoned with, but reasoning with her, getting an oath to keep her from closing the Veil, and persuading her against any of her plans for me didn't seem like it would happen, although I kept a smidgen of hope that I was wrong.

Xavier's eyes narrowed as if he was trying to recall something. "She kept her hands in her pockets, clutching something like a lifeline," he muttered. "I figured it was a weapon which would be useless against us." Seeming to find the absurdity in that, he slumped into himself.

We exchanged glances, nodded, and headed upstairs with Xavier reminding us that he would need food later. They decided on a rotating arrangement that excluded me.

CHAPTER 13

Madison stared at the destruction of Mephisto's home, Clayton next to her, his hand making smooth circles over her back as he escorted her into the house. The rictus on her face wouldn't ease and I was sure she was going to come back with a handful of hair with the way she roughly twisted her curls. Cory looked at the damage from the door. We'd cleaned up, but the floors seemed off and had remnants of blood stains on them, or perhaps it was my imagination. Dust clung to the air. And we kept finding shards of glass and splinters of wood that we'd missed while cleaning. Mephisto's home looked and felt like the site of unspeakable violence.

They followed us into Mephisto's office, and we told them everything that had transpired.

"So, you have Xavier, a renowned member of the Southern vampires, hostage in your basement," Madison concluded.

"Hostage doesn't seem like the right word," I countered.

"He's only eaten twice today despite exerting himself in the fight, which I'm sure is keeping him in a state of malnourishment. He's cuffed with a zirconium brace with a sleep spell bound to them, divested of his free will to leave," she recounted with a grimace.

"The way you say it seems a little judgy," I quipped, earning me a dagger-sharp glare.

At the mention of Xavier's name during the recap, she'd sucked in a ragged breath, exposing the gaps in my vampire knowledge and their hierarchy. She had a visceral response at the mention of Lilith. Short, shaky breaths continued throughout my retelling of our interactions with Damia and the ease with which she disposed of the vampire while keeping us locked in the *adligatura* circle. By the time I'd concluded, she had plastered on a tight smile but her calculating eyes were peak Madison. She was trying to figure out what she should do next.

"You haven't found out what Damia was holding?" she asked. While waiting for Madison and Cory to arrive we all had drawn a rendition of it and the markings, then assisted Benton scrolling through his library of books and searching through the magical objects in their possession that looked similar. We hadn't discovered anything. Madison looked at the drawings, and her brow hiked at one of the pictures.

"Did she have more than one object?" she asked.

"I don't think I got a great look at it," Kai said, defending his drawing, a flush hitting his cheeks and nose.

"I couldn't find anything," Benton told her.

"It could be an elven object," I speculated. An object with the ability to perform magic that had a true effect on gods. Was this the real reason Malific wanted them dead when they declined becoming tools of destruction for her?

"That would make sense, along with how it responded when Dr. Sumner attempted to take it. Would the response be the same if it was Erin?" Cory asked.

"I don't know. I should discuss it with Nolan," I suggested.

"If she closes the Veil, what is the likelihood of you

finding a way to work around it?" Madison asked the group but kept hopeful eyes pinned on Clayton.

They ruminated over the question for a long time. From the furtive looks exchanged, I speculated they were chatting with each other as well.

"I don't know. If she's using an elven spell, I'm not sure we could manipulate it. If we're locked in because of our link to Veil magic, we may be able to find a way around it," Clay speculated.

Eventually. He withheld the word, but it was loud in his body language and the comforting look he gave her.

Madison offered a tight-lipped smile as if she was holding back the other question that had settled in my mind as well. If we could find a way to close the Veil and keep them here, would they choose it?

Neither one of them asked, and when I caught her eye, she shook her head. I figured she thought it best to give them time to think about it. They'd just gained entry; were they willing to lose it again?

I gathered the drawings. My stone was the most accurate, whereas Clayton's depiction of the markings on her hand and arm was better than mine. "I'll let you know if I find out anything new from Nolan."

"I'll go with you in case you run into Damia again," Mephisto suggested. Clayton fell in step with him.

I shook my head. "If she was going to do something, she would have done it earlier. We've been given a reprieve, although I'm not sure for how long. It would be best if you stayed behind to continue to research. Split the work to be more efficient."

He knew I was right but was reluctant to agree despite it being the most pragmatic option. After several moments, he reluctantly nodded.

In the car, Madison's fingers drummed against the steering wheel as she drove.

"They seemed rattled by Damia," she acknowledged after a long stretch of rigid silence.

"I am, too," I admitted. "You had to see how effortlessly she used her magic."

"You think it's all from the stone?" Cory asked from the back seat.

"I don't know. The disdain she had for the Huntsmen makes me nervous. She wants them gone—"

"And you dead," Madison's tremulous voice interjected.

I inhaled a breath. "As retribution for Elizabeth and Fabian's deaths. She was having an internal struggle. I'm not confident she wouldn't quickly change her mind and decide to kill me. The scariest thing is that she may be able to do it with the same ease she killed the vampires."

"Wildcards are the hardest to deal with," Cory said, directing his attention out the window. Etches of worry could be seen in his profile. "Did you get the impression she's impulsive?"

"I have no idea what to think about her. She didn't seem to be, but she was determined to close the Veil."

"She's not wrong about the Veil," Madison said. "Life would be easier and safer for us if the Veil was closed. But—" She ended with a sigh.

I filled in what she left unsaid. We didn't want Mephisto and Clayton gone. I didn't want any of them gone. And if Damia could be reasoned with and the Huntsmen left behind, we had no idea what their choice would be.

When Madison looked at me, her expression held the same uncertainty that I felt. Hopefully, Nolan could offer us the necessary information, so we'd never have to ask.

Nolan greeted me with an empathic hug. Surprisingly, I didn't stiffen from it. The display of affection felt right, and I let it linger. He maintained contact with my hand, stepping away while giving me a sweeping assessment.

"It's bad." He frowned, stepping aside to let Cory and Madison pass us.

I nodded.

"Do you know of any objects or talisman that would enhance elven magic to the point it works against gods?" I asked.

His brow furrowed with confusion. Then I explained my run-in with Damia.

"Damia." He breathed out. "It's been a while since I heard that name."

"You know her!?" Cory shrieked, his voice heavy with relief.

"I know of her. Elizabeth..." A heavy sadness filled his tone at his sister's name. It was hard to look at him, so I let my attention drift to the living room and the changes he'd made since my last visit. It seemed cozier, giving me the impression that he was planning to stay for a while. "She had a complicated relationship with Damia. Fabian as well. Fabian was reluctant to allow her to live at the Havenage but eventually conceded."

"Why were they reluctant? She's not a full elf?" I asked. That was typically the reason one was denied. Half-caste weren't considered valuable, especially if they were mixed with human. I assumed it had more to do with keeping a concentration of power than protecting them from those who wouldn't be completely loyal.

"No. Elizabeth didn't trust her," he said. "I suspected it wasn't just distrust but envy as well. Damia is a full elf, but her understanding of magic exceeded Elizabeth's. Her magical knowledge and abilities were where Elizabeth was the most talented, earning her favor with the elves and Fabian. Damia was born here and grew up hearing of the brutality of the Veil and Malific's role in causing us to flee. It appeared she was consumed by the ideology that power led to senseless violence. Showed inability to view it through a nuanced lens. She, Fabian, and Elizabeth shared many beliefs but different values."

One belief they didn't share was my existence. Elizabeth wanted me dead. Fabian wanted me alive if he could use me as a tool.

Nolan grew quiet. I wondered if he was ruminating over the value and trust he'd put in Fabian only to discover the lengths he'd go to for power for himself and the elves. Fabian's intentions may have seemed noble initially, and maybe in the beginning they were, but they became entwined with nefarious actions and manipulations that voided any good in his initial goodwill.

"Fabian's doubts about Damia were warranted. I believe that within three months of living in the Havenage, she left. Elizabeth was told that Damia had stolen a great deal from the elves, but never went into detail. They've been searching for her for nearly five years. She was skilled at being elusive. She must be feeling emboldened now," he said with a small smile. Although he didn't seem to accuse me of anything, I felt liable. Had the presence of Elizabeth and Fabian been the only thing keeping her in the shadows? But I couldn't help but believe taking the elves' magic had incited her into behaving this way.

"You have no idea what she's taken?" Cory asked.

He shook his head. "It would be best to ask Sanaa, she was closest to Fabian."

"Is she now the leader?" Madison asked, slipping back into her role as STF agent.

Nolan's lips pulled into a tight line at remembering that Madison's role consisted of more than just being my sister and ally but also an important figure in the Supernatural Task Force.

I nudged her hand as a silent request for her to stop. The

conflict on her face made it apparent she wanted to but needed the information. Nolan, despite his newfound relationship with my family, had wanted to live in the Havenage or at least have a relationship with the elves.

"We should talk to Sanaa," Cory piped in, cutting the uncomfortable tension.

Nolan nodded. "Would you like me to go with you?"

I shook my head, wanting him to have distance from the situation if it ended poorly.

Cory drove toward the Havenage, noticeably preoccupied, several times looking from the road to me, his mouth parting slightly before closing when he reconsidered what he wanted to say.

"I can't remove their magic again," I admitted, responding to the suggestion I thought he was debating to make. "Asher made it clear I could never use Ms. Harp again, nor do I want to. That isn't an option. Even if it were, I don't know if Xavier's family of vampires will retaliate. I don't want to leave the elves defenseless."

"Drop her ass off in Blose Chasm," he snapped. It was another unhelpful suggestion, making it seem as if opening a magical purgatory was as simple as opening a door. There was a magical sacrifice required for that. Not only would I have to convince Damia to follow me into the Chasm, the cost of using it was magic that wouldn't be returned to me until she died or was removed from the place. And I'd need another elf to close the Chasm for me.

His unhelpful suggestions were coming from a place of desperation and frustration of being met again with magic far more nefarious and complex than that of witches, who at one time had the advantage and were at the top of the hierarchy—from their perspective. Although I stood by my belief

that mages and witches were the same thing, different brand-
ing. Just colas with different packaging, witches earned a
level of recognition and respect because of their abilities.

"You know that's not possible. First, we need to locate her.
Then convince her to follow me into the Blose Chasm. And
then get another elf to agree to reopen it for me to exit. I think
getting an elf to trust me, let alone help, may be impossible."

They'd leave both me and her there and say good
riddance to the problems that had fallen at their door.

"What if Damia killing the vampire with a spell isn't
exclusive to her but something all elves can do, and we've
just not been aware of it?" I speculated. It was an ability I'd
kept hidden. Just like my ability to reverse vampires made
me a target, the knowledge of such an ability would make
elves no end of a target.

"If she can do that, do we wonder about her other abilities?" Madison pondered.

Needing to satisfy our curiosity, I called Nolan. It took
him several minutes to respond, and I knew he was going
through every possible spell and combination to provide the
answer.

"Mortem spell requires consent. All spells that require life
or death need consent. It's a failsafe. I've gone through a
combination of spells that would be available to full elves
and can't think of one," he said.

I knew that all too well when Fabian used it to lock
Mephisto and the others in the Veil and used the threat of
Madison's life as leverage to get them to agree.

Nolan's voice held deep concern when he told me to be
careful going to the Havenage. He knew I was going into
hostile territory.

Damia used a death spell on the vampires. She had to be
an exceptionally talented manipulator to get them to agree
with that. Death spells needed to be created with sigils. I

hadn't noticed any on them, which made me suspect she'd found a loophole. The more I discovered about Damia, the further out of my league I felt.

Cory parked far from the perimeter of the Havenage, giving us time to prepare to combat the repulsion spells on hyperdrive that surrounded it. Cory, Madison, and I sighed collectively getting out of the car, our bodies stiffening, readying for the onslaught of mental and physical manipulation we'd endure. I didn't know why they didn't just put up a roadblock. Each step toward the area increased the nausea and sharp pangs that shot through me. An ominous feeling of harm enveloped me, shivers ran through my body, and dark eerie images flickered in my mind.

"I hate this place so much." Cory's voice was tight with disgust as he struggled with the repulsion spell. Madison grunted her shared sentiments. Her face pinched with each hesitant step.

"Go back."

I heard Sanaa before seeing her. An illumination behind her blurred my vision and gave her an ethereal appearance. Once my eyes refocused, I trailed her as she moved toward the car.

"You are breaking our agreement," she said, stopping a few feet from the car, a disapproving frown beveling her lips. Eyes that once looked at me with warmth and a bit of understanding were cold and unforgiving. "Do you honor any of your agreements?"

Ouch. It led me to believe she'd learned of the situation between Landon and me. How far had that information traveled?

"I wouldn't be here if it wasn't necessary. Your help will ensure that the elves are protected."

"Ah, so you're not here to protect us. Our safety is predicated on helping you."

"Contrary to what you all seem to want, she is an elf," Madison spat out.

"Quarter-elf," Sanaa corrected. "She has more of her"—she sneered—"other half than us and that is where she's derived her morals."

These discussions about my lineage were just annoying, especially coming from the hypocrisy crew. My patience was thread thin and about to snap.

"Damia killed more than ten vampires with a spell. There is no way that will not go without retaliation. I need to find her."

A slow smile curled her lips. "You've met Damia. That had to be an interesting interaction."

"Why?" I asked.

"You two remind me of each other, great power and conflicting interests. She holds our safety in as little regard as you do. I have no idea why you are here." She studied my face, and I ushered all expression from it. Stepping closer to me, her eyes narrowed. "What did she do to you?" she asked, a hint of amusement in her tone.

I was reluctant to tell her, because knowing that Damia was "undecided" on whether I should live wouldn't encourage help from Sanaa. She waited with anticipation as I decided what to tell her. I opted for the truth, telling her everything, including me reversing vampirism for Dr. Sumner, which piqued her interest and earned me a look of admiration mingled with apprehension.

"Landon just decided to attack your friend with no cause. It's shocking that you didn't retaliate after such an egregious act."

I swallowed, tempted to withhold the information and curry favor. Whether she helped me or not, it would not be because of deception and would give me insight as to where I truly stood with them. Without a doubt, Damia was a situation that should concern her as well.

So I gave her the necessary details about the debt I incurred to save Dr. Sumner and my desire to prevent Landon creating vampires that might become a societal problem and the exchange of that debt for the Obscuro Mors.

"Obscuro Mors?" she asked.

I was really hoping we could just brush over that part.

"It will destroy the vampire line of the one staked."

Her eyes widened and I expected one of her backhanded insults about my depravity, me being a monster, or narrow focused. Or the plethora of other shortcomings she'd managed to see in me and Nolan while ignoring theirs.

She made a motion with her hand, encouraging me to continue. I told her everything from the attack of the vampires, Damia fixing Dr. Sumner, and enclosing us in the *adligatura* spell with minimal effort to hold it up while using another spell to kill a vampire.

"Were the Huntsmen with you?" she asked.

I nodded.

"They were kept in the circle as well?"

I nodded again.

She sucked in a ragged breath. A look swept over her face that led me to believe I'd lost her to Damia. Everything seemed to come down to the Huntsmen and the ability to subdue them or get rid of them. Both seemed equally desired.

"What did the object look like?"

I pulled the pictures from my pocket, sans Kai's depiction, and handed them to her. She studied the drawings for a long time while I watched her for any signs of recognition.

"This was once in Fabian's possession, but I don't believe he ever discovered its abilities. It was an item he'd found. I guess she's figured out how to use it. I always believed Damia was talented enough to be desired as an ally but too precarious to be of any use."

"What do you mean by that?" Madison asked. Sanaa raked a look of contempt over her.

"She cannot be trusted. I do believe if she had the ability to remove magic from the world, even at the risk that some would die, she'd make that choice. The times I've dealt with her, she fixated on the exploitation of power. From a superficial perspective it seemed admirable until you realized the wide lens through which she considers the exploitation of power and magic. Shifters' and vampires' supernatural abilities to hear and move is considered exploitation of power. Wynding. Binding spells and wards. Calling demons." Clearly Sanaa didn't have a problem with it. "Defensive magic. In a simplistic and naïve way, wanting magic to only be used sparingly and for good is admirable. When shifters and vampires use their supernatural abilities to save someone, is it exploitive? There lies the issue. She doesn't see how self-limiting she is, and the mere fact that she believes she should be the magistrate deciding that makes her dangerous.

"We've distanced ourselves from her. But now I see she has abilities that make her dangerous to many people. If she can do that to vampires, to your Huntsmen"—she made sure to add a healthy helping of derision to the word—"and even help your friend, do you not wonder about all her capabilities? The fact that she hasn't decided whether you should live should be of some concern to you."

Some. I'm terrified.

"You think she's really dangerous?" Cory asked.

"You don't? She has figured out a way to use a magical object that had been in Fabian's possession for years. Using it as a paperweight would have served him better than it just being packed away. I don't know the name of this object. I do believe it is elven, but a lot of our history is lost, hence Fabian's inability to use it."

"She has the final Black Crest grimoire, too."

Sanaa looked to the sky and sighed. "I may be able to find her, but I will need an oath from you, Erin."

"An oath for what?"

She looked away, taking slow measured breaths as she stood in contemplation. Her eyes breezed over Madison then Cory before falling on me. "I'd like the Obscuro Mors. I have no intention of using it but having such an object would give us an advantage I'd like. Seeing that you were willing to give it to someone who'd use it more freely than we would, I don't see where that should be a problem. And it is my understanding that you have the Mystic Souls spell book. I'd like that as well."

"No to the book." It should be no to the stake as well. But at least with the book of powerful spells, I'd be able to figure out a way to make the stake useless.

After a long moment, she conceded. "My last request must be honored in order for me or any of the elves to offer assistance."

"That is?"

"Damia is talented, but we both agree she is dangerous, correct?"

I held my answer and waited for her to borrow Cory's suggestion and drop her off in the Blose Chasm.

I choked out a breath when she said, "I'll help you find her, but you will be tasked with killing her. And since you have a history of fulfilling your promises with trinkets of your choosing, I will require a blood oath to guarantee compliance. One that puts your life in jeopardy for failure to comply."

CHAPTER 14

"That cannot be your answer. You want Erin to act as your executioner because you don't trust Damia. What the fuck is wrong with you?" Madison bit out.

"Do you really believe that Erin has the moral high ground on this?" Sanaa challenged.

"Abso-fucking-lutely. Damia is a slight issue and now you want her dead. How long will it be before you're recruiting someone to take Erin out?" Cory snapped. His face was flushed with anger. After taking some steps back, he bit his lips before releasing a long sigh.

He looked at Madison, seemingly wanting her to do something like send them all to Stygian without so much as a trial. Shoving a frustrated hand through his hair, he moved his attention away from her to the surrounding landscape.

Was it the new role or was this who she really was, and I'd somehow missed it?

The uncomfortable silence became heavier with each passing minute before Sanaa broke it with a heaved sigh.

"Although I don't agree with those you've decided to form community with or chosen as allies, you have them. You have a connection and a desire to protect them. Despite your question-able moral compass, there is a level of rationale to it. I can appreciate the choices you've made and the actions you've taken to protect those and adhere to your belief, even when I was once a victim of that action. I would go as far as to say you can be reasoned with. Did you get any of that from Damia? Who are her alliances? It is not her kind. Who does she care about?"

She let her words settle with us. Shaking her head, her lips pressed into a tight line. "You said she killed the vampires with ease, using a spell. You can't believe that a person with skills like that is not a threat. Can you confi-dently believe she can be reasoned with? She killed the vampires because they didn't keep their promise and she didn't trust them. Did they promise not to hurt you, or was that her expectation that she imposed? Now she's debating on your life. What if she has a spell to kill you with the same ease? You made a promise to Fabian to do no harm to us. You violated that and we were hurt by that broken promise, as was she. She knows you have the ability to remove our magic —do you not think she sees you as someone who has exploited their magic? Broken promises? Does she see you and your ilk as untrustworthy?"

Flashing before me was the disdain for Dr. Sumner when he attempted to take the object from her. *I see that you can't be trusted, either.*

Sanaa waited several moments for a response which I hadn't even given a second thought. My mind was in a whirl of thoughts trying to figure out how to deal with Damia and further responses from the visiting vampires. What happens when the group doesn't return? Then there was Xavier. What do we do with him?

Once she realized that I wasn't going to agree to assassi-nating Damia, she nodded and started toward the Havenage. "Does palladium work on elves?" I asked.

"No, and even if it did, it wouldn't be the answer to the Damia problem." It could be a temporary one.

"How can elven magic be restricted?" I asked.

She laughed. "If you want my help with Damia, you know my requirements."

"What happens when you consider me a threat that can't be reasoned with?" I asked when we were shoulder to shoulder as she made her way back to the Havenage.

"Don't insult me by underestimating my understanding. I know that I'd never incur your wrath so long as I leave your sister, the witch, and that vapid beast you've chosen as a partner alone. You don't bother mine, I don't bother yours."

With that she moved quickly toward the entrance of the Havenage.

***

Our collective quietness in the car seemed to be a tacit agreement that we wouldn't even entertain Sanaa's request with a discussion. The uncomfortable silence remained as we drove home. Cory dropped me off first with reports that he wanted to do research on his own and that he planned to speak with members of his coven. Madison was going to go to work to find out more about the object Damia possessed after taking pictures of the drawings I had and the markings on her hand.

I quickly ate some food and pulled out all my spell books, including the Mystic Souls, while I waited for Mephisto, who'd be staying with me while his home was being repaired.

CHAPTER 15

Yesterday, I'd rested against Mephisto's chest, his comforting arms wrapped around me as he occasionally nuzzled at my neck and pressed soft kisses over my temple and cheek. It did nothing to diminish my mind from fixating on the events of the day before. I was repulsed by Sanaa's request that I kill Damia. When I told Mephisto of Sanaa's demand, I was met with his stoic unreadable face. I didn't know if he'd expected it or didn't care.

Don't hold me to the morals of this world.

Now he had been noticeably withdrawn into his thoughts. Along with everything we'd discovered about Damia, Mephisto was absorbed by the new finding of palladium's ineffectiveness against elves. He was concerned that even their information about elves was flawed.

Contrary to what Sanaa believed, finding a way to restrict elven magic would at least provide a temporary solution. So, we left the research of the stone to Benton and the others, and redirected our search for a metal that would restrict Damia's magic. We were an hour into our search when my phone vibrated with a text notification. Alex wanted to meet me.

"Did he say why?"

"No, but I should meet him." The drawings that I kept on the coffee table triggered an idea. "The shifters have an extensive collection of magical objects. Maybe they have this."

That piqued Mephisto's interest, although it wasn't just the possibility of finding the stone but also intrigue about the shifters having possession of objects that weren't in his own collection.

When I responded, Alex quickly sent me a location and time.

***

Seated on the bench at the small park where Alex had asked me to meet him, I kept reviewing the curt message in which he didn't offer anything but the request to meet. Mephisto stayed behind to continue our search. Before I left, I could see the effort he put into removing his worry about me leaving again. Damia had debated about whether I'd live, whereas she was quite decisive about closing the Veil and sending the Huntsmen away. We acknowledged I was probably safer than he was from her.

The longer I waited for Alex, the glummer I became, wondering if the meetup was on Asher's behalf. Had something happened to Ms. Harper? Or had he heard about Damia? If he had, Asher and his pack's reach was more impressive than I'd imagined. Would he intervene? The elf wasn't a threat to anyone but me and the Huntsmen by proxy.

Alex approached holding a small bakery bag and a chocolate mint milkshake. I looked at the drink and smiled, wondering who'd revealed my weakness for it. Taking a long drink from the shake, I rummaged through the bag and took out the croissant and picked at it.

"You wanted to talk?" I said between bites when he sat next to me.

He nodded but didn't immediately start speaking. Instead, he picked up some of the napkins that had fallen and walked them to the trash, lingering for a beat before returning with a forced smile.

His nervousness was making me nervous. "What is it, Alex?" I asked, shoving the croissant back in the bag and ignoring my drink.

"Cory's lease is up next month," he blurted. He shook his head, ran his hand through his hair, frowning. "This is so stupid," he mumbled to himself. Then he stood up and stayed there for a few moments before pacing in front of me.

I was used to so many descriptors for shifters: arrogant, jerk, part-time assholes, annoying, dogmatic, but never a nervous bundle of goo. And that's what he was. I stepped in front of him and gently touched his hand.

"What is it?"

"I've never been rejected before, and I feel like maybe…is it too soon…would he?"

"Do you want to live with Cory?" I guessed.

He nodded and I laughed. The unexpected burst of sound caused him to flush.

"Alex, his closet is divided by color and season. He has a hand vacuum in most of his rooms to 'handle those little messes'. He enjoys the smell of bleach and lemons. He's only going to allow the decorative pillows to be out of place for so long before he's aligning them," I said. I didn't want to discourage Alex, but I'd stayed with Cory on many occasions and his face became more punchable each day.

The list simply brought a smile to Alex's face. "I know that already. He seems to enjoy his space, and he's never lived with anyone." The ruddy color on his cheeks darkened as he plopped back on the bench.

He's afraid of rejection.

Returning to my seat, I waited until his eyes met mine, then smiled. "It's you, Alex. I don't think he'll say no. *But* it's like a buy one get one free situation with Cory. You get him, you get me." My grin widened.

"I know. Depending how often you visit, I can increase cleaning service."

"Hey. Rude. How messy do you think I am?"

"I'd rather not answer that, and you might not want to pose that question to Cory, either."

"For someone asking for my blessing, you're awfully mouthy," I teased.

His brows scrunched together and he smirked in a way that gave me a glimpse of the shifter that fit all the descriptors. "Blessing? I was asking your opinion because I didn't want to put him in an awkward position to feel pressured to say yes. I don't need your blessing."

"You can pretend like you are requesting my blessing," I said with a haughty jut of my chin. I extended my hand to him. He stared at it. "Do it like that ridiculous, in Cory's words, 'classic' mafia movie he loves so much. Take my hand and ask for the blessing," I instructed, doing such a poor imitation of the character Alex cringed.

"First, that 'classic' mafia movie is *The Godfather*. It's a classic for a reason because it's a great movie. The characters kiss the hand of the Godfather, as a sign of respect and submission. I'm not submitting to you, Erin."

"Fine." I rolled my eyes and made a face as he fought back a grin. Anything that challenged the loyalty to the pack, even in fun, wasn't taken lightly. Asher referred to me, Cory, and Madison as a pack and regarded our trio with the same respect and understanding he would a shifter pack.

The slight flush remained on Alex's face. It had taken a lot for him to come to me and make himself vulnerable enough to ask the question. I wanted Cory to say yes. Excitement briefly caused me to forget the secondary reason I didn't mind abandoning my research to meet with him.

Opening my crossbody bag, I pulled out all four pieces of paper, unfolded them, and handed them to him.

"In your collection of objects, have you seen anything like this?" I asked. If I could get my hands on the object, I might be able to figure out its limitations and how to nullify the magic in it. The only thing I was positive of was that Damia had bonded to it. If the bond could be broken, it would render her weaker. Probably even divest her of the ability to kill vampires willy nilly. Or me. And possibly remove the threat of closing the Veil, too.

He studied each one. "Well, we don't have a cat," he said, handing me back Kai's drawing.

"Don't look at the object." Kai had done a horrible job recreating the thing itself, but his copy of her markings was excellent. After several moments of examining the paper, Alex frowned.

"Why are you looking for this?"

"The elf who has this wants to kill me, or rather she's deciding if I should live or die. And after watching her kill several vampires by whispering a spell, I'm convinced she might be able to do that to me as well."

"Damn," he said on a breath. The flicker of unease was easy to see in his eyes. Alex didn't want me dead, but I knew his overt display of concern was heavily influenced by his feelings for Cory and the devastation he'd feel if Damia succeeded.

Sensing his turmoil as he decided how much to reveal to me, he excused himself and made a phone call, reminding me of issues his relationship with Cory would face. Pack loyalty. His phone call only lasted moments before he returned.

"I think we have something similar. It's a different color, but the markings are similar, perhaps even identical. I'll need to see it against the picture."

Trying not to be overly optimistic, I stood ready to leave but groaned at the sight of Elon, Dallas, and an unknown third approaching. Alex quickly moved in front of me, adopting a protective stance, lips furled into a sneer.

This was going to go badly.

"I got this," I told him. Easing him back took more effort than I expected. Shifters had deceptive forms. Their movements always denoted they'd have slim, lithe bodies, which was contrary to how they were really built. They were solid muscle and seemed to grow roots into the ground when they didn't want to move.

Dallas's deceptively amiable smile gleamed as he fixed me with soft gentle eyes that accompanied his relaxed casual movements. I refused to be lulled into complacency and the belief that he was innocuous or that his presence near me held no danger.

I was starting to dislike him even more because of that. In that sense, I considered him more harmful than the other two. Elon and the other vampire didn't pose that deceit. Their approach coaxed you into donning a weapon, finding a place to hide, or preparing a magical assault. You weren't going to stand there and do nothing while violence in a tailored suit approached.

Foolishly, I did, because the park contained enough people for them to behave and not compel them all to forget whatever they may have seen, despite it being illegal as hell for them to do such a thing.

"What?" I asked when they were a few feet away.

Their eyes slipped to Alex. Their expressions hardened. He'd probably gone primal or was challenging them to give him a reason to do so.

"Alex," I said under my breath but keeping my eyes on the trio.

"Landon would like to see you," Elon said as if that was enough for me to pack up my things and follow.

"Then Landon should have come here to see me," I challenged.

Letting out an exasperated breath, the third vampire—who must have been new to everything—grabbed for me. Within seconds, Alex had snatched him by the neck and thrown him to the ground, positioning the vampire's head in a manner that gave the knife Alex held secured in his other hand easy access.

Since I'd had a similar reaction and magic had blasted from me, sending Dallas and Elon several feet away, I wasn't in a position to chastise him.

But his reaction signified that the pack was involved, which made things more complicated. When I gave him a look that indicated such, he shrugged. "I thought he was reaching for me," he responded in a flippant tone that made clear he'd put no effort into making it sound convincing.

"Such a violent little minx." Landon's amused voice carried over the sounds of people in the background speculating and gawking at us.

"Release him," Landon demanded of Alex, who didn't move.

"It's okay," I whispered. Alex let the vampire go.

"That's enough," Landon snapped at the vampire who looked ready to retaliate. He waved Dallas and Elon away as well, and within seconds they were gone, still leaving a small crowd of onlookers.

"Perhaps we should leave," Landon suggested.

"I'm not going anywhere with you."

"That is fine, but we seem to have drawn an audience."

"Or witnesses, which will be good for you all. Your vampires will want their witness accounts during the trial for your murder." I treated him to a dark grin.

His boisterous laughter confused the small crowd who'd managed to keep their distance and were only able to gather the crux of our discussion from body language.

His dismissive laughter pricked at my ego. Despite all that had happened, Landon wasn't afraid of me, nor did he see me as a threat.

"I thought we were having a truce."

"Then why did you send your muscle—no, your assassins—to retrieve me?"

He chuckled. "They're the only ones I trust to bring you back alive. Others are holding you responsible for what was done to me. They seem to be the only ones who seem to understand the nuances of the situation. It was to protect you," he said.

"What do you want?" Since the interaction had lost its fervor, the crowd had dispersed.

"The woman who visited my *home*, what is she?" he asked.

Home? Perhaps it could be described as that until one visited the basement. The house of horrors was the only applicable description.

"Which woman?" I inquired. He glared at me. We didn't look for surveillance cameras, but it wouldn't have been implausible for him to have them. Why? Did they watch the torture? Or was it just for monitoring the prisoners locked away in the dungeon? I pushed away the disturbing thoughts that were creeping into my mind. Landon had always seemed kinder and tolerant toward me. My history of dating vampires but rejecting him piqued his interest and his yearning for the conquest. His intense curiosity about me only fueled his fascination. I dealt with the mild version of him, which made me forget that he was the subject of many macabre stories and historical accounts. Warnings about him were not without merit. And Landon was feared by many. He wasn't chosen to take Ramos's place because he was a docile people pleaser, it was because he'd done what was necessary to be a feared leader.

His tilted, narrowed eyes landed on me hard. "Is she like you?" he asked.

I shook my head. He stepped closer, acutely watching me, searching for a lie. He ignored Alex who'd adopted a defensive stance.

"You saw what she did to the vampires?"

He nodded. I didn't think his midnight eyes could get any darker, but they did, darkening to an inky abyss. "And I witnessed the things she did to you, Mephisto, and the others."

"Do you have a copy of the video?"

He nodded, confirming my assumption about surveillance.

We could see everything from a different vantage point. Get a better look at the object she held, the markings on her, and the spell she used on Dr. Sumner, too.

"May I see it?"

"Well, aren't you amiable now?" he taunted. "That is the reason I sent my vampires for you."

"They couldn't tell me that you had information you needed to share opposed to demanding I give you an audience? You knew that wouldn't work, especially where we are now."

"Where are we, Erin?"

My forgiveness threshold was lowering by the minute. "I don't know. What you did to Dr. Sumner was indefensible."

"What you did was unacceptable." Anger rose in his voice and warped his gentle smile into a sneer. "You denied me what you had promised."

"Do you think I would have agreed to that if I'd known that was what you wanted?"

We were face to face now and I put my hand up to ward off Alex's intervention.

"You would have had to or watch your friend die because of a tenuous belief you had about the vampires we would have created."

Taking a step back, I let his words linger, giving him time

to process what he said. And feel some form of shame for using my desperation to his advantage. There was none. Mephisto was right: Landon had exploited my desperate situation and obviously didn't see a problem with it. His expression remained unchanged. There wasn't a single moment of self-reflection or regret.

"You shouldn't have taken advantage of the situation," I stated.

"Then you shouldn't have called me. Instead, you should have depended on the human services, as I recommended," he retorted.

"You weren't ever concerned about the type of vampire you could have created with me?"

He shrugged. "Not really. If they became problems, they would be dealt with. But I am capable of cultivating talent."

There wasn't any reasoning with him, and I didn't feel inclined to do so.

"Once I have Xavier, I will send you a copy of the video," he informed me, turning and walking toward the parking lot.

"Xavier?" I said to his back.

"Yes. I want him in exchange for the video."

He wanted the vampire responsible for abducting and hurting him. Was this request to protect Xavier and get him away from us, or did he have nefarious intent?

"You can't kill him," I blurted, earning a sneer of surprise from Alex and Landon.

"I'd advise you to take Lilith's words to heart," Landon rebutted.

Responding to my look of confusion, he said, "Did she not reprimand you for interfering in vampire business? I think she was quite clear about that. I share those sentiments. You would have saved yourself a lot of trouble if you'd practiced that from the start." A dark cast washed over his expression.

I simply nodded.

Alex had agreed to get me the object, but I hadn't made it out of the parking lot before I received a call from Asher.

You couldn't wait fifteen minutes, Alex.

"Asher," I greeted.

"Erin," his response a low growl of incrimination. "Alex is worried again."

"He should meditate," I proposed.

Asher's deep, graveled laugh was absent of any amusement. "Erin?" he challenged.

"What do you know?" I asked.

He filled me in on everything that Alex had relayed, including my interaction with Landon. I had to give it to Alex, he was efficient at providing information in great detail in a short amount of time.

"How can my pack help?"

"If you have the object I showed Alex, that would be very helpful."

There was a long silence before he spoke again. "Is that all?" Doubt clung to his words.

"For now it is. I am not in a position to decline any help. If I need more, I will let you know."

"Do not hesitate. Okay?"

"I won't." Before we ended the call, I said, "Thank you, Asher."

His low growl of laughter absent of any humor returned. "You can thank me by giving Alex peace," he countered.

"I'm sorry my impending death is making Alex's life so hard, because it's easy breezy for me," I shot back.

He scoffed and slipped in a hasty goodbye before ending the call.

CHAPTER 16

When I returned home, Mephisto was still working on finding metal magical restrictions for elves. I updated him on my visit with Alex, skipping over the Cory cohabitation details and going straight to my interaction with Landon.

"So, we give him Xavier," he said.

I nodded but he sensed my hesitation.

"What?"

Images of the dungeon flashed in my mind every time I considered giving Xavier over to the disgruntled and wrathful Landon. It gave me pause and I relayed my concerns to Mephisto. As he nodded his understanding, nothing about his mien or expression led me to believe we shared that concern.

The kiss he pressed to my forehead felt warm and comforting. I sank into the hug he gave me and stayed there.

"The vampires have to be in the room for the spell to work," he surmised when I stepped out of the hug and refocused on our immediate threat and Damia's capabilities. "If that wasn't the case, the other vampires, including Xavier, would have been killed as well. It's not a global spell."

Well, that information was something. It wasn't like the

spell done with the shifters. Using Asher, Sherry, and shifters from the Veil, Elizabeth was able to imbue them with the same resistance to magic that the shifters in the Veil enjoyed.

"How confident are you that the pack has the object comparable to Damia's?"

"Confident enough to want it. I'd put the chances at greater than fifty percent. If that doesn't work, maybe Asher will let me explore his exceptional collection," I told him.

"How exceptional? Do you think it will be worth me looking at it?"

"No. It will make you wistful if he has items you don't possess. And he won't sell it to you."

"Will he sell it to you?"

I shook my head.

"They don't have magic that would allow them to use the objects," he asserted.

"As long as it's in their possession no one else can use it, either," I countered.

He considered the advantages, but I didn't think it was a convincing enough defense to keep him from wanting to at least see the collection.

Mephisto slipped back into his research, leafing through additional books that weren't from my collection. I wanted to follow up on several ideas that had come to me during my drive home.

The peculiar object in Damia's possession seemed to be the source of most of our troubles. I wasn't confident that her closing the Veil and removing the Huntsmen was linked to the object but would be achieved with a spell. It led to me looking for spells that could be manipulated into doing that. I hadn't found anything.

Mephisto took a break and repositioned himself to get a better look at all the spells I'd attempted to weave and variations I'd put down on paper. I had created a list of magical abilities I determined Damia possessed and counterspells to block them. He pored over the information, which included the reasoning I'd scribbled off to the side.

One of his arms wrapped around me, pulling me into a hug. He kissed my cheek and then the top of my ear. "Undeniably Erin," he whispered into it.

"In what way?"

"You're so resourceful and bright. You've harnessed whatever you've learned and improved on it."

"Yeah, but at what cost?" He grew silent waiting for me to continue. "If I had acquired my magic and kept it simple, I don't think things would be like this."

"How would you have dealt with Malific, Fabian, Elizabeth? Don't denigrate yourself for having to tap into a darker side of your magic to protect yourself and those that you love. There shouldn't be a penalty for that."

But there was. There always would be.

My phone chirped before I could respond. It was a message from Landon with the video attached.

"He sent me the video!" I said, surprised and wondering about his change of mind.

"That's because he was given Xavier."

"I'm going to figure out a way to get in on the chat group."

He flashed me a challenging smile. "If you discover how to do it, we will welcome you in it."

"What if we need to question Xavier?"

His wry smile deepened as he studied my face. "We won't. For the past two hours, I watched your internal debates, and they would have gone on for more hours because you are torn and desperately want to distance yourself from your mother and not give anyone reason to compare you two." He frowned. "What you did to get back at Fabian and Elizabeth has weighed on you. And your decisions and actions are filtered through that desire. I saw the way you looked when Clayton said you were the villain in the elves' story. It hurt you. He didn't say it to hurt you. It's a harsh truth. I'll do what I can to make sure you don't feel that way again. When you are unsure about making the harsh decisions, I will."

Grinning, he kissed me lightly on the lips. "It doesn't bother me to be the villain in the story as long as it's not in yours."

I could make the hard decisions, but it did bother me how dark and cruel I needed to be with Fabian and Elizabeth, even if I was matching the cruelty of their actions.

I constantly questioned if I could become Malific, and thoughts of nature vs nurture troubled me.

We watched Damia interact with a bound Dr. Sumner in the upstairs half of the home, under the watchful eye of Lilith, Annalise, and six other vampires. When she neared him, he reared back and struggled with his binding while she whispered soft words of assurance that didn't ease his discomfort.

She invoked a spell that spiraled silver all around him, and with a rote hand movement casting another spell, pulled it away from him. His face reflected confusion when she unbound him and invited him to stand. He looked around the room of horror and then to the vampires and finally returned his attention to Damia, scrutinizing her and her ears that she hadn't bothered to glamour—or perhaps she had, since only those with elven blood could see them even when they were glamoured. Mephisto confirmed that they weren't glamoured.

"How do you feel?" she'd asked. Her voice was soothing and held an avid interest.

"Fine," he said, backing farther away from the crowd.

"What did you do?" Lilith asked, inching closer to Damia, who was rightfully wary of her closeness.

"Spells. You wouldn't know it if I told you."

"Can the vampire reversal that Erin performed be replicated?" she asked.

"Not by anyone else," Damia provided with a strained voice.

"Would she be able to perform the spell you just did to make them fully human?"

"Yes."

Like Sanaa, Damia was quite economical with her words or had lost interest in the vampires since she'd achieved her goals. Damia's arms crossed over her chest, keeping her focus on Dr. Sumner who she appeared to want to question more but was refraining from doing so with the vampires present.

"Find Erin and get rid of her and anyone who protects her," Lilith directed the vampires. Annalise sidled in next to her in silent agreement of the order.

"If Xavier is alive, bring him back," Lilith ordered.

"No," Damia asserted softly. She turned to Lilith. "Our agreement was for me to stop Erin and her guards. I did that. And you agreed to leave her alone. Just like Erin undoing vampirism to save a vampire you were owed wasn't her decision to make, Erin is not yours to deal with. I offered my assistance to fix the situation."

"Fixing the situation would entail Dr. Sumner being *our* vampire." Lilith closed the distance between her and Damia. Knowing Damia's abilities and Lilith's fate still made me feel like I was watching a horror movie where the plot twist was yet to be revealed.

"What resources do you need to make that possible?" Lilith asked.

I suspected Lilith wouldn't be opposed to seeing the result of a vampire sired with an elf as a consolation.

"None. It's not possible. Erin and I are different." Damia had read the same thing in Lilith's expression. "Nor will I be used to change him, either. He didn't agree to being changed and I won't allow it." She looked over her shoulder to Dr. Sumner for confirmation.

He nodded.

"You won't allow it?" Lilith scoffed.

Damia ignored Lilith's mockery. "I made things as they were. Whatever deal Landon had with Erin will remain between them. They must figure out what is mutually acceptable. Since he's escaped from you all, he has the right to do so."

I liked the Damia in the video. She could be reasoned with and didn't seem like the unbalanced, disloyal elf that Sanaa wanted to be rid of.

Being reminded of her failure to kill Landon caused Lilith to draw back her lips, exposing weapons that she appeared seconds from using. She managed to find patience, relaxing her lips and forcing a tight smile. "Erin's guards, I'm not familiar with their kind. Are you?"

Damia's eyes slowly roved over her, then moved to Annalise and around the room as if she was seeing everything anew. I spied the object in her hand, but there weren't any markings on her hand. Without answering Lilith, she turned her back on her in a dangerous show of dismissal. Damia's mouth was moving, but I couldn't make out the words. The familiar markings laced over her fingers and hand.

"I agreed to help you with Erin and her guards, not to be your educator. Dr. Sumner and I are leaving now." She waved for Dr. Sumner to follow. They hadn't moved far before Lilith was in front of Damia, her hand cuffed around Damia's neck.

She gasped a strangled noise.

"It wasn't a request. Who. Are. They?"

Damia made more noises in an effort to speak. Lilith's hold on her loosened. The fatal mistake caused her and the other vampires their lives. Damia whispered the spell and made a few movements with her hand. They dropped where they stood, and seconds later they were given a true death.

Dr. Sumner cut off his scream and backed so far away from Damia he fell into the chair where he'd been seated earlier. Wide-eyed, he looked as if he was anticipating he'd be next.

"I have no plans to hurt you," she said. "You will need to stay here. Erin will come get you soon."

He nodded. "What did you do to them?" His question was a result of shock and the lack of knowledge. He knew exactly what had happened despite needing a more comforting answer.

She whispered a few words and made more movements with her hand, enacting a spell that secured him to the chair.

"I have no intention of hurting you," she repeated. "But you need to be here so that Erin will come. I'd like to speak to Erin, and if I let her pet go, I won't have that chance."

Dr. Sumner had the same response I did to him being referred to as my pet. He sneered at her, which only made her laugh.

She wiped away some dust on the floor as if it wasn't the remains of the vampires she'd just killed. Seated comfortably on the floor, she appeared to be moving further away from reasonable Damia to scarily unbalanced Damia. She offered him a warm smile.

"You know what she is, don't you?" she asked.

He didn't respond. I wasn't sure if it was to protect me or because he was still in shock.

"She's the daughter of a ruthless god, Malific, and Nolan, a foolish elf who seemed to have made all the wrong steps in an effort to protect the world from Malific. But I believe his intentions were pure." She said the words aloud, but it felt like they were meant for herself. She studied her hands for a long time before lifting her eyes to meet his.

"They should have never lifted Erin's magical restrictions," she mumbled, canting her head and leaning forward to scrutinize him. "Is she able to go through the Veil?"

"I don't know what that is," he responded softly, earning a look of doubt and a frown.

He looked so troubled it made watching their interaction difficult. But I focused on what I'd learned so far: She needed to engage the magical object with a spell. I assumed she didn't keep it engaged all the time because the markings would give her magical boost away.

"That doesn't seem like the truth."

Dr. Sumner closed his eyes, probably wrangling with the idea of sharing my information. He'd been the person I felt free to discuss everything with, and I had. He knew me better than anyone, or rather, in a way no one else could.

She examined him for a while in silence and he did the same with obvious apprehension. Several times his eyes dipped to the object in her hand.

"Are you better off knowing her?"

The question shocked him into an open mouth surprise. But the answer came immediately once he'd composed himself. "I am."

She gave him a tight smile, but I couldn't determine if she believed him or not, nor why it was important.

Without saying another word, she left, leaving Dr. Sumner visibly confused.

The number of times I'd watched the video of Damia was inching toward obsessive, to the point Mephisto left to get us a late dinner. Despite what I'd learned about her handling of the object, I had no more insight into how to deal with her. She was kind and gentle with Dr. Sumner, even when she transferred him from upstairs to the dungeon. Her interaction with him in the dungeon was in a second attachment that missed his transfer to the basement. She was vocal in her refusal to put him in the torturous-looking metal chair with the straps and left him there for several minutes while she looked for an acceptable chair. And she apologized several times for having to restrict him with rope.

When Dr. Sumner asked why she didn't use her magic to restrict him as she had upstairs, she simply responded with, "I need my magic." So, there were some limitations even with the object. But it wasn't enough. She still had the ability to secure an *adligatura* and cast a spell for true vampire death simultaneously. Finding out that she could only do two powerful spells instead of three wasn't the game changer I'd wished the information was.

From the hours of watching the video, and the questions Dr. Sumner asked that she'd answered, I knew two things for sure: She was a strange one, and she had every intention of closing the Veil and locking the Huntsmen away in it.

I stared at the phone as if it were a venomous snake when Landon's name flashed on the screen.

"Yeah," I answered.

"Were the videos of any use to you?"

"A little," I admitted.

"That isn't encouraging," he said.

He eventually broke the stiff silence. "What she did to the vampires, is that exclusive to her or are all your kind able to do that?"

"If I had that ability, I would have nuked you and the visiting vampires when they attacked me," I said.

"I see our cease of hostility isn't going well," he shot back with a hint of amusement in his voice.

Despite his attempt to be aloof at the prospect of dying with a whisper of a spell, it had to be weighing on him. "I believe that for her to do the spell, the vampires have to be in the same space with her."

"I gathered that," he said, "but that is still not enough. I let

Xavier see the video. We've established a truce so we can deal with this elf." His sentence ended abruptly. Too abruptly. He wanted to add more but had decided against it.

Oddly, their established truce allayed some of my concerns. I believed that Mephisto had given Xavier over to be tortured in their dungeon and it bothered me. It was on the same level as allowing the fae to kill Elizabeth. I was no less culpable for their actions. In fact, I was the initiator. My alarms were going off regarding the missing information.

"And?"

"It's good that she's the only one with the ability."

"Don't be coy with me," I urged.

"As if it needed to be said. If all the elves had the ability, it couldn't be allowed. If you and Damia exist, there are others. I'd make it my business to be preemptive if that were the case."

Even as a potential recipient, I understood the rationale. How could vampires exist in a world where they had to be in a constant state of anxiety that with a whisper of a spell from an elf, they'd meet true death.

"If you watched the video, you saw the object in her hand. I believe that is the source of her ability. I don't like her having that ability any more than you do." That was a half-truth. I didn't like that she could use the *adligatura* against me and gods. Take away her ability to kill vampires, and I take away that ability as well. "Don't act on anything, please. Give me forty-eight hours."

"To do what?"

"To fix our Damia problem."

"Is she *our* problem, Erin?"

She was a lot of people's problems, including the Huntsmen.

"Yeah."

"How so?" I'm sure he'd watched the video as many times

as I had, if not more, and her questioning of Dr. Sumner had to have piqued his curiosity, but I'd leave it unsatisfied.

"Just give me the forty-eight hours. Do you have any more information on her?"

"Nothing more than what is in the video. But I'll press Xavier. I suspect you want a way to find her?"

"Yeah."

"I'll see what I can do."

With her ability to harm vampires, I wouldn't have to remind them not to confront her. I pulled up the video of Damia again and zoomed in close on the object in her hand before calling Alex to ask him if I could get their magical object.

CHAPTER 17

The next day, expecting Alex, who had texted me, to meet me at the Northwest Pack's compound, I was surprised to find Asher and Dr. Marisol Reyes waiting, regarding me with cynical interest. Dr. Reyes was standing at Asher's side. I wasn't sure if she had accepted the invitation to join their pack or was still trying to determine how to deal with Ms. Harp. Asher's hand gently placed at her lower back as they let Mephisto and me into the compound, and his use of her first name, led me to believe she may be a new addition to the pack and that their relationship had become more intimate.

Asher and Mephisto leveled stony dark looks at each other. Marisol and I stood back, taking in the tension-laden assessment. At one time, I had been at the root of the animosity that they held for one another. I'd been displaced by the annoying desire for dominance. I frowned at the display. A wolf and grizzly weren't likely to be friends in the animal kingdom or in the living room of the Northwest Pack's compound.

"We appreciate your help," Mephisto managed to say, breaking the icy silence and smoothing over the edge of contention between them.

"No problem. I hope this can be an equal exchange of services," he said, directing his attention to me, which explained why he'd met me and not Alex.

"What services?" I asked, trailing behind him and Marisol as they led us downstairs to his impressive vault. At the landing of the stairs, Mephisto managed to mask the curiosity he'd displayed when he requested to accompany me. As a staunch collector of unique, highly sought after, and deadly magical objects, both legal and illegal, he was curious about the pack's collection. I had assumed he gathered them as a means to return to the Veil, but his interest in Asher's collection, despite his free access to the Veil, had proven otherwise.

Asher led us through a narrowed corridor to an eight-by-ten vault. In the vault, surrounded by steel-reinforced concrete, Mephisto's guarded expression relaxed into an appreciative regard.

Asher moved through the various shelving until he stopped in front of one. He lifted a garnet-color box, opening it to reveal an ecru-color stone similar to the one Damia had. Mephisto and I stepped closer to examine the markings that were very like those that covered Damia. Similar but not exact, which wasn't encouraging.

"Where did you get this?" Mephisto asked.

"Do you need that information to use it?" Asher challenged.

"Just curious."

"Then I choose not to satisfy that curiosity," Asher said, handing me the box.

"If I use it and it is undamaged, I will return it to you," I promised.

He shook his head. "It's yours." He returned to the shelving and picked up the rolled vellum that had been next to the box. "Perhaps this will help."

When I opened it, all the apprehension I felt was chased

away by the Elven language on it. Although still a novice at reading Elven, I could tell that it was history and information about the object. I was about to ask where he got the information but figured I'd be met with a similar response as he gave Mephisto. It was in my possession and that's all that mattered.

But I hoped he'd let me return and that we'd come to an agreement that would allow me possession of all the elven magical objects, or at the very least full access.

"What do you need from me?" I asked.

He looked at Marisol, who nodded. "It's Ms. Harp." Her pensive look scared me.

"What's wrong with her?"

If using her as a conduit made things harder for her with the full moon, I wouldn't be able to handle it. Frustration roiled at the idea that something was wrong with Ms. Harp, and they hadn't revealed it until now. There was a full moon three days ago. I should have been informed then.

Keeping the foreboding feeling at bay was becoming a huge task I was failing as Mephisto and I trailed Asher and Marisol to the home the pack had provided for Ms. Harp. She answered the door immediately, offering me a welcoming smile and Mephisto a forced one devoid of the warmth she extended to me. The aroma of rich, dark roast coffee with notes of cocoa and almonds mingled with the scent of Kahlua wafting from the large mug she held.

No one needed to elaborate on the changes in her. They were obvious and staring back at me. Feline eyes. Topaz eyes housed pupils like the slits of opening curtains. So intense and soul piercing it was difficult to hold them. I felt their pull and they were just as predacious and sharp as the other shifters.

"Two days ago, Sherrie attempted to shift her again. Ms. Harp still couldn't attain animal form, but her eyes changed to what you see now. A shift reversal made her peculiar eyes disappear, so we had Sherrie keep them like this."

Marisol had moved closer to Ms. Harp, examining her again with a frown. Ms. Harp stepped back several feet with a stealthy grace she hadn't had before. She was an anomaly: the result of a cat shifter and a witch contradicting all rules of magic when it came to shifters. Their magic trumped all. Having a child with a shifter ensured you'd have a shifter whether you were witch, mage, or fae. That abnormality was what piqued Asher's interest. But when he discovered Ms. Harp suffered physical pain and cognitive issues during the full moon, he set his sights on finding a way to help her.

"How was your full moon?" I asked her, noticing her heightened irritation at the discussion about her without involving her.

"Fine. Not like the rest. This one"—she pointed to Marisol—"just wants an excuse to study me. I'm different. We know that. I'm old and fine. Do something else with your time." She gave her a playful glare. "I'm sure there's plenty to study with him"—she pointed to Asher—"or you can just spend time with him."

"I transferred here for you."

Ms. Harp snorted and took a long drink from her mug. "Okay." She let out another roll of laughter as she headed toward a comfortable-looking recliner.

I had no doubts that Dr. Marisol Reyes's transfer was motivated by a multitude of reasons and not solely because of Ms. Harp or her relationship with Asher. Her time with the pack had exposed her to rare magic and unique situations that had captured her interest.

"Nothing like this has ever occurred before?" Marisol asked me.

"It was my first time using that spell."

Her eyes trailed over me with intense scrutiny. "Your magic is chaotic and fascinating," she offered, her voice laced with wonder and trepidation.

She wasn't wrong.

"You all can stop worrying. I don't have any pain. My eyes are gorgeous. And…" She made an exaggerated show of turning on the TV and finding the many court shows she enjoyed, "I'd really like some *me* time."

Despite her dismissal, she held our attention. For several beats we all watched her in silence as if waiting for her to complete her shift. Or do something that would devolve this situation into more chaos.

Sensing that she continued to be the subject of interest, she twisted in our direction, frowning. "Carry on," she instructed with a shrug.

Asher and I exchanged glances in silent acknowledgment of Ms. Harp being a constant evolving enigma. A shifter who couldn't shift had now transformed into a human with feline physical characteristics. From my observation, it didn't seem to be a hindrance.

"Has she performed any magic since the changes?" I asked, wondering if she had any similarities to Dr. Sumner.

"No," she shouted from the living room. She had enhanced hearing already, despite pretending she needed a hearing aid.

"Besides her eyes, is there anything different?"

"She doesn't use her cane," Marisol interjected. Asher and I smiled.

"She never needed it," I pointed out.

"Rude. I used it sparingly."

"Because you didn't need it in the first place," I spouted my challenge.

Glaring at me, she dismissed me and my response with a flippant wave of her hand.

"I've missed you," I said. "I think you should move back."

"I can't. *He* won't let me." She shot Asher a look before snuggling back in her recliner and increasing the volume on the tv. Asher's lips pressed into a seam as he attempted to hide his laugh.

"If you wish to go back, it is fine," Asher said.

Leaning forward, she gave us all a searing look. The home the pack had provided was nicer than her apartment and everyone catered to her. The pack adored her, and Asher was amused by most of her antics. She wasn't going anywhere.

"No," she huffed out. "You know I don't like to be a bother. And moving would be too much trouble for you all and I wouldn't want that."

She said it with a straight face.

"Is that right?" he shot back with a grin.

"Of course it is. I know how busy you are, and it would be so inconsiderate to add that to your long list of responsibilities."

"If nothing else, I can count on you to be considerate and the easiest of my responsibilities," he responded, the laughter he'd suppressed reaching his eyes.

"You're welcome," she touted before taking a long drink from her cup.

After moving my attention from the dramatic septuagenarian with poor self-awareness, I considered Asher for a long time. He was still watching her.

Moving closer to me, he said, "I think she's okay, but will she stay like this?"

Mephisto broke his silence. "I believe she will." He looked at me, reluctant to say it but needing to. "Magic will never be exact, and you can't confirm that it was only elven magic that she held when she was used as a conduit. It's obvious that the magic had an effect on her. I suspect it happened when the spell was reversed, which may explain the difficulty with it."

The memory rekindled the frustration and anguish

Marisol and Asher exhibited during the spell casting. Their eyes snapped to mine; uneasiness stifled the room.

I agreed with Mephisto in believing that Ms. Harp would be fine.

Relief flooded Asher's eyes for a few seconds before his brow drew together after several moments of thought. "Shifters like her are a possibility now?" he mused.

"No. As long as our children don't have children with a shifter, or an Arch-deity, or ask a shifter who can't shift to be a conduit for magic, it should be fine," Mephisto answered.

My breath caught and my legs didn't want to hold me up. *As long as our children don't have children with a shifter?* I hadn't thought further than agreeing on a date to celebrate our anniversary, boundaries to our working relationship, and how much clothing we should leave at each other's homes.

I hadn't considered anything as definitive as children or marriage. Based on the looks I was getting from everyone, I was failing at masking my inner conflict.

Finding a few strands of composure, I fumbled out my supporting thoughts of Mephisto's response. Through the existential haze, I managed to finish my conversation with Asher and Marisol, thank Asher for the gift of the magical stone, and give Ms. Harp my departing words. She in turn regarded me with concern. Before I could move away, she tugged my arm and beckoned me to move closer.

"I believe it was a hypothetical, not an expectation. Calm down, okay?"

I nodded, a response that seemed to be the only thing I could manage. Mephisto had undeniably rattled me.

"My comment about our children unsettled you?" Mephisto asked once we'd entered my apartment. We'd ignored the conversation in the car. I knew it was a topic that would inevitably be introduced again. I had hoped at a later time.

Placing the newly acquired stone and vellum on the coffee table, I plopped onto the sofa under his inescapable focus. Keeping his distance, he relaxed against the wall, waiting for a response. When his expression broke into a sadness I'd never seen on him, I moved to him, hugging him and resting my face against the soft fabric of his shirt.

"No, it didn't," I said, pulling away to look at him. My finger traveled along the sharp lines of his cheek. "It didn't unsettle me. I hadn't thought that far ahead and was surprised that you had."

He considered my response, then took my wandering finger and pressed it to his lips. "I think about you and us a lot. I can't help but think about the numerous debates I've had with Kai, Clayton, and Simeon about you. The times they've accused me of being short-sighted and foolish for you, and I realized there's no one I'd rather be that way for. I've lived a long time and absolutely no woman has aroused such intense and complicated emotions in me. Yes, I've thought about a future that involves more than we have now. Whether it will be marriage with children or just us together forever."

"Marriage and children with you didn't come to mind, not because I couldn't see it with you," I admitted softly. "I couldn't imagine it with anyone. A lot of my life was spent with me spiraling and believing I was a death mage. I thought something was wrong with me because I couldn't control my magic desires. Then I found out my origins and became a target with even more baggage and issues. My life became even more complicated."

His arms tightened, comforting me in a way I hadn't realized I needed. "Many of the complications were a result of you existing here, and I wouldn't change that for the world. I want you here. And to be with you. Marriage and children are something I considered because often I wasn't sure it was possible for me."

I kissed him, long and hard. "I didn't know that we could be possible," I admitted.

"Such pessimistic thoughts, my demigoddess," he whispered against my lips, his hold not allowing any distance between us.

"Or practical thoughts," I countered. Our eyes went to the stone. "I need the threat of you being locked in the Veil and taken from me gone and to be able to spend time with you without worrying that someone is plotting to send you away. I love the time I've had with you and I want more." Tugging his arms from me, I laced my fingers with his in a tight hold. "I'm tired of magic being an albatross."

"Magic isn't a burden. The people you've encountered have made it that way." His thumb gently stroked the skin of my hand. "Let's make it so that it's not. Let's deal with Damia first and then the others so we can have our time to be us and just be together," Mephisto said.

"I don't want to kill her, just stop her."

He sighed into the nod. "Stopping her is the first option."

"Our only one. We need to stop her."

He smiled at me. "If anyone can do it, it will be you."

I wanted to share in his confidence. Even having an object that might make it possible, I wanted more assurance. I needed more assurance.

I must have been wearing my thoughts in my expression, as he kissed me lightly on the lips and said, "It will happen."

The next kiss felt like it sealed a promise that I desperately wanted and needed. We stared at each other. I could feel the internal battle in his touch and his intense gaze whether to leave at that moment to prevent the vampires from going after Damia or spend some time with me. The uncertainty shifted to longing.

He lifted me and carried me into my bedroom. Lowering

me onto the bed, his body hovering over mine, I felt ensnared by his dark eyes that held the complexities and the simplicities of our relationship—our lives.

"I love you, Erin," he said.

"I love you, too."

His kiss gave a declaration that exceeded his words. The gentle press to my lips deepened, exploring my mouth, nipping my lips and teasing them lightly, drawing a low moan from me as his hands slid under my shirt, gliding over my skin. He removed my shirt, leaning back and taking in my exposed skin. Quickly yanking off his own shirt, he tossed it aside. His body pressed over mine, covering me in a molten warmth. Light touches sent tingles of heat coursing through me, igniting something deep and fiery. Straddled above me, he held my eyes as I traced my finger along the hard lines of his sculpted chest, caressing the delineation of his abs.

Taking hold of my hand, he extended one of my fingers, laving his tongue seductively over the tip. The deviant glint in his eyes had my breathing coming in fast clips, wanting to feel that sensation over other parts of my body.

His need exceeded mine quickly. With a flick of his fingers, the clasp of my bra came undone, and he tossed it aside. My panties received an aggressive tug, the material ripping off me in pieces. The turbulent hunger in his gaze wandered over my body and made its way into a hard, devouring kiss. He cupped my breasts, his fingers creating tantalizing circles over my nipples until they were painfully hard. The sensation sent ripples of pleasure through me and a craving for more.

I moaned against his lips and writhed at his touch. Desperate fingers digging into his shoulder, arching into him, craving more. He complied. Pulling away from the kiss, I couldn't make out the deep rasped whispers said against my skin as he dragged his teeth on a delicious path all over me, alternating between kisses and caresses with his tongue. His touches became more urgent and fervent. His whispers of "demigoddess" felt reverent as his exploration of my body continued until his face was nestled between my legs. My fingers laced in his hair, I writhed and moaned as his tongue thrust into me, deft fingers running over my clit. Tantalizing strokes matched my desperate whines at a steady rhythm, coaxing more pleasure from me until the room was a cacophony of moans and breathless pleas.

He moved on top of me, his body molding perfectly against mine. Spreading for him, I took hold of his hardness, stroking his satin skin, enjoying the sounds of his heavy breaths of desire for me. The heat of his need was sweltering against my skin.

I pulled him into a kiss. Guiding him into me, I moaned against his lips as I felt him entering me. There was no movement, allowing me to bask in being filled by him, the pleasure of our raw and primal connection.

His hips started to rock in a slow, gentle, rhythmic motion that exploded into deep and commanding thrusts as we sought our pleasure. His fingers pressed firmer into my calves, raising my legs and saddling them to his sides, deepening his strokes. The sensation of him moving deeper inside me was delicious perfection, taking me to new heights of bliss. We crashed into the climax. My body trembled as his shuddered into the orgasm.

Repositioning, I rested my head against his chest, basking in the afterglow of sex. I found solace in the steady rhythm of his heartbeat. Things felt like they were at a standstill with his fingers interlocked with mine. The complexities and simplicities of our relationship seemed symbiotic and harmonious. There was peace.

Despite the chaos in my life, I wanted to stay there next to him, in our own little world.

"I wish we could stay like this," he said, his tone sullen and apologetic.

"We have a few hours. Then we need to figure out how to use our new acquisition."

He brushed back my hair and kissed me on my forehead. "I'll leave that task to you and"—he searched my face—"Nolan?"

I nodded. I had every intention of asking for Nolan's help with the translation of the vellum and possibly with our new object.

"I will be watching the vampires. Because there's no way Landon's going to honor your forty-eight-hour request. I want to respect your wish to keep Damia alive," he said, rolling out of the bed. It was obvious that he was adhering to my wish and not that he agreed with it.

"Thank you."

He shook his head. "I don't know why you need it to be this way. But you do and that's all that matters. I'll do what I can to make it possible."

He kissed me again, a touch filled with reluctance and urgency. Sharing the desire to stay together but understanding we couldn't simply indulge in more leisure time. Before he made it the short distance to the bathroom, he'd looked over his shoulder several times at me. I nodded my encouragement for him to go on. Minutes later he'd showered and gave me a long lingering kiss before he headed out to shadow Landon and the vampires.

CHAPTER 18

Mephisto had called me earlier to inform me that the vampires hadn't found Damia but neither had the Huntsmen. I suspected her location was warded or under a cloaking spell.

While Mephisto and the Huntsmen kept an eye on the vampires, I dedicated my time to figuring out my new acquisition while waiting for Nolan to return my text requesting his help. It had been two hours since I called him. The call went to voicemail. I left a message and sent a text. Figuring that he was doing his own research, which would probably be of some help, I was reluctant to keep calling him. He'd worry. I wasn't getting far with the vellum and grabbed my phone to send him a picture of it when I saw a string of missed texts from Dr. Sumner that made absolutely no sense.

Reading them again, I debated if it was accidental, until he called. Before I could greet him, he said, "Damia, what an unexpected visit. What brings you by my office?"

Shit. I snatched my phone, rushed to my room, and grabbed a double-edged karambit, secured a knife to my leg, and chalk as a rush of ideas ran through my mind. Not wanting to put Dr. Sumner's call on hold or risk Damia finding out I was listening, I muted the call, searching through my drawers until I found a burner phone I'd stowed away. I called Mephisto from it, but it went to voicemail. I left a quick message letting him know what was going on.

Then I called Cory. When he answered, I wasted no time. "Damia is with Dr. Sumner at his office. Meet me there."

"Meet you there? Are you insane? Wait for me and we go together."

"I don't have time to wait. I need to get there as soon as possible."

"Why, to make it easier for her to kill you? This is a horrible idea," he admonished. "She's debating whether to keep you alive and seems to have an odd infatuation with Dr. Sumner. Between the two of you, who do you think is likely to survive an encounter with her? We have no idea of the extent of her abilities or the object's capabilities. Stay there."

"We have her. If I can secure the *adligatura* spell at the entrance, I can hold her there. I'm calling Asher to see if he can meet me," I told him. "We can apprehend her and then go from there."

"I am going to kill you if you die!" he snapped.

"That seems like a perfectly sound decision," I shot back, ending the call and listening to more of Dr. Sumner and Damia's conversation.

It was a benign interaction during which he offered her a list of things from coffee, tea, biscotti to cookies and nuts. What, did he have a small market there? He even half-heartedly offered her vodka, tequila, or bourbon.

"I'll have the bourbon," her soft voice answered.

It caused him to ask, "What?" in a sharp voice.

Her laughter was a sweet, melodic lull. "Bourbon."

There was silence and then Dr. Sumner offering her a drink.

"You're not going to have one?"

"I don't drink," he responded.

"I don't think that's the truth." Her soft voice held an edge to it.

"I don't want to drink while I talk to you," he admitted. "You helped me, and I want to show my appreciation by giving you my undivided attention. Alcohol will diminish my ability to do that."

Brilliant. These very tactics were the reason I didn't trust him in the beginning. Although it made me apprehensive, based on the lightness in her response, she felt differently.

The long stretch of silence made my heart race. Privy to sound and not visuals, I was at a disadvantage and unable to effectively gauge the situation. Was this the calm before the storm or just straight up violence?

"Damia, what brings you here?"

"I don't know," she admitted. I could hear the lack of certainty in her voice.

"Okay," he said softly. "Tell me what's on your mind. You seem distracted."

Unable to get hold of Asher once in my car, I sent him a text and another to Cory to bring Alex. Then I refocused on the conversation, speeding through the streets to get to Dr. Sumner's office, and parking as close as possible to the building entrance.

At his door, I quickly scribbled the sigils for the *adligatura* and waited a few feet away, listening to Dr. Sumner try to pull useful information out of her without coming off as too intrusive. She ignored his question about where she lived, responding that it was a place where she felt safe and admitting she'd moved twice because Fabian had discovered her home.

"You didn't feel safe with Fabian?" Dr. Sumner asked.

It took a long time before she answered. "His visits weren't sincere. They weren't to check on my safety or well-being. They always had ulterior motives. He was using his visits as an excuse to search my home. There were things he wanted to take from me."

"The Black Crest grimoire?" Dr. Sumner provided.

"Yes. He wanted to destroy it and I was confident he'd sacrifice my life to do so. I decided it was best that my living space wasn't so easily discoverable."

"Clever. Now that I'm aware of your kind, I can't help but be completely fascinated by it." The gentle intrigue and compassion in his voice was disarming. It would have annoyed me during our initial sessions because I mistook it for insincerity. In my warped mind the more sincere it sounded the more disingenuous it was. "In this world of magic and technology, how do you keep from being discovered? I'll admit, I envy that ability."

"You don't have elven magic, so it's not possible." Her response held a tinge of skepticism.

"I'm assuming it's not something you're willing to perform for a fee?"

"No."

"That's understandable." His voice remained gentle and affirming. "And the stone in your hand, did he want that as well?"

You're the best. But I couldn't help the pang of discomfort at his manipulation.

"Of course, because I took it from him. He didn't know what it was and had spent years trying to discover its use. It took me a month to figure it out."

"What is it?"

Another long stretch of silence had me leaning into the phone with anticipation. Just when I'd given up hope, she said, "Tenebrous stone."

"It allows you to kill vampires?"

"It allows me to do a lot of things by strengthening my spells and giving me the ability to perform dark magic. But it has to be used sparingly. I've spent time learning all that it can do because it is necessary and to make things right."

"What do you need to make right?" he asked.

"Us. Not just the elves but restore the balance of it all. The Veil needs to be closed. Elves and gods cannot coexist. Demons have their own realm; they should stay there. I will make that happen. Balance will be restored."

"You are afraid of the gods?"

More quiet, but I heard the click of glass on a table and wondered if she had taken a drink to ignore the question or to give her time to consider her answer.

"Yes. I don't fear them because they are more powerful than we are but because they are crueler. So are the inhabitants of the Veil. Great power and cruelty are never a good combination. I can't destroy the Veil and its occupants, but I can ensure that we never interact. They bring out the worst in us.

"Fabian was cruel because of them. His disdain for the gods and desire to be stronger than them made him that way. He hid it well," she said softly. "I realized his intentions were never good. He presented them so that he wouldn't look evil. His ways were indistinguishable from Malific's. He wasn't as violent but just as harmful by wielding his magic and deceptions as tools of destruction. Just like Erin."

"You believe Erin is evil?"

I started to despise the quiet.

"I believe she's Malific's daughter with elven blood."

"I've grown to care for Erin as my friend. I don't see her as Malific's daughter but a victim of circumstances," Dr. Sumner eased out softly. "I've dealt with Mephisto and the others, and I don't see cruelty."

"You wouldn't because you aren't a threat to them. Would a lion ever need to prove to a rabbit they are a threat? The rabbit knows the lion sees them as food, and they act accordingly. It is not the same with elves and gods, which is why they need to live separately. I will fulfil Fabian's wishes. I owe him that since he made it possible for me to do it. But the elves won't live as Fabian and Elizabeth wanted—as ruling magic that subjugates others. I will destroy the Tenebrous stone once I'm done with it."

"You recognize that Erin is both elf and god. What becomes of her?" Dr. Sumner asked, a nervous hitch in his cadence.

"I don't know," she admitted. "My indecision bothers me. I don't wish to make her pay for the sins of her mother or the foolishness of her father. She's been a tool for so long, I fear that she's now a weapon of chaos. She must live as an elf if she is to remain."

Remain had dual meanings. Remain in this realm or remain alive?

"If Erin is evil, or rather a weapon of chaos, then how are you different?" Dr. Sumner challenged. My heart raced, fearing he'd crossed a line that could put him in danger. Despite trying to convince myself he'd be able to read the situation, I still considered Damia volatile.

"Perhaps we should ask her. Have I given you enough time to contact her? She should be here by now. Thank you for your help." Her voice rose as she called my name.

I ignored her.

"I'd considered visiting her at her home, but you are useful collateral." Her voice maintained that benevolent undertone that seemed to be reserved for Dr. Sumner.

It took everything in me not to rush in and keep her from hurting him.

"I don't feel like collateral, or even a hostage, with you sitting across the room from me," he said, letting me know that he wasn't in danger.

"I have no desire to hurt you, just use you to get an audience with her. Please don't force my hand to do more."

I had no idea how to deal with a person who was both volatile and calculating.

"You're not cruel, Damia. You and Erin share many similarities and goals. You both wish magic to exist and be used without hurting others. No hierarchy or abuse of it. You're different than Fabian in that sense. And better than Elizabeth because she never saw Erin as an individual but only as an extension of Malific. Elizabeth believed Erin should pay for the 'sins of her mother and the foolishness of her father' and the only thing that kept her from killing Erin was the promise she made to Nolan. She was cruel to her at every chance."

The silences were going to be my destruction.

"Erin is different but just as precarious, and she has aligned herself with the gods, which is where I fear her loyalty lies. She took our magic for them. Can the elves trust her?"

I'm precarious. I'm kettle, how are you doing, pot?

"Would that be your concern if she hadn't interrupted your magic?"

"She didn't interrupt our magic, she took it. Left us defenseless. She didn't care that the Havenage was left vulnerable to the world."

Emotions are an unreliable narrator, and I had allowed mine to dictate how to handle Fabian and Elizabeth. I was the villain in their story as much as Fabian and Elizabeth were in mine. But the elves were willing to throw me to the wolves on Fabian's behalf.

This was an entire mess.

"Erin, please join us," Damia said.

I stilled.

She exhaled an exaggerated sigh. I heard movement. The door was snatched open and she looked for me as I pressed my back against the wall, out of her line of sight. Occupied with searching for me, she didn't notice the sigils for the *adligatura*. I gave her a magical nudge, enclosing her in it. Damia's face was ruddy as she landed a tempestuous glare on me the moment I stood in front of her.

"It's a weak circle," she berated.

I couldn't help but smirk at her insulting me while restricted in the circle that, despite her efforts, held her captive without use of her magic.

"Strong enough to render you magicless," I shot back. A frown beveled her lips, and she looked down, examining the markings that surrounded her. Lowering herself to the ground, her fingers closed tighter around the Tenebrous stone, but the markings of their connection were gone. She pushed against it and mumbled her discontent when she was nudged back.

"Do you not know how *adligatura* circles work?" I asked.

She stood and glared at me. Whether she'd acknowledged it, she was becoming what she believed she hated. Powers now enhanced and stronger than most, she seemed to have forgotten she could be vulnerable. Before I could make that point, a sharp pain seared over my shoulder, grazing my skin. I stumbled back several feet, pain blurring my vision. With several blinks, I cleared my vision enough to see a man approaching me from the east entrance of the building, holding a gun aimed at me, the tell-tale glint of gold signifying their straddle between animal and human. Shifter. But Asher's shifters would never attack me.

The pain resolved some, leaving a tear in my clothing but no wounds—well, at least not a bullet wound.

———

Dealing with shifters meant battle would be fought with steel and ingenuity and not magic.

"Move," the gun-wielding shifter demanded of me, his gaze sliding from me to who I figured was his target: Damia. The hit from the butt of the gun made me lose my concentration and drop the magic surrounding the circle, and she swiftly stepped out of it.

"Come with me," the shifter demanded of her. A sheaf of arrogance spread over her smirk. The Tenebrous stone's marking returned to her hand and she made several movements with one hand, sending a fiery sphere in his direction. It hit him and dissipated over his body, not even causing him to break his stride. Shock fell over her face, and I realized she hadn't been aware of the shifters' magical immunity when in human form.

Fear quickly eclipsed her haughty expression. She scanned the area, her face twisted with panicked planning. Inching back, she reached behind her for the door. Two more shifters appeared, moving with their customary lethal grace as they closed in on us. Narrowing the distance between them, the first shifter with the gun grabbed for her. Damia slammed her hand holding the magical stone into the side of his head, I wrenched the gun out of his hand, emptied the clip, and tossed it aside. The quick motion unbalanced her, sending her falling back into the opened door. I kept my attention on the shifters coming up from the opposite direction. Three at the other entrance that led to the parking lot, and two a few feet away, slightly obscured by the building.

Dr. Sumner stepped around Damia and sprayed the fire extinguisher in a semicircle, getting the shifter closest to him and the one just a few inches from me. With the shifters' vision obstructed enough, Dr. Sumner smashed the canister into the shifter closest to him. The shifter yanked it from Dr. Sumner, then delivered a punch so hard it sent him into the wall. He recovered faster than I expected. Not used to an opponent who moved with deadly precision and grace, the front kick Dr. Sumner delivered missed. Another strike from the shifter brought Dr. Sumner to his knees, blood flowing from his lips. Undeterred, from his position on his knees, Dr. Sumner struck the shifter in his stomach. The shifter groaned.

I wanted to scream, "Fuck decorum, punch him in his family grapes." I fought to win, violating all rules of propriety, not thinking twice about a nut punch or a tit strike. Not only was it painful, it was shocking as hell to the opponent and gave me a time advantage.

The shifter nearest me moved to Damia, close enough to yank her to him. He hesitated for a fraction of a moment, his attention drawn to the Tenebrous stone. It made me wonder if acquiring the stone was the greater objective. It had to be Landon who'd given them the information that it was the source of her magic.

Seeing his target, Damia cradled it to her chest, whispering several words. The markings unraveled from her hand, along with the stone.

The shifters standing with annoyance at the disappearance of the stone gave me the opportunity to grab my double-edged karambit. A figure eight advance put the shifter on the defensive, retreating to prevent being cut by the sharp blades and putting distance between him and Damia.

They definitely weren't part of the Northwest Pack, which meant they were the rare lone shifters. Because lone shifters weren't under the financial umbrella of a pack, they did a lot of freelance work. The ones in our area tended to have a tacit agreement between them and the packs not to violate pack rules. Me being viewed as a friend of the pack would prohibit them attacking me. From the slight accent of the first shifter and their unfamiliar faces, it was safe to assume that they were visitors or employed by Xavier and the attack condoned by Landon. Mephisto was right; he wasn't going to give me forty-eight hours.

Damn. I never would have expected saving a person who wanted me dead to be on my Bingo card. But there it was. For a fleeting moment, to my shame, I considered how drastically easier life would be without Damia.

But I would protect her because I couldn't let her get hurt or worse. Xavier wanted worse, I was sure.

To let Damia and Dr. Sumner get into the office, where they'd be safer, I had to give them space from the shifters. Quickly changing direction, I dropped to my knees and slashed the shifter's thigh. He stumbled back, transferring his weight to his uninjured leg and kicking me with it, striking me at my temple. Color flashed before my eyes.

He'd heal quickly, and the only way to stop that was to get silver in him. My blades were carbon steel. Him advancing toward me put me on the defensive as he adapted to my movements, which weren't nearly as fast as his.

I made a show of turning and running away. The shifter going after Damia ignored her for the opportunity to grab me. His outreached hand was met with the blade slashing into his palm. Cursing, he stumbled back. I couldn't tell if Dr. Sumner and Damia took advantage of the moment of distraction. I hoped they had. I'd definitely made myself the target.

Listening to the steps pounding after me, I couldn't determine if it was all of the shifters, excluding the one I'd just injured. Sprinting to the other side of the building, I sank against the side of it. Invoking my cloaking spell, I wrapped myself in a veil of invisibility.

My heart was pumping so hard, I could feel it in my ears. In an effort not to give my location away, I calmed my heavy panting. I had the advantage of the sounds of the city, which, though there wasn't nearly as much traffic as I'd like, was likely enough to distort their senses.

Carefully listening for lithe footsteps, I clutched my karambits closer. I sneered at one of the shifters who arched his back before his body twisted and contorted into a wolf, trotting off to track me down. He'd probably assumed I'd used magic to put more distance between us. Once he lost my scent, he'd return, but that left me just three shifters in human form to deal with.

Without the use of silver, I'd have to be quick and brutal, inflicting injuries that would require more recovery time or require them to shift to their animal to assist with the healing process. I lunged at the oblivious shifter who'd caught my smell but not the sight of me. I made deliberate slashes into his back, causing him to unleash an involuntary growl of pain before collapsing to the ground writhing in pain. I severed his Achilles tendon and quads, exacting the greatest amount of damage needed to ensure he'd heal but only with time. His body shuddered and jerked as he changed to his jackal form. The other shifter, who'd seen his partner assaulted without signs of a body, raised his nose to the air. His eyes narrowed in my direction. Moving toward me, he pulled leaves from a small bush he'd passed. He charged in my direction, throwing them in hopes they'd fall over me, allowing him to home in on my location. I lunged to the ground and rolled away, letting them fall over the recovering jackal.

His laughter wafted through the air, a smirk settling over his lips. He enjoyed the challenge. If he were part of a pack, he'd probably be the Alpha. They were a twisted bunch, enjoying a challenge and a worthy adversary. Cool, I'd take compliments where I could get them.

"They want you, too, but you aren't a priority. I guess we'll be exceeding their expectations." His hostile hungry glare made me wonder if it was more than the challenge but the payoff. He glanced over his shoulder where Damia clawed and punched at the burly shifter who was carrying her to a car.

Where was Dr. Sumner? I had to shelve my worry and hope for the best. My mind raced, trying to figure out a way to get to Damia and avoid the shifter who was locking in on my position.

Damia wasn't going without a fight. As they neared the car with a driver at the wheel, her hands made rote movements. The car windows exploded, sending shards of glass everywhere.

The pompous shifter looking for me cursed under his breath at the explosion, and I used the opportunity. He could only estimate my location whereas I had a direct hit. When he inhaled the air and smiled, I knew he'd got a lock on my scent and had a better idea.

He changed direction, which put him directly in front of me. I lowered enough to miss his extended hand that attempted to grab me, spinning until I was at his back, delivering similar injuries to those I had inflicted on the other shifter. He was defiant in succumbing. A front kick sent him crashing to the ground. Snarling in the direction he figured I was, he glared, panting and finally giving in to his need to change in order to heal.

Turning away from him, I was met with a fist slamming into my face from a woman I hadn't seen before. Another kick to my torso came moments later from the other direction. I assumed it was the shifter I'd lost sight of. I crashed to the ground, losing hold of my weapons. The woman's eyes brightened at what had to be her ability to see me. Grabbing my leg, she tossed me a few feet from my weapons. I returned to standing as swiftly as my pained body would allow, quickly assessing the situation.

Two shifters, ready to attack. I tried to invoke the cloaking spell, but it dragged on me, feeling like I was lifting an anvil. I was magically close to depleted. Things went from bad to worse when I glanced toward the car but found an empty space and shards of glass. Despite Damia's efforts, they'd taken her.

The woman was closer to my weapons. Her shifter speed and agility would ensure she'd get to them first.

What were the orders for me? To bring me in or kill me? Considering how the other shifter handled me, I assumed it was to apprehend me. But I didn't think the vampires would be too disappointed if the shifters disposed of the woman who could reverse vampirism. The woman's lips kinked into a taunting smirk. I charged with all the energy and anger I could muster. Moving just before we collided, I shifted to the right, grabbed a handful of her ponytail, and used it for leverage to toss her over my hip. Her solid build made it impossible to stay standing. We grappled on the ground, exchanging poorly aimed blows. Rolling to the side, I accepted the onslaught of blows drilling into my body, waiting for an opening that eventually came. A left jab into her throat shocked her. Reflexively she grabbed it, and I came to a half kneel and elbowed her in the nose. Struck again and again until I saw blood and watery eyes. I stood and kicked her in the crotch.

Crotch kick. Hell yeah, anyone can get it.

Snatched by my shirt from behind, I was about to turn when I heard a crack and the assailant wail in pain. Turning, I saw Alex standing over the shifter who was cradling a broken arm.

"You don't come to our city without letting us know, and you damn sure don't touch ours."

Technically, I wasn't theirs. Asher said I operated as my own pack, but he'd extended courtesies to me that I doubt many shared. I was a friend to the pack, and that was enhanced by a series of other associations. Cory was Alex's and I was Cory's. It was personal and the main reason Asher butted in far more often than I wanted, because my problems involved Cory and ultimately affected Alex.

"Erin!" Cory called my name, allowing me to miss another bone being broken. Cory's face fell at my appearance. "Oh shit." He rushed to me, concern quickly turning to anger.

"The blood's not mine," I said confidently. I wasn't sure. But I could feel my lips swelling. It hurt when I moved my face. My body ached everywhere.

Alex had leaned down to the writhing shifter, his voice low and ominous. "When you heal, stay down or you won't heal so quickly the next time."

He made his way over to the shifters who'd shifted to heal. He snatched up the jackal by the scruff, holding his gaze to his.

"Change now," he demanded of them both. When dominant shifters spoke, something in their demand made it hard to ignore. It went through the body, strongly coercing you to comply. Even Cory winced and shivered as if warding off the feeling.

Walking to the wolf lying on his belly, Alex's glare intensified, seemingly more insulted by his presence as a wolf than the jackal. Alex cuffed his hand at the back of the wolf's neck, pressing him firmly against the ground. Leaning down, Alex said something to him that from my distance was a series of baleful growled words. The wolf struggled helplessly against him before relaxing and tucking his head into himself, I assumed in a show of submission. The woman who'd I grappled with earlier then received Alex's attention. Defiant, she stood, shoulders rounded, brow quirked in a challenging gesture.

A serrated chuckle came from him that hinted—no, promised a level of violence no one wanted. He beckoned her with the crook of his finger. She didn't move.

He let his eye travel to the wolf man whose arm and leg

he'd broken. "I won't let you heal until I'm ready," he warned. Color drained from her face and the defiance wavered before completely falling. She moved closer to the other wolf.

"Should I be turned on or scared of Alex right now?" Cory asked.

"Scared. The correct answer is scared." Because the brutal menacing man in front of us showed so few traces of Alex, I wasn't sure he was still there.

"I don't think that's the right answer," he countered.

Even with my strength zapped I mustered enough to playfully jab him in the stomach. "It is. What is wrong with you? Why are you like this!"

"I'm just saying it's kind of sexy."

I didn't have time to go down that rabbit hole of nonsense.

"Damia," I squeaked, looking in the direction of where the car had been.

"Mephisto has her." Cory looked at his phone, I assumed to confirm.

"I need to check on Dr. Sumner and get my phone."

Alex urged us to leave him with the shifters. As we left, I saw him making a call, probably to Asher. I had no issue with staying out of shifter business.

I ran back to the office and found Dr. Sumner frowning and gently pressing a compress to his face, where bruising was starting to show.

"I'm glad you were able to come," he said weakly.

"Thank you." I moved closer to examine his injuries.

"I'm fine." He nudged my hand away. "How's Damia?"

"She's with Mephisto."

He relaxed and made an attempt at a smile, but the pain didn't seem to be worth it. "Good." He studied me for a moment. "She's not your enemy." He offered a small smile at the doubt in my expression.

"Were we listening to the same conversation?"

"She wants the Veil closed and your friends gone," he said decisively. Despite being aware of my feelings for Mephisto, I believed he wanted the Veil closed as well.

"She said she'd destroy the Tenebrous stone once it closed, and I believe her. You may not agree with her concerns or the means she chose to achieve them, but there may be something to what she said."

"I don't want to lose Mephisto."

"I know." Again, I was hit with a determined response devoid of emotion. His eyes softened and he gave me another weak smile. "She can be reasoned with. You may be able to change her mind."

He sounded confident. I was hopeful, but doubt was firmly placed in me, too.

"I see that shifters have entered the fight," he said grimly.

"Not ours. They're from Lilith's territory."

He nodded. "I gathered. Nevertheless, they're in it. The vampires have every reason to be desperate, and although you may try to resolve this situation without any losses, I feel some will be inevitable." He quickly closed the distance between us, shocking me with an unexpected hug. His body folded around me, cradling my hand to him, warmth enveloping me. It was so tight that my body moved with the sigh he expelled. "Don't be one of the losses."

He pulled away and looked at Cory who'd managed to retrieve my phone that I'd left outside near the side of the building. His discomfort with Dr. Sumner's display of affection had him examining my phone.

"I'm going to take a short vacation. I'll have my phone with me. Contact me if you need me." His eyes invited us to leave but his request for me not to be "one of the losses" lingered in his eyes.

Giving him a hurried goodbye, I looked back at him before he closed the door on us. I attempted to push down the guilt that was threatening to rear its head.

This is not my fault. I said the unconvincing mantra over and over.

Like hell it wasn't. But reliving the incidents of the past wasn't going to change anything.

I would fix it, and I would have Mephisto here with me.

CHAPTER 19

Mephisto texted us Clayton's address, where they were holding Damia. The car that had driven away with Damia was parked on the side. Behind it was one of the Northwest Pack's ostentatious SUVs. I recognized two shifters that Asher had sent as guards on one of the many occasions he'd inserted himself in my life.

"If nothing else, they are efficient," Cory acknowledged.

"That and they're very territorial." I knew that; I'd just never experienced it to that extreme. It was always a good reminder that being on the opposing side of their more questionable qualities and impressive resources wasn't good. Appreciation of being in alliance with them made itself felt.

The property surrounding Clayton's home stretched for miles before a neighbor's home came in sight. He didn't have the same security measures as Mephisto. We didn't have to deal with codes or gates.

Cory's mouth parted at the striking architecture of the home before us. The pewter brick–color home with sleek black aluminum–framed floor-to-ceiling windows gave it contemporary masculine elegance. Smooth light gray stones, meticulously arranged, created a pathway to the front door.

Alluring aromas wafted from the blooms of unfamiliar flowers. Large trees surrounded the home, giving an extra layer of privacy.

Madison answered the door, dressed in her work clothing. "When Clay called, I took the rest of the day off," she explained. From her dejected look, she was likely questioning the security of her job. She sighed, frustrated hands washing over her face. "Damia's refusing to speak to anyone. She'll probably talk to you." Madison's assertion lacked confidence.

"Go back to work. I'll fill you in on everything and if I need your assist, I'll let you know."

She shook her head. "I need to be here. I'm going to need to push for the elves' visibility because they aren't making an effort to do so themselves. Damia is a wildcard. Your abilities and hers are no longer a secret and you're both at risk."

"I gathered that when the shifters attempted to abduct us."

She sighed. "That's an issue, too. The shifters here have done a great job hiding their newly acquired immunity. In fact, from what I saw it wasn't flaunted by any of the shifters. However, even with their discretion, it hasn't gone unnoticed and a lot of questions are being asked." Her fingers wrapped around a tuft of curls and her eyes flattened with distress.

"Let them speculate. The only people who know the truth are the shifters from the Veil, Sherrie, Asher, and us. Magic is nebulous and always evolving." I shrugged. "As far as they know, it's just another evolution."

The Supernatural Task Force had squashed all knowledge of the fae with animancer abilities, which led to me having to help the shifters' magic immunity. Elizabeth wasn't around to disclose it, and I was confident that the elves wouldn't offer the information. I suspected that the shifters reluctance to expose themselves was rooted in them wanting to keep their new abilities quiet. That lack of knowledge was a tactical advantage. Damia had experienced it today.

Giving a noncommittal shrug, Madison's eyes traveled over me. I had done my best to clean up in the car, and Cory's magic helped with the pain, but I had strains and aches that his magic didn't seem to alleviate. I suspected a fractured rib. I was a little over eighty percent sure there weren't any torn ligaments.

"Let me guess, you look worse than it is?" She glowered, her tone laced with a glib snark.

"Exactly." I flashed her a grin which she acknowledged with a shake of her head and a request for us to follow her.

Abruptly, she looked over her shoulder, catching several of my careful steps. "I guess the limp is just a new gait pattern?" She tossed out her concerned observation with an edge of irritation.

"I'm fine." I sped up a little to give her arm a reassuring squeeze while getting glimpses of Clayton's captivating home and the serenity of horticulture, from the expansive windows in his home that were diametric to the clean lines and bold angles and hues of gray, black, and taupe.

We passed his large kitchen with luxury black stainless-steel appliances that appeared unused. Sleek matte charcoal gray cabinets lined the walls and complemented the polished black granite double island. A splash of color came from hints of copper in the marble backsplash.

"There is absolutely no way he cooks in this kitchen," I said.

Cory stopped to take it in. "This room belongs on Instagram or Pinterest."

"Does he use it at all?" I asked.

"He cooked for me once. The kitchen nicely reflects his cooking abilities," Madison provided cryptically. Her lips beveled into a small frown at our coaxing looks. "It was edible," she said, after several beats searching for the right words.

The living room was adjacent to the kitchen. Walls, painted in a soft shade of greige, served as the backdrop for a plush, inviting charcoal-color sectional and accompanying barrel chair seating that looked equally comfortable. The hardwood floor was complemented by a rug. A handcrafted wood table was in the middle of the room; Kai's work, I felt sure.

"Damn, I need to work on building a better friendship with Clayton," Cory said, poking his head into the home theatre where we got a preview of the unique artistry of charcoal gray paneled walls adorned with ornamental sconces, their soft golden glow adding a touch of warmth to the dark room. Madison maneuvered around us to turn on lights, revealing hidden LEDs in the intricately designed molding and a collection of plush, oversized reclining leather chairs arranged in a tiered formation. Each recliner was equipped with a built-in cup holder and a small foldable table. The centerpiece of Clayton's lavish retreat, the screen, stretched from wall to wall, dominating the space with its sheer magnitude.

"Hypocrite," I mumbled once Madison closed the door and we continued to follow her through the audaciously large home. From the number of snide remarks and teasing he'd lobbed at Mephisto, I'd expected Clayton to live in a modest cottage.

The impromptu tour was a welcome distraction from my chaotic mind that was trying to devise a plan to deal with Damia. The abduction attempt and the discovery of the shifters' total magical immunity, if she somehow linked it to me, might sway her completely to seeing me as big of a threat as she viewed the other gods.

Venturing through the home, we were given an even more in-depth look at Clayton's modern sanctuary from the sculptural pieces, made of brushed metal and positioned strategically throughout the rooms, to the expressive home décor and unique art. Several items deviated from the consistent style of the home, which I assumed were Kai's addition. Despite being beautiful, they didn't quite fit the aesthetics.

At the back of the house, I found the Huntsmen lined near the wall, leaving ample space between them and the noticeably disgruntled Damia who was seated on the sofa in a sunken second living room, or whatever Clayton would call this room to prevent him admitting he had more than one living room. Entering the space, I pinned Clayton with a very judgy look. His lips tightened into a line, and a glow crept over the bridge of his nose, forehead, and along the hollow lines of his cheeks. His shame made holding my eye contact hard, and he quickly tore his eyes from mine.

Before I could move farther into the room, Mephisto had closed the distance between us. "Erin," he breathed out. Cupping my face, he examined it before leaning back to give me a full body assessment.

"I look worse than I feel." I repeated Madison's words from earlier. She frowned but held her comment, which came with some effort based on the way her teeth gripped her bottom lip.

"That's doubtful," he countered. I'd caught a glimpse of myself in one of the mirrors in the house and made an effort now to usher away anything that reflected the fatigue, soreness, and pain I felt.

Mephisto returned his hand to my face, his thumb moving lightly over my cheek and gently tracing over my lower lip. "Are the injuries on your face the worst of them?" he asked.

They were the worst he could get to see without going under my clothing. He appeared to have gathered that from my expression. He nodded, slowly. Moments later, the familiar menthol feeling moved gently over my wounds, easing the throbbing pain. Pressing my lips together, I didn't feel the swelling that had made them lopsided. I hadn't mastered healing wounds. That was an intricate part of magic that witches didn't possess but gods did. It was a skill I needed to work on. I wondered if it would be the same when self-administered as it was with Mephisto's warm hands caressing me. The way his magic cradled me in a familiar and soothing way and the comforting way it molded over me accompanied the feelings he invoked in me. I loved him. With him standing in front of me, it felt like the world dropped away and it consisted of just us. A feeling I'd never felt nor thought I would.

"I think my ribs are broken and a bullet grazed my shoulder," I admitted, glancing at the affected shoulder. He nodded, inched closer, slipping both hands under my shirt, splaying his fingers over my ribs and treating me to another course of his magic. He applied a similar treatment to my shoulder. The absence of pain as I breathed or made minute movements was welcomed. Leaning forward, I rested my head on his chest.

"Better?" he whispered.

"Better." I hadn't realized that my hand was fisting his shirt and he'd enveloped me in a hug.

Cory's forced loud coughing broke the bubble, making me aware of the disgruntled elf with an agenda seated on the sofa.

"Are you okay?" I asked Damia.

She shrugged. "It was expected that the vampires would retaliate, I just never thought it would be with shifters. A flaw in my expectations." She gave me an accusatory look. "I hadn't realized they are immune to magic in both forms, but I could tell from your expression you were aware of it." Smirking, her brow hitched, waiting for a confirmation she most definitely didn't need.

"Yes."

"Knowing you and your friends' closeness with the local pack"—disapproving eyes snapped in Cory's direction before returning to me with fierce accusation—"am I wrong in assuming you were involved in that?"

Withholding my answer, I waited for her to provide evidence to support her assumption.

"Once the elves discovered that your magic had been restored, Fabian found me. He wanted me to align with him, Sanaa, and Elizabeth to rein you in. Elizabeth said you were causing havoc with your magic. I just didn't know it was to this extent."

I scoffed. "Elizabeth gave them their immunity."

For a long moment Damia scrutinized me with a critical eye in an attempt to read if my response was a lie.

Losing my patience with her, I said, "How can you believe the things Elizabeth and Fabian said about me despite your distrust of them and their hunger for power? You know they would have sacrificed your life if you stood in the way. You can't be 'the justice and the balance needed in a world where magic exists' if you're dead."

"Can't be it if my magic has been confined, either," she shot back, revealing the oddly misshapen manacle on her wrist. As small as her wrist was, it had obviously been a struggle to get it on her, because on the other arm was the brace used to induce sleep on the vampires.

"That's what we were doing when you couldn't get in touch with me. Benton and I returned home to find out more information about magic restrictions for elves. Rhodium is the only thing that came up with the elves," Mephisto whispered. Something in his voice felt off, as if he wasn't confident in the information.

"During the commotion of getting me back, I found myself here with these on me. I guess no one wants me to use my magic," Damia said.

"No, we don't want you trying to kill Erin," Mephisto snapped. "You already know if there is a choice to be made between you two, what it would be."

She studied Mephisto for a long time, then looked at me. Her head canted as confusion suffused over her expression. "I don't get you two. Not at all."

"Sounds personal," I shot back. "Our relationship is not something for you to *get*."

Damia's expression turned amused, a wide smile spreading over her face. "You're right. I have no obligation other than to correct it. I don't want you dead. If anything, you're misguided. I'd like to help you. You've earned that much from me. We work together to mend the elves, make them whole and not as in Fabian's vision. Something new and beautiful. It won't be possible if we must worry about becoming prey."

I gritted my teeth at the small twinge of sorrow I felt for this woman, because it wasn't about power. But she was aggressively unaware of the flaws in her plan.

"You want me to mend the elves and ally with you after you lock away the man I love?"

Her mouth parted, disgust flitting over her expression. Then sorrow that was unequivocally directed at me. She shook her head, showing the same dismissal of my declaration of love as one would a child with a crush. Relaxing back on the sofa as if this was a casual visit and not some strange hostage negotiation situation, she said, "My mind hasn't changed on gods and elves living together, and it won't change because of your *love*. It can't happen."

"You expect me to deny the other parts of me? I can't do that. Should I be cast away with them?"

She shrugged. "I hope you won't. But you seem quite attached to your beast, so I will leave that up to you and hope you make the right decision. With them gone, you won't be nearly the menace you are believed to be. He brings out the worst in you." She shot the group of men a castigating look. "I'll bring out the best in you. *We'll* bring out the best in the elves. We have so much work to do. But I've come to respect many aspects of you. And Dr. Sumner likes you. He seems good."

We stood in silence for a few moments, the weight of Damia's words hanging in the air. The tension in the room was palpable.

"What have *we* done to the elves to warrant us being cast out?" Kai asked. Of the men, he had the least menacing look because of his cherubic features. When it came to magic wielders, looks were often deceptive.

"Should you be given an opportunity to do unspeakable and possibly irreparable damage before something is done? History is the best foreteller," Damia countered.

"You're basing it on the history of one person," Clayton pointed out. He kept his voice low, but aggravation steeled his comment.

Damia's lips curled into a contemptuous smile. "And those who have come from the Veil have caused havoc here and returned. I don't believe you all are any different, just better at hiding it."

"Should we be flattered by the exceptional credit you are giving us? We've been here for over fifty years. If we were as menacing as you believe us to be, at least one vile act could be traced back to us. Surely you have that information to share," Simeon offered.

Damia held his probing gaze for a long time, defiance in her expression. Refusing a response, she returned her attention to me.

"Before we were forced into this realm, we were responsible for apprehending the worst of our kind. We don't want those capable of great harm moving freely to hurt others or leaving the Veil," Kai provided.

Damia seemed unmoved.

Madison said, "I agree that the Veil should be closed." Her admission didn't surprise anyone except Damia, whose eyes widened. "Erin remains here and so will they. I don't know if you don't have a response for Simeon or you're being evasive, but I can assure you they are not a problem. As someone who shares your concern about the free travel of the occupants of the Veil, they have been a help to Supernatural Task Force. I want to work with you to restrict all travel except theirs. Wouldn't it be advantageous to have the men tasked with apprehending the worst of their kind the ability to come to this realm and help if necessary? Or even share their knowledge and resources? They've proven on many occasions to be assets, not liabilities."

A slow-roving, derisive smile curled Damia's lips before it erupted in a wave of laughter, making me revisit my impression of her tottering between sanity and insanity.

"I didn't answer Simeon because his question didn't deserve a response. I know what they are and what they are capable of. I won't be responsible for the imbalance their presence causes, nor the destruction they could exact on a whim, because of your fallible belief that they are more of an asset than a liability. I am confident that the elves can be resources and could help. Erin's existence is a consequence we must live with. I am giving her a choice. I think that is more than kind and an adequate compromise. The Veil will be closed with Mephisto and the others within it without any option to return."

Mephisto sneered his frustration, his eyes narrowing at Damia. "You think you can just send us away as if we are mere trespassers?"

Damia's challenging gaze remained steady under Mephisto's glare. "That is precisely what you are. Interlopers. Your magic doesn't belong here. You know that we can't coexist. I won't allow it."

"You won't allow it?" Clayton scoffed.

Snatching her gaze from Mephisto she withdrew into her thoughts. "It shouldn't be allowed. You can't deny what happens when we live together."

I knew she was referring to what my mother had done to the elves.

"This isn't up for debate," Madison snapped, moving closer to Damia. "You seem to possess the same sense of superiority and entitlement as Fabian—"

"You believe I deserve his fate?"

"No. I believe you need to get off your high horse and work with us. Our goals align more than you think."

Damia inclined her head, her features softening ever so slightly in acknowledgment of Madison's words. Her penetrating gaze remained so intense that Madison began to fidget. "Can the shifters' immunity be changed?" she asked, removing her attention from Madison and staring at the blank wall, making it apparent that the discussion about the Huntsmen had ended. "That isn't the way things were. We need things returned to normal."

Omitting that I also knew the spell, I said, "Elizabeth performed the spell that gave them their immunity to magic."

Damia nodded, her expression a mélange of frustration and determination. "Why would she do such a thing? There was no advantage to it. In fact, we are now at a disadvantage when it comes to them."

Her eyes darted from face to face searching for answers. It landed on me where it stayed. For an excruciatingly long time, we sat in the dimly lit room. The weight of uncertainty was making me more frustrated by the moment, and I could feel in the air the disdain for the volatile elf.

Considering whether her knowing the events that led to Elizabeth performing the spell would make the problem better or worse, I decided it wasn't information she needed.

Before I could speak, all emotion vanished from Damia's face as if she'd come to the conclusion that I'd played a role in it. Whether correct or not, the determination on her face said it all. She planned to find a way to remove the shifters' total immunity, and with the help of the Tenebrous stone, I wasn't confident she couldn't.

Damia slid off the sigil-covered brace first and placed it on the cushion next to her. "I've given you all enough of my time, and we've made our stances known. I'm done," she said softly. She looked at the clock. "You have three days to leave willingly. After that, the Veil will close. It is up to you whether you leave freely or are forced out."

I opened my mouth to speak, but she held up a dismissive finger. "We're done." Reappearing in her hand was the Tenebrous stone, the sigils lacing around her fingers. A taunting smile broke through her stern expression. "It needs to be pure rhodium."

No one moved, watching as she sliced a finger over the rhodium metal manacle, breaking it open and looking at it with disdain as it fell away from her wrist.

I considered lunging at her, snatching the stone despite the image of Dr. Sumner's response flashing in my head when he attempted it, ending it all with a sweeping act. It would be futile if I died during it.

"Erin, what is your decision? Do you choose to leave or stay?"

"I'm staying and they will be allowed to freely move between here and the Veil," I asserted. I agreed with Madison on allowing them a way to breach the locks of the Veil.

She responded with a placating smirk. "Allowing them to travel through the Veil will leave the opportunity for others to do so. I won't allow it, and since you have not made the decision, I'll make it for you. You will stay, but they will leave. I will make it so."

And with that she was gone.

CHAPTER 20

The tension was palpable after Damia's abrupt departure, everyone's focus on the sofa that held the powerful elf. With seventy-two hours to stop her, we didn't have a lot of time to ruminate.

Madison and I caught each other's gaze. We were faced with the reality that the question we'd put off so long needed to be answered.

"If we can't stop her from locking the Veil, but we do discover a way to keep you all here, are you okay with that?" Madison asked the group of men.

Her question was met with an unsettling silence.

"Give us time to think about it," Clayton said.

It wasn't as simple as a yes or no because nothing was concrete. Even if they'd agreed to stay, if we couldn't figure out a way to do so, it was a moot point. Stopping Damia remained the primary goal.

Once I'd given Madison the information about the Tenebrous stone, she returned to work to search whether she could find anything that could counter it. She didn't seem hopeful. Magical objects confiscated by the Supernatural

Task Force were linked to witch, mage, or fae magic. She was convinced that the Tenebrous stone was solely elven magic.

Cory didn't wait for an assigned job and indicated he wanted to track Damia with Alex. The shifters needed to be involved because their magic immunity was at risk. Clayton, Simeon, and Kai returned to Mephisto's to assist Benton who had been unsuccessful so far, and in his frustration had convinced himself that Damia wasn't just an elf. I disagreed. She was just more skilled than anyone he'd encountered and had the extra boost from the stone.

Mephisto told me he'd return to my home in hopes of learning more about the object I'd acquired from the shifters but wanted some time with the Huntsmen. I assumed he wanted to discuss Madison's question or to be angry without an audience.

I hated that a newly acquired magical stone about which we knew nothing was our best hope.

Before Nolan arrived, I showered and stood in the middle of my bedroom, a towel wrapped around me, damp hair brushed against my shoulder, the heat of the kiss Mephisto placed on my shoulder chasing some of the chill off my damp skin. I'd been surprised to find him waiting for me after I got out of the shower.

Planting another kiss on my neck, Mephisto's arms closed around my waist, pulling me against him. The soothing feel of his magic moved over the aches and pain that I'd ignored.

"Pure rhodium," he whispered his disappointment. "We couldn't get a lot of it on such short notice to make a manacle. Pairing it with palladium seemed logical because I remain unconvinced that palladium doesn't have some effect on elves, even if it's minor."

I nodded in understanding, easing toward the new ecru-color stone, my finger tracing over it.

"What if this stone does nothing? Then what?" With a ticking clock, I wasn't sure if I should be savoring every moment with Mephisto or fighting like hell and using every second to stop the clock. I despised that there was a part of me that wished I hadn't intervened when the shifters attacked Damia.

Sensing my thoughts, Mephisto said, "You did the right thing helping her. She's proven far more competent and capable than we gave her credit for. I believe she would have gotten away, and you withholding help would have made things worse."

He sat on the bed, pulling me to him, cradling me to his chest, kissing my exposed skin. The idea of me losing him made my heart ache. His face grew serious as he looked at me.

"What?" he asked.

"You all didn't answer Madison's question. I know we're focusing on stopping Damia. But if we can find a way to keep you all here, we won't be restricted by her timeline. Let her close the Veil, and we work on figuring out a way for you to circumvent the restriction. If that's not what you all want, we focus solely on stopping Damia."

He nodded, giving me an understanding smile that I didn't expect. "If closing the Veil is in play and us having to live here permanently is the only solution, then so be it. I told you it wasn't the same when we returned. I'm sure eventually things would have returned to normal, but it had been off for us. It didn't quite feel like home. Perhaps it's because our interaction here is different. More..."

"Domesticated," I offered in a taunt. They were forced to be their base selves in the Veil. They didn't have to be like that here, and I wondered if they found some solace in that.

"No." He nipped at my shoulder. "I still want the freedom

to navigate both realms, but we had to admit that it might not be where we belong most of the time."

My mouth parted but the words wouldn't immediately come out. Eventually I managed a raspy, "Are you sure? Is everyone okay with that? Even Kai?"

Kai being restricted to land was an ongoing concern for them. They worried about him, and often he looked like he was suffering; it was heartbreaking for them to watch.

He nodded. "We wouldn't have come to the decision if he hadn't pushed for it. He suffered so much we didn't want him to go through that again. When you suggested finding a way to keep us here after the Veil was closed, he told us about a small town he'd found that allows him to fly to take the edge off and where he'd not likely be discovered. The area near the vampire's dungeon is an option, as well. Those are both places where he could spread his wings and fly without drawing attention to himself. It's not ideal, but if this is where we stay, it will be enough for now, although we'll continue to search for something that will meet his needs."

I understood what was left unspoken. If they couldn't find that, they were willing to expose their existence to give him that freedom. I'd do whatever I could to protect them.

"Clayton's a given. He seems quite enthralled by a woman who slapped cuffs on him and threatened to have him arrested."

"You really are going to have to let that go," I teased as he clung to the umbrage of Madison at the end of her patience dealing with Asher and Mephisto who seemed to be having a measuring contest when I was missing.

He laughed. "As long as Simeon has animals he can interact with, he's happy." I remained convinced that Simeon dealt with humans out of necessity, not desire.

"Once we returned to the Veil, Benton didn't seem as happy as he used to be. It was apparent he was happiest here.

I suspect he will eventually request to be unbound from our magic to live the remainder of his life here."

Mephisto's admission—or was it a concession—gave me some relief, easing tension that I had been carrying since our encounter with Damia.

Resting against him, my mind raced through any options available to us. The likelihood of reopening the Veil was possible, but it would take time. It was doubtful the gods could hide from Damia, but I couldn't figure out how she'd evict them from our realm. Where could they be hidden where she couldn't touch them? Jerking up, I turned to face him.

He studied my face, his thumb strumming over my cheek. "What's going through your mind?" he asked, a hint of amusement in his tone.

Changing position until I was straddled on his lap, I said, "It might be the worst idea ever, but it's a solid one. I'm not sure what spell she'll use to remove you, but it must be able to detect Veil magic. If your magic can't be detected, you can't be expelled." He looked less entertained and optimistic than he had moments ago. "Blose Chasm. We keep you there while she closes the Veil."

The hopefulness disappeared and his eyes darkened. His thumb languidly stroked my cheek in a sympathetic strum that made me lean into his touch. Lifting my chin until our eyes met, he kissed me deeply. My towel loosened when I wrapped my arms around his neck. His warm hands flattened against my back.

"What are the requirements for the Blose Chasm?" His question was a sobering douse of cold water that I didn't want.

"Magic," I whispered. "It requires the sacrifice of magic."

"Exactly," he said gently. "If it's for me, Clay, Kai, Simeon, and Benton, that would require the magic sacrifice of five elves, and someone to close it."

"Their magic will be returned once you leave the Chasm, right?"

His small smile lifted the corners of his lips but didn't reach his eyes. "Do you really think you could convince six elves to do that?"

"Five," I corrected. "I'd sacrifice it for you."

"I don't want you to."

"I could probably get two. There are so many things I could barter to get two."

"So, I can stay here and the others are locked away?"

I hated that my desperation had placed a hopeless sorrow in his expression. I despised that, once again, a misguided elf was forcing us into making hard decisions. Children and marriage, how could I even think of those things when the threat of Mephisto being whisked away and locked in the Veil was a possibility?

"Then we stop Damia. That is the only option." Looking at his expression was too hard, so I stood. I could feel his assessing eyes on me as I quickly dressed. Looking over my shoulder at him, I got a pensive smile laden with a darkness and determination that didn't bode well for Damia.

"She'll fail. You will all stay here. The Veil will be closed, and we'll find a way for the five of you to navigate between both," I asserted with unsubstantiated confidence. Nothing in the quiver of knowledge, magical objects, and/or current situation lent to it being feasible.

The critical issue remained: Damia was a magical powerhouse with abilities we couldn't grasp. It made her very dangerous, and she'd decided the Huntsman had to leave. She left no room for negotiation. I gave another hopeful look in the direction of the stone and the vellum next to it when my phone rang.

Rolling my eyes at Landon's number, I answered.

"Erin," he hissed out. "Have you not learned any lessons

from the past few days? Stay out of vampire business! This is my last warning."

"Thanks for the confirmation. This is my last request. Give me forty-eight hours. Based on what happened today, how likely are you to be more successful than me?"

"The pack got involved," he snapped.

"And they'll get involved again. You realize she wasn't the only one they wanted?"

The silence came abruptly, shutting down whatever he had been about to say. "What?"

"Stop trusting *them*. Xavier doesn't seem any more trustworthy than Lilith, and unless you want to end up like her, I'd give me that time. Damia won't strike first, but if you attack her again, more vampires will die."

"I can't give you that time. We are trying to stop a woman who can kill us with the mere whisper of a spell. This cannot go unaddressed."

"It will be addressed. But I want her alive and you're giving me the impression that you don't. Drop that plan."

"My ego has been shelved for the greater good. I advise you to do the same."

"It's not my ego that's making the request. I wasn't lying when I told you she wanted me dead. I didn't save her to curry favor. I will stop her, and she won't be able to hurt the vampires either. But—"

"But nothing, Erin. I will not leave this to you. I can remove the bounty on you, but if you intervene again, I won't protect you."

"Protect?"

A short sharp silence lingered, then he said, "Your abilities are a concern, which is why they wanted you as well. Stand down. Your actions today are going to make it difficult for me to even plead for your life."

Mephisto took the phone from me. "It's not Erin's life you need to be worried about. She asked for forty-eight hours.

Give it to her and make sure no vampire comes near her. If she so much as loses her balance and gets a scrape dealing with your vampires, I will be the problem that you and Xavier do not want."

"I don't respond to threats," Landon snapped.

"What about promises? Because that's what I'm making. Don't come near Erin, her family, or her friends because I'll deliver the punishment you deserve." The low ominous promise was all he gave before ending the call.

Thinking it was Landon when the phone rang again, I was prepared to keep Mephisto's energy in responding to him. It was squashed when Nolan told me he was just ten minutes away.

CHAPTER 21

Nolan arrived with a satchel of books, papers, small magical objects, and a determination that mirrored mine. He read over the vellum, seemingly losing the plot on the reason he was here.

"This is absolutely fascinating," he said, his eyes scanning over the words. "We are an ingenious group," he whispered softly.

He'd never be accused of not loving elves, and I adored that about him. While telling him everything about Damia, I admitted that part of me felt foolish for not taking more drastic measures with her. I was glad Mephisto had returned home to help the others, giving me time alone with Nolan.

"She is misguided," he agreed. His voice held a paternal concern. "You are proving more than anything that you are not like Malific. When you win and Damia's alive, others will see that, too." He looked at me with soft eyes. "That's what you want, isn't it?"

I nodded, blinking back the tears starting to form.

"Do you miss being able to interact with them?" I asked.

"Of course. But they made their choice. I have you and that's better than the Havenage."

That was a beautiful lie and I appreciated it.

Learning Elven was about survival because the ability to read it enhanced my magic. But Nolan enjoyed it for the sheer breadth of elven history it provided. One that could have been lost.

"Why are we so incredibly ingenious?" I asked.

"Didn't say incredible," he teased, brushing a few strands of my hair back. I smiled at the touch and took hold of his hand.

"Our magic seems to always have a contingency plan." A trauma response for being nearly rendered extinct. Sitting next to Nolan, I felt the connection and the rationale behind his desire to be invited to the Havenage. It provided an opportunity to commiserate about their history and survival.

My intentions were never clearer as to why I hadn't taken the easy route with Damia. Misdirected, definitely unbalanced, but she didn't want power—she wanted safety. In her mind, the people from the Veil posed a threat to that.

Nolan tapped the stone. "This is a Lexis stone, a counter to the Tenebrous stone."

"Will it undo her binding to the Tenebrous stone?"

His face grew grim with a deep frown. "We might be ingenious, but we're not very direct," he admitted. "It says here it will be the light to the darkness. It is a shield to the sword."

"A shield to the sword makes more sense. If the Tenebrous stone is ever used for harm, I'm assuming it will shield that from happening," I speculated.

Turning the words over and over in my head, the only thing I could think to do was bind myself to the stone as Damia had and do a reversal spell in the hope of rendering them both useless. In turn removing her boosted magical abilities. I expressed my hypothesis to Nolan who considered it for so long that I was expecting him to disagree with me.

"I think you are mostly right. I don't think a reversal is

the right thing, though." He wrote a spell out and I looked at it and reared back quickly.

"I don't want to do that!" Memories flooded back of Elizabeth manipulating me into binding myself to Malific, causing us to experience the same thing. Malific used it to torture me. I couldn't do that again. I refused to be bound to Damia.

Taking my hands in his, he said, "I'd never risk you, Erin. You have to know that." His warm hands slowly eased the panic away. Earnestness and caring soaked into his eyes and expression. "Erin," he said softly, "you do know that, right?"

"I know." I inhaled a shaky breath. And asked on the exhalation, "What do we do?"

Nolan was so meticulous in his preparation, rewriting the spells phonetically from Elven for me to use and moving items out of the way as if he expected a magical burst that would cause damage. Tasks complete, he stood in the middle of the room, his face contorted in thought.

"Are you really willing to close the Veil?" he asked.

I nodded. "Not just to placate Damia, but Madison's life would be easier if it's done. My concern is that it may prevent Mephisto and his brothers returning to their home. And it could possibly take years to find a way for them to negotiate the lock to return to the Veil. Mephisto says that they would be fine with it, but I hate that they have to make that choice."

"Erin, you can't save everyone from living with inconvenient and unfortunate outcomes. Do your best to do the right thing. Closing the Veil is the right thing. Them living here is the right thing. Preserving Damia's life is the right thing," he asserted.

The relief of his words eased things some. He moved to the satchel he'd brought with him, pulling out a notebook and a small object. After flipping through the pages, he brought it to me. "She had figured out a way to close it."

It seemed to hurt him to say Elizabeth's name. He looked away as he continued. "I believe she had every intention of closing it with you in it." His eyes returning to the paper, he pointed to another part of the spell. From what I gathered, it looked like a summoning spell.

"How did you come to that conclusion?" I asked.

"That is what you'd be called in Elven. Since you are the only one of your kind, this is specifically for magic like yours." He pointed to a word in the spell. His perceptive eyes watched me as I took in the new information. Once he'd determined I was okay, he provided, "This closes the Veil."

He pulled out a pencil, marking off part of it. "Just this part. Nothing more."

Agreeing, I tried to process the information he offered and how it had to affect him when he found these spells. I assumed it was when he cleared out Elizabeth's home after finding out about her death.

Flipping through the spells, I speculated whether this was something else that needed to be destroyed. Damia planned to destroy the Tenebrous stone, and I planned to do the same to the Lexis along with Elizabeth's book of spells.

"Destroy the Lexis but not Elizabeth's spell book. Let me keep it. Please." Nolan had learned to read me very well in such a short time. Or perhaps we had so many similarities that he understood me because they were things he would have thought or done.

I trusted that he wouldn't use the spells, and because of his limited magical abilities, some of them couldn't be performed by him alone. These items were the remainders of his sister and showed both her brilliance and flaws.

"Of course."

Smiling, he directed me to the cleared center of the room. "Invoke the spell and bind yourself to the Lexis," he instructed. "Get a feel of what it can do. Become familiar with how it feels."

Thankfully, the spell was short and didn't require the use of blood. Which made it dangerous because it could be invoked quickly. I'm not sure how ingenious it was that any rando could possess and use the spell. I hoped the ease and speed of use was because of the Lexis's purpose and because it was important for it to be accessed quickly. Maybe the Tenebrous stone required more difficult measures to invoke it.

Reciting the spell, the stone warmed in my hand and invisible fingers secured a hold on me.

"Are you okay?" Nolan asked.

My only response was a curt nod as I felt a complementing magic blend with me, a new placid surge of power moving through me as clay-color markings crawled over my fingers. I understood why Damia displayed such unwavering confidence because the flood of magic felt omnipotent, exceeding the god and elven magic I possessed. I felt thankful that Fabian never learned how to use it. And it drove home the belief that the magical objects the shifters had in their possession needed to be curated.

While I reveled in the new power, Nolan's speculative concerned expression turned on me.

"I'm okay," I confirmed. "*But* promise me that if I waver on destroying the Lexis, you'll do it."

"Of course."

I needed to see the extent of the stone's abilities.

"Stay bound to it," he said as he quickly scribed the *adligatura* around me, and when he attempted to invoke it, a simple reversal spell by me wiped away the sigils. Nolan's eyes widened and he gave me a triumphant smile. This was a shield and a companion object to the Tenebrous.

An idea triggered. I invoked a locating spell hoping the stone would immediately look for its alternative companion. A light jolt ran through me. I breathed through the dark and abrasive magic that seemed to bind to the magic from the

Lexis. They were distinguishable, equally powerful. I knew I had latched on to the Lexis's companion stone—the Tenebrous.

I followed up with an unbinding spell, hoping it would remove the magical link from Damia and my stones. I speculated that by maintaining the unbinding spell, we both would be prevented from having access to the magic.

The markings on my hand lightened but wavered. When gold emblazoned the stone, a shock ran through me and then an explosion of pain. A tug that evolved into a vicious ripping as if the stone was struggling to unbind itself from me. Ignoring my door rattling violently and enduring the torment, I continued the cycle through the spells.

The door flew open, revealing Damia who stormed in, her face twisted into a rueful scowl. The onyx markings on her hand and fingers were now soft gray as they pulled from her.

"Stop it." Her demand sounded more like a wounded entreaty as the gold marking emblazoned and started to fade. Damia's empty hand covered the one holding the stone, drawing attention to the moon ring on her opposite hand. Moon rings prevented shifters shifting and were solely used by them. It was the closest thing that she had to a shifter other than one with her. No one could convince me that she wasn't trying to use the Tenebrous to remove the shifters' magical immunity.

"What are you doing with that ring?"

"Balance," she panted out, struggling with her hold on her Tenebrous stone. It wasn't a direct confirmation, but clearly I'd interrupted her performing a spell that involved the shifters, and because she considered their total immunity an imbalance, she was probably working to change that.

I shook my head, continuing to recite the spells, watching the markings unravel from us. Desperation and panic washed over her features. A large candle soared in my direction, and I dropped to my knees to prevent it hitting me. More objects careened in my direction. Nolan, who'd escaped her notice, blocked them with his magic. Rage and unfettered determination had become Damia's driving force.

She lunged at me the moment I stood, surprising me with a strike on my cheek. The effort to maintain our bindings to our stones had us exchanging haphazard strikes and blows. Grappling on the floor, Damia demonstrated unexpected fighting skills that forced me into fight or flight mode. Accepting the strikes to her side and body I delivered, she pounded on my hand with her fist, cracking the moon ring in the process when it connected with the exposed stone. When a piece broke from my stone, she huffed and gave me a smile of satisfaction.

"You can't beat me," she panted out. "I can't allow it."

Untangling from me, she crawled away and stayed on all fours, taking a few beats before she stood. Eventually she gave me a quivering victorious smile. Slowly backing her way to the door, she kept her eyes on me the entire time. Whatever strength she could muster, she used to scuttle out the door. Magically depleted, she wasn't able to Wynd.

Cursing, I took in the condition of the Lexis, knowing the damage would render it useless to unbinding her. My first instinct was to go after her, but sanguine stains left behind on the stone kept me from doing so. Our exchange was a victory for both of us. I could now find her anywhere and I'd figured out a way to stop her.

Grabbing the Lexis, I stored it safely and then rushed for the door.

"Where are you going?"

"To the Havenage. I need to chat with Sanaa."

CHAPTER 22

I wasn't surprised when Nolan invited himself along for the excursion, and as he sat silently next to me, I only got slight indicators of his feelings from the side glances he'd given me that reflected a myriad of emotions ranging from incredulity to horror. My idea wasn't as ambitious or haphazard as it seemed when it initially formed. The closer I got to the Havenage, the more confident I felt. Perhaps it was from the nod Nolan gave me, which probably was just an indicator for me to proceed with telling him, but I took it as an encouraging, "You got this. There is no way it will fail."

Parking at our usual spot at the Havenage, I prepared for the onslaught of pain and compulsion from their wards. Looking at the distance between it and the pending deterrent, I mused.

"I wonder if I can bring the ward down?"

"That's not a great way to ingratiate yourself, and whether you believe it or not, you will need that," Nolan advised. He took my hand and gave it a squeeze. Our deep sigh was nearly in sync before we traipsed to the entrance. Before we could make it a few feet, Sanaa advanced toward us, her face pinched into a disapproving moue.

Her pointed look trailed from me to Nolan and returned to me.

"Have you changed your mind?" she asked.

"No, I'm here to change yours," I said.

A sardonic grin broke into her steely expression, diminishing the optimism I'd held moments before.

"Damia is a gifted and dedicated practitioner. If your goal is strength, you want her. And as the provisional leader of the elves, do you want your desire to kill your own to be known? She's a misguided problem and is ruled by the desire to protect elves and return the unbalance she believes was made. Is that different than what you want? Welcome her back into the fold, show her that you don't want power but protection of the elves, and you will have her loyalty," I offered.

Her expression remained unyielding.

"You will have her," I went on, "the Black Crest grimoire, and the other elven items stolen from Fabian." I considered adding the objects that the pack had, but I wasn't sure I'd be able to get them.

Her cold expression warmed as she considered my proposition. "And what do I have to do?"

"Restrict my magic and close the Veil."

I had her undivided attention.

***

I'd made so many deals, promises, and concessions, that if I failed, it couldn't be said it was for lack of trying. The Veil would be closed as Madison, Damia, and Sanaa wanted. When the elves went before the committee to register, they'd have their involvement in closing the Veil as an attribute of why they were an asset and whittling down any concerns some may have about them. Despite the effort put into it, I still had to convince my friends and the Huntsmen.

With Nolan, Mephisto, the Huntsmen, Madison, and Cory the room didn't seem crowded, but the heightened emotions made it feel suffocating. The room was silent after I relayed everything, but the glares shot in my direction and rebuttals left unspoken raged in the room. Clayton's arms were wrapped around Madison, his chin resting on top of her head. An adorable position that I was sure was an affectionate restraining hold. Her narrowed eyes and hostile glare confirmed it.

"Has sleep deprivation made you lose all sense?" Madison finally proposed in a brittle whisper. "How could you make these deals without letting us know? Why would you even visit Sanaa without us? Do you know how badly that could have gone?"

"I'm glad someone said it," Cory said from the sofa, fiddling with his hands as if looking at me was too difficult.

"Damia is going to send everyone who doesn't belong here back to the Veil and close it. They agreed to stay if the Veil is closed. I needed a way to make sure they could."

Madison didn't look surprised by the news they were willing to stay, just angry that I'd done this without them and had put myself in a situation that could have gone wrong.

Looking at the little homing device, I felt confident in my plan, which I'd needed only because of Damia's determination to destroy the Lexis by any means. Disregarding the protection of her blood during the fight, Damia had given me a means of tracking her anywhere.

"I'm calling it. Drugs. The strong stuff. How else can she explain this level of delusion?" Cory chimed.

The strain on Mephisto's face was heartbreaking. He wanted to defend the indefensible. To him, the easiest solution was to lift all protection I'd granted to Damia and let fate handle it. The vampires definitely planned to kill her. At this point, one mention of what she planned for the shifters and they'd probably become an additional threat to her. I could give them her location and be done with it all.

But I didn't want to have a hand in her murder. There was only one way to fix this and to do so, I had to put my life and future in the hands of the elves.

"It's not delusion. I won't be helpless. I'm reverting to who I was for a short period. It's the only way I can take her magic and break her bond to the Tenebrous stone. She can't close the Veil without it."

All eyes went to Nolan with the expectation that he had the ability to change my mind.

"I don't like this, but it is the best option. She won't be as she was because the magical restriction is temporary. Of course, I will help with the spell," Nolan offered. His contribution didn't seem to offer the relief he'd expected. Despite his proficiency, he was noticeably lacking in magical strength compared to full elves.

"So, Sanaa and whatever cabal of elves she brings with her are going to open the Blose Chasm and keep the Huntsmen and Benton in it while someone closes the Veil," Cory challenged.

"Then you plan to allow Damia and Sanaa to close the Veil?" Kai asked, caution heavy in his voice.

I nodded. "I don't want to take Damia's magic, but if she doesn't agree to protect you all against being locked in the Veil, then I will. Sanaa will only help if she's allowed to close the Veil. To do so, she'll have to use Elizabeth's spell. It doesn't matter whether it's Damia or Sanaa who performs the spell. Anyone who belongs in the Veil will be pulled from this realm and locked there."

"Except us," Clayton added with a broad smile. I appreciated the confidence he displayed was an overcompensation for the lack of it coming from Madison.

"And Sanaa was able to convince the elves to help place us

in the Blose Chasm, sacrifice their magic, and release us?" Mephisto asked.

It was the third time he'd posed the question, and the answer hadn't changed. I nodded. Fabian had warned me that magic would be diminished after opening the Blose Chasm, but I was proof that wasn't true. And I suspected, as with most things when it came to Fabian, it had been a form of manipulation.

"Only if you all allow an oath that prevents you all hurting anyone with elven blood."

He'd waved that away. I wasn't sure if it was due to his confidence that he'd find a way to circumvent it or that he had no intention of making the oath. He'd only wavered when Sanaa requested that the oath be signed immediately before the Blose Chasm was opened.

"But why allow them to be the ones to close the Veil? Why not you?" Cory asked. I knew Cory didn't care who performed the task. He was being driven by spite, a quality that amused me often. But this time it was an obstacle. His lips downturned into a rigid frown. "You're giving too many concessions to Sanaa and will be perceived as weak."

"A lion doesn't have to convince anyone they are a predator," Clay said. He'd used some variation of that when I tried to flex being a demigod and he gave a subtle—well, it wasn't that subtle—reminder that he was a god. I smiled at him. Of all the people in the room, I never expected Clay to be my hype-man. He might not agree with my decision, but he was becoming my staunchest supporter because of Madison. I'd take it any way I could get it.

Madison looked as if she was seconds from hauling me away to a sequestered room and pleading her position until I agreed to rejecting most of the plan.

"It's a good-faith show. Allowing them to close the Veil will make them feel proactive in it because they've been harmed by the occupants of the Veil," I said.

"You trust Sanaa?" Simeon asked. His deep-seated skepticism was unexpected.

I made a face and rocked my hand side to side. "What would be the advantage of leaving me without my magic?"

"Because she dislikes you," Cory rebutted.

"She doesn't dislike me…"

"That's it. Start the intervention now." Cory came to his feet. "I'm Googling the process. Someone grab her to make sure she doesn't escape."

I laughed because I had no other choice.

Nolan said, "You can trust her. She's not Fabian or Elizabeth. Contrary to what you've been exposed to, elves prefer to keep to ourselves. We will choose peace over war. Erin is offering peace. The Tenebrous stone will be destroyed, making Damia less of a concern to us all. If things go well, Damia will rejoin their community. It will make her less likely to become a problem in the future."

"What if they're willing to sacrifice the five elves' magic and keep them in the Blose Chasm? We have no way to counter it," Madison challenged.

"Then it seems like you'll have to trust us," Sanaa's raised voice said from the other side of the door. Opening it, ten elves spilled into the room.

"I'm not feeling very trusting," Madison admitted.

"Are you feeling pragmatic?" Sanaa asked. "If we work together, we all win. Damia's tenacity and knowledge will be a benefit to us." I speculated that she was counting on Damia's presence also giving her access to the Black Crest grimoire. "I don't wish to fight with Erin, nor will the elves be subjugated by her. Betrayal by either of us will have consequences that neither of us will like nor truly benefit from."

I rolled my eyes, wondering if this was going to be the extent of my relationship with the elves: distrust, poorly concealed hostility, and threats.

Seeing my response, she tacked on, "You have our word. If you trust us, we will trust you. I have no desire to be in a war of attrition or to gain a Pyrrhic victory. That's why we're giving Damia the option to join us. It'll be the same result. The Veil closed. The Tenebrous stone destroyed."

CHAPTER 23

Without time to waste and everyone seemingly onboard, the blood Damia left on the damaged Lexis was used for the location spell. After finding her whereabouts we all filed out of my apartment. Before I could leave, Mephisto took hold of my arm.

"I love you," he whispered. I stopped in my tracks to look at him. The anguish in his voice had me turning and searching his face for answers. Had I missed a flaw or obstacle in my plan?

Cupping his face, I said, "I love you, too."

Our eyes locked.

"What's going on?" I asked.

"I know that you being without your magic is going to be hard, and I appreciate everything you've done for us. For my brothers."

"You've made sacrifices, too. Your willingness to stay here despite limited prospects of returning to the Veil."

His small, conflicted smile revealed his feelings about how the Veil didn't feel like home to him or the others anymore. He may not have seen the loss of the Veil as a sacrifice, but it was his foundation and held memories, and not being able to visit it even if only for nostalgia was going to be difficult.

"Are you afraid?" he asked.

"Yes," I admitted. "I want it over and to shed the weight of being Malific's daughter. And in the process, right some terrible wrongs. I hate that the Veil is closing but it will give so many peace of mind. It'll remove the fear that another person like Malific could come through it."

"There was no one like Malific," he said.

Sadly, he was right. Even the Huntsmen didn't possess the narrow focused, virulent violence, chaos, power-lust, and thirst for vengeance that she possessed. Acts so terrible nothing seemed to undo the abhorrent view the elves held of gods and even demigods.

"Do you believe Damia won't be a future problem? Are you being led by your heart or your mind?"

"Both. Because nothing exists without both. Even in sheer violence, emotions exist. It's inescapable. I'm pragmatic and I believe Damia is, as well. If she can't be reasoned with, then I'll be forced to be cruelly pragmatic. If that doesn't work, I'm going to crotch kick her."

His deep melodic laugh broke through the tension. "Because my Erin loves a good dirty fight."

I nodded. "And it's so unexpected when dealing with a woman. The WTF face they give me makes it all worth it. It makes me happy," I quipped.

His face grew serious. "That's what I want for you, Erin. For you to be happy. For *us* to be happy."

"That's what we'll have," I said, leading him out the door. Happiness, less drama, peace, and my ability to see our relationship past a date that didn't erupt in chaos or get tainted by impending problems. Once we had that, I'd never take it for granted.

Finding Damia in a tiny, dilapidated home in the middle of nowhere surrounded by barren land was unexpected. The grass near the home was scorched and I had no idea why. Failed spells? Or was it from the previous owner? The small white house with the unkept steps, unstable-looking wrap-around rails, and neglected garden showed Damia for what she was: a woman on the run. Possibly an erratic woman on the run. Hopefully she was tired of it. A few homes in similar condition were located a few feet away on each side. The distance offered privacy, but from the looks of them, I wasn't confident any of the homes were occupied.

We'd parked several feet away and walked the remainder of the way. My traipse was slower than the others' because despite agreeing to have my magic restricted again, I wasn't looking forward to it. The memories of the emptiness and longing knotted my stomach. Nolan slowed until we were in step.

"It won't be for long. The moment we can, you will get your magic back." His paternal warm voice felt more like an apology than a statement. It held a guilt I doubted he'd ever let go.

I directed my attention to the two elves who worked with astonishing efficiency to create the *adligatura* around Damia's home. They were so practiced, I made note to be careful around them.

Mephisto, Benton, Kai, Simeon, and Clayton were clustered a few feet away, similar unreadable looks on their faces that I was sure took a great deal of effort to maintain. They didn't want to be without their magic, but once they entered the Blose Chasm they would be. Similarly, the five elves who were sacrificing their magic to place them in it worked hard not to display too much emotion. Magic wielders hated when their magic was suppressed. I knew its complete absence was going to be a challenge for them all, and I felt that unease and raging influx of doubt and worry that clung to the air, making the area feel dense. I know we all wished there was a better way.

Nolan kept his back to Sanaa while he combined the ingredients for the magic restricting spell. Mephisto, Clayton, and Cory sauntered over, creating a barrier between him and Sanaa. Nolan had already refused to give her the invocations for the spell until it was needed to be performed. If she didn't have knowledge of the spell, she wasn't going to learn it from him, nor the necessary ingredients.

Detaching from the situation, I waited until my finger was pricked and linked with Sanaa and Nolan. A spark of energy curled over me followed by a light dusting of warmth that eased over my arm. Swirls of black and gold meshed together and floated over my skin, leaving the shape of the raven on my wrist.

"Hello, friend," I said bitterly. Nolan quickly retrieved the spell from Sanaa's hand as she reiterated that once I stepped into the house, I only had ten minutes before the *adligatura* was disabled and Damia would have access to her magic. Hopefully in that time she would have made the choice to work with us.

The door swung open before I could knock. Damia glared at me, her hand clenched over the Tenebrous stone, but no markings covered her skin. I started the timer on my phone.

"I was not expecting you," she said as I pushed my way past her. She was a great magic practitioner but a terrible liar. Her tone indicated that she'd been waiting for me for a while, probably from the moment she lost her magic and the connection with the Tenebrous stone when the *adligatura* was raised.

She didn't allow a lot of distance between us, matching my steps, keeping keen eyes on me. "I shouldn't have broken your stone," she whispered.

I nodded.

Closing her eyes, she took a long deep breath, fatigue evident in her posture.

"You're narrow focused and you will keep making mistakes because of that," I told her. Her eyes tracked me as I slowly paced the floor to gather my thoughts and to take inventory of the room and any nearby weapons or anything that could be used as one. There weren't any. But she'd used the Tenebrous stone as a weapon before, so I kept a cautious distance from her.

Exposing my wrist to her, I asked, "Do you know what it signifies?"

She glanced at the raven and nodded. "Nolan used you as a way to restrict Malific's magic. That's the sign of the restriction."

"I'm able to borrow magic from others. Most magic wielders are connected to their magic, and if they're without it for a long time they die. That's not the case with elves." I stepped closer and glanced at my timer. "In less than five minutes, I'll be able to take your magic. I don't want to do that to you. My own life has been filled with my options and autonomy being taken from me."

I took her intent listening as a good sign. "We'll close the Veil, but my friends stay here. And yes, they are my friends and the man I love. You won't send them away because you've attributed the wrongs of Malific to them. Then we will destroy the Tenebrous stone, as you indicated you planned to do once the Veil is closed."

"That won't restore the balance."

"You're looking for perfection in an imperfect world and it can't happen. You gave me the benefit of the doubt, and I want to extend the same to you. But you know what I'm capable of. Don't push me to it. End this now, and you'll have the protection of the elves, because they want you. Sanaa wants you to help the elves form a strong community, improve their skills, and be aptly capable of protecting themselves if necessary. Most of all, she wants peace. I think that's what you want, too. Believe me, you want their alliance because it means protection for you. You've pissed off the vampires. Whether you no longer have the ability to kill them with a spell doesn't matter. The Huntsmen will also be an obstacle to their vengeance. For your safety, I urge you to create as many alliances as you can."

Flitters of defiance reared up in her expression. Time was ticking away. I inched as close as I could without her noticing.

"I make these concessions because I don't believe you are evil. Misguided? Yes. But it's because you just want to be safe. Fabian and Elizabeth were cruel and misguided and made it their goal to hurt me. I didn't enjoy doing what I did, but it became evident that I needed to. They were never going to let me be."

Surprisingly, I found understanding in her look. She was a woman with a mission, and I was slowly unraveling it.

"It seems more like a threat than a concession if my only choice is to concede and do it your way or have my magic taken," she complained.

"We're going to debate about semantics? The Veil will close. A functional level of balance will be restored, and you will have the protection of the Huntsmen. They've agreed to an oath that will protect those with elven blood."

"What about the shifters?"

Girl, you are getting on my nerves. I blew out a breath. "Once the Veil is closed and the Tenebrous destroyed, you're welcome to try to return them to their previous state. But shifters tend to mind their business until you mess with them. Then they take great pleasure in destroying you for fun. Do you want to invite that level of chaos into your life? They're still vulnerable to silver, so they have limitations."

A small challenging smile lifted the corners of her lips, and I could tell that she was thinking how to create a spell that would mimic silver. Damia was a talented menace, one the elves would need to rein in to prevent future conflicts.

She was lost in her thoughts and seemed to have forgotten I was standing in front of her. She hadn't given me an answer and I needed one.

Time ticked away.

"What is your goal, Damia?" I pressed.

Her expression hovered between defiance and accepting defeat. "For us not to live with the fear of extinction." If her words and demeanor were to tug at my emotions, she'd succeeded.

"Then you win because it won't happen. Not at the hand of gods. And no one else is as powerful as you are. This is the time to grow a strong community with little sacrifice. If you have to be forced to do this, no one will trust you and you will still lose."

The minute notification vibrated in my pocket. I feared that once she had magic, I'd have to act quickly and take away her choice and any autonomy.

She opened her mouth, but the words wouldn't form.

"Do you accept?" I pushed.

Too many things happened at once: The timer ended, the markings skated back up her arm, and I snatched her to me, prepared to give her the *kiss* when she said, "Okay."

Then her lips started to move, and I started to grab her, but she held up one hand to stop me. When the spell was complete, the markings unraveled from her hand and fingers and she handed me the Tenebrous stone.

Staring at her unexpected offering, it took me a moment to react.

"I'll need it back to close the Veil."

Blinking, I'd assumed that would be performed by Sanaa and Damia, but I was confident Sanaa would give that task to Damia without any objections.

"Follow me," I said.

All eyes had turned to me before fixing on the compliant Damia. Sanaa didn't have a problem with Damia closing the Veil despite it denying her access to Elizabeth's spell, which was in Nolan's possession. He'd agreed to provide it prior to closing the Veil.

I handed the Tenebrous stone to Cory whose face relaxed. It seemed like he wanted to drop to his knees in relief. Madison hadn't relaxed at all, splitting her attention between the cadre of elves a few feet away and the Huntsmen and Sanaa and Damia.

"Return it," I demanded of Nolan and Sanaa in a tone harsher than intended. So used to having magic, I felt like an empty husk without it and hated how satisfying the prospect of taking Damia's magic felt. This was the only way that guaranteed I could take her magic and unbind her from the Tenebrous stone.

I didn't want to go back to my former self, and I knew I'd devolve into Damia if my magic was withheld for any extended amount of time.

My command didn't seem to be perceived as harsh, but I must have seemed manic because Nolan was in front of me and Mephisto behind, abandoning the group of elves tasked with opening the Blose Chasm. The warmth of Mephisto's chest radiated across my back. It was nice but it wasn't my magic. Once again, Nolan was protective of the ingredients and the spell as he and Sanaa returned my magic. Relief settled over me along with a number of things. I could trust Sanaa and I didn't have to resort to my poorly formed plan B that involved a great deal of violence.

The Veil needed to be closed next. Sanaa handed Cory the paper with the oath she'd written up. After going over it, Mephisto, Simeon, Kai, and Clay read it.

"Why is Erin excluded?" Mephisto asked.

"You're in a relationship with her," Sanaa said cryptically.

His brows inched together at her response.

"This oath will prevent you all from hurting us in any manner—harm is not always physical." She gave a dismissive wave. "I thought I was being kind by not obliging you to behave in a manner that is inconsistent with how you behave in relationships."

I scoffed at the thinly veiled insult and prediction of me being hurt by our relationship.

"This is an oath of intention. Her name can be added without any issue," Mephisto said.

Sanaa pulled out a pen, prepared to add my name, which I stopped. "I trust their intentions toward me. Don't need an oath for it."

They smiled. Cynicism inched into Sanaa's sneer as she returned the paper to Cory.

"You all think so poorly of us yet do not adequately protect yourselves from us. A witch cannot bind us to this oath because their magic doesn't affect us. Only elven or god magic can bind us to the oath," Mephisto told Sanaa.

Damia and Sanaa each took a sharp intake of breath at the realization that they would have gone through this and not successfully protected themselves from the gods.

Mephisto's actions may have been viewed favorably and earned some trust, but it hadn't changed their demand of the oath. They had left Benton's name off the oath, excluding him from the agreements the Huntsmen would be obligated to. I thought they had made a mistake when drawing it up, but they confirmed that it wasn't an error before performing the spell to bind the Huntsmen to the oath. They'd declined to add him; none of the elves seemed to view him as a threat. They were mistaken, but I kept my opinions to myself and performed the oath binding spell.

Cory glared at Damia's hand outstretched for the Tenebrous stone. Still apprehensive, he waited. With a nod from Sanaa, the elves opened the Chasm. None of the Huntsmen displayed any concern or apprehension entering the realm that would render them magicless. Madison and I shouldered enough concern for everyone. My hands balled at my sides and Madison chomped at a thumbnail.

Dividing my attention between the sealed realm and Damia, I watched her bind herself to the Tenebrous stone again. Her lips moved fervently invoking the spell to close the Veil. A spell that was significantly shorter and more efficient than Elizabeth's. Iridescent light covered her body, her pupils became pools of onyx, and the pulling energy that flooded the area made me lock my legs to stay in place. And when the world became dark for just a few moments, I looked at Madison's strained face that said: *How do we explain this?*

I shrugged. *We don't.*

Panting, Damia dropped to her knees, although the fatigue didn't dampen her smile of satisfaction. "It's closed," she whispered. Looking out over the barren land, I no longer saw the openings. It had become part of me, seeing the entries to the Veil. And now the Veil was gone.

Not giving Damia time to become reacquainted with the Tenebrous stone, or to reconsider her assurance that she'd destroy it once the Veil was closed, I asked for it. And felt a surge of embarrassment at how quickly she relinquished it. Misguided woman.

Pulling out the blade sheathed at my leg, I used the handle to crush the stone into pieces. Periodically I glanced at Damia, expecting her to stop me or show some signs of caring. There wasn't any. Sanaa turned away from my condemnatory look that effectively said, *And you wanted me to kill her?*

"Open the Chasm," I said, because Sanaa was still looking away from me and taking too long to make the command. My heart slammed into my chest at her hesitation, gripping the knife tighter in her hand. Nolan had eased closer to her, and Cory had turned an assessing gaze on her.

She huffed. "I have no desire to be at war with you, Erin. Failing to release them ensures that we would never find peace." She nodded her head in the direction of the elves who still had magic, and they opened the Blose Chasm, allowing the men to walk out. The moment Kai's feet were on the other side, he took to the sky. Kai was going to be a problem if the Huntsmen planned to maintain their clandestine life. Between the world darkening for a little less than five minutes and a winged man, the world would be abuzz for a few days.

"Is she about to have a cardiac event? Should we call someone? That's not an appealing color," Cory whispered, nudging his chin in Madison's direction.

Madison gathered her composure enough to walk over to Sanaa, a white envelope in her hand and the official seal of the Supernatural Task Force.

"As acting leader of the elves, you have been officially summoned to declare your existence to the committee and register."

Sanaa glowered at the letter then turned her glare on

Madison before accepting it. Opening it, she read over it slowly. "I will be there," she said.

Madison clasped hands with Clayton, earning a disparaging look from both Sanaa and Damia. There may be a tentative truce between them and the gods, but they'd never be accepting of relationships with them. Madison headed toward her car, giving Kai, who had just landed a few feet away, a warning look and made her way to the car with Clay. Simeon, Kai, and Benton departed after. Cory, Mephisto, Nolan, and I remained, although it was made clear Sanaa and Damia wanted to be left alone.

"Nolan, will you stay?" Sanaa requested. He looked at me, suppressing a smile. I gave him a small wave and left.

Several feet from the car, Mephisto released my hand. Quickly scanning the area, I found him standing just a few feet from Damia, gripping an arrow in his hand. Damia crouched on the ground, her body rising and falling as she took ragged breaths.

I ran toward them, seeing Clayton and Madison hurrying back toward her. The person advancing took another arrow from their quiver and aimed at their target on the ground. My magic hit the aggressor in the chest. She wailed as she lurched back several feet before crash landing. I was ready to deliver the same response to the crossbow-wielding man several feet away who was approaching with determination.

"Careful, Erin," Mephisto whispered. "They're human."

Damia stood, surveying the area, her face flushed with anger. "Human?" I didn't understand why her voice sounded so pained.

"Humans want me dead?" she whispered.

I hazarded a glance back at her and the disillusioned expression on her face. She and I didn't share the same outlook on humans. They were unpredictable at best and inconsistent in their views of the supernatural. They seemed to fear them while having an unhealthy fascination with magic. And even a desired proximity to it, perhaps to covet it or abhor it. But attacks like this were rare.

"They're not working under their own volition," she said, delivering another push to the woman I'd disabled when she stood again, exhibiting the same determination as the cross-bow-wielding man. Assuming by the choice of weapons they were hunters, we surmised they were hired. Four more people appeared from the house to our left, which I had thought abandoned. They swiftly moved toward us sporting compound bows.

The elves who were waiting for their magic to return to them after the closure of the Blose Chasm, found refuge behind the elves that had magic. Sanaa directed the elves to hold the humans using magic, giving us the opportunity to disable them physically. Controlling the strength of magic was more difficult.

Damia's expression was a mix of sorrow and fury as she realized that the advancing humans were controlled by a vampire. I was willing to bet that her realization was compounded with the knowledge that there was never true "balance" and safety, especially when faced with the conflicting situation where she wished to preserve the life of her attacker because they weren't working on their own.

Simeon rushed toward the group. As the immediate threat, I assumed the weapons would be turned on him, but their target was set; no one else seemed to exist. That was the problem with a vampire's compel: There was no nuance to it. If a target was made, they were the only person who existed to them. At least Landon hadn't directed them to hurt or kill anyone in the way. But his motives had definitely changed, and he no longer wanted Damia apprehended. He wanted her dead.

Kai and Benton followed Simeon's lead, engaging the humans with the compound bows in a fierce struggle. Kai moved swiftly, his movements fluid and graceful, as he grabbed the soaring arrow before it could get anywhere near Damia. A quick swipe of the human's leg sent him crashing to the ground. Benton used the distraction of another to lunge at him, tackling him and taking away the bow. He moved with the efficiency of a trained fighter as he locked the human in a hold where he held him. The man struggled and eventually eased into unconsciousness.

As chaos erupted around us, Cory's eyes blazed as he advanced toward us, his lips murmuring a spell. Before he could unleash his magic, I yelled, hoping he could hear me through the chaos.

"Stop!" I yelled. "They're not acting of their own free will."

He continued advancing.

"They're being controlled by vampires," Madison yelled.

Too focused on his target, he didn't hear and I was forced to give him a magic nudge. It was just to get his attention but pushed him harder than expected, making him faceplant into the ground. Quickly recovering, he looked at me. I rushed to him, explaining the situation.

"Landon is an asshole," he growled, teeming with frustration. "He couldn't give you forty-eight hours."

I glanced at the time on Cory's watch and sighed. "Technically he has," I acknowledged, although he hadn't truly honored my request because he had been looking for Damia all the time.

Clayton weaved through the arrows, catching some and leaving the ones that clearly were going to miss Damia. She darted toward her house. Seeing that help wasn't needed, I followed her into it. The elves already inside had gathered some items.

"Do you have ingredients for a slumber spell?" I asked Cory who'd come in after me.

He shook his head. I gathered the hodgepodge of items they'd gathered that would work for restraints.

We returned to find two of the humans rendered asleep,

the others being held by Kai, Clayton, Simeon, and Mephisto while Benton watched carefully over the sleeping humans. Sanaa's face was twisted into a scowl, taking in the scene and periodically looking down at the formal request for her to make an appearance. I got the impression that Madison was going to have to escort her to it.

Madison seemed to have come to the same conclusion. "If you want peace and to live freely you will show up. Don't make your appearance be made under duress."

The undercurrent of challenge eased into Sanaa's narrowed eyes before she looked again at the scene before her and the humans being restrained. After several moments, she agreed with a small nod.

CHAPTER 25

With Clayton by her side, Madison waved away our invitation for her to accompany us to Landon's with the humans.

"I need plausible deniability with this," she said, grumbling more things under her breath. We all were likely included in her remarks of displeasure, curses, and annoyed complaints. It was more than just the issues with Landon; she probably wanted to get to the office to determine if today's events had created enough of a splash that she'd need to start preparing the necessary PR spin.

After recognizing that the single-focused efforts of the humans were going to lead them to hurting themselves to get loose and return to attacking Damia, we decided to put them under a slumber spell. The bound humans were split up and placed in the two SUVs, their weapons stowed in the trunk. We stopped by Cory's to gather the ingredients for a slumber spell, which he immediately performed.

At Landon's home, Mephisto and I approached together. If we needed assistance, Mephisto could signal the others without Landon noticing. Elon let out a surprised gasp, baring his teeth when Mephisto rendered him immobile against the wall, a stake inches from his heart, seemingly waiting for Elon to give him a reason to use it. Anger filled Elon's eyes but his lips relaxed, hiding his fangs.

The thud brought Landon out of one of his rooms. He was met with me flinging a sphere of magic into his chest. The next one sent him crashing against the wall with enough force to leave small cracks in it. He shook off the disorientation from the assault and found the blade of my karambit pressed against his neck.

"You used humans to carry out your dirty work. You jackass!" I pushed out through clenched teeth. The blade pressing into his skin was causing a rivulet of blood to run down his neck.

He blinked. "What?"

His obvious confusion threw me off. His arrogance would never allow him to deny his involvement if it were true.

"Damia was attacked today, using humans. And we had to intervene to keep them from dying for it."

His expression grew blank before it was overtaken by flashes of irritation. His body radiated anger. I moved away to give him room to seethe and stand.

"I would never do that. My plan for getting rid of her if you failed was far more sophisticated than sending humans," he scoffed.

Mephisto appeared next to me, his hold still on Elon. He shoved Elon toward Landon. Elon was prepared to strike at Mephisto, when Landon commanded him to stop.

"I'm assuming if you knew of the attack, then the Damia problem is handled?" he speculated in a strained voice, his ire heavy in it.

I nodded, pulling out a small piece of the Tenebrous stone that I'd kept for myself. Wiping away the blood from his neck, he eyed the small piece of stone that had caused so much trouble.

"The humans?"

"In the SUV under a slumber spell," Mephisto said.

"Xavier," Landon called, his voice raised slightly. I wouldn't have heard it at that volume, but Xavier did. Sauntering in with a glass of sanguineous liquid, his graceful movements were self-assured and languorous, which only fueled Landon's anger. He yanked the karambit from me and hurled it at him. Xavier missed being impaled by a fraction. His discarded glass painted the walls crimson. Mephisto eased me to him, both of us satisfied that Landon wasn't involved.

Xavier recovered from the attack only to have Landon slam him against the wall, holding him by his neck. "You found her and didn't share this information with me?!"

Xavier didn't need to breathe but Landon's hold prevented him speaking. He choked out a few words and Landon's grip loosened enough for him to speak. "You're too cozy with this elf-woman. I did what I determined you wouldn't." He sneered. Quite brave of him seeing that Landon looked as if he wanted to behead him.

"Forty-eight hours. How dare she make demands of us," Xavier scoffed. "And you listened!"

Not to be pedantic, but he didn't. He was looking for her, too. He just wasn't successful in his attempts before I found her.

Landon tossed Xavier to the ground and hovered over him. "This is where I live. Where I entertain. Where I feed. And you dare to mess things up for me by compelling humans to do your work?"

Xavier was just as shocked by the slap as I was. A punch you get—it's heated and is a volatile response. A slap is insulting. I'd never been slapped before and was a million times positive I'd be more offended by it than a punch.

"Get out of my house!" Landon demanded.

It wasn't until Xavier didn't move that I realized he was speaking to us. Mephisto and I didn't like his tone. We didn't move. He looked at us, and it was apparent he couldn't contain his anger enough to say it any more pleasantly.

"Leave the humans here and I'll make sure the compulsion is lifted and they are returned safely."

"Do not feed from them," I said.

"They will be well taken care of," he provided. The same courtesy wasn't going to be extended to Xavier.

Elon, Dallas, and the unfamiliar vampire followed us to the car and gathered the people, who were groggy from the spell. The slumber spell lifted and once they gained their senses, they became difficult to manage, causing the vampires to quickly compel them to relax. Their efficiency supported my skepticism about them adhering to the rules prohibiting compulsion.

CHAPTER 26

Two days since the Veil had closed and I was still enjoying the banality of our days. The first day we'd spent at Mephisto's home in bed, ignoring the contractors working on his house, only resurfacing to eat. The second day we enjoyed a movie, a trip to the bakery afterward, and a stroll in the park. It had also been two days since we'd left the humans with Landon, and our quiet stroll was being intruded upon by me worrying about their well-being.

"Call him," Mephisto urged when I expressed my concern.

"What, Erin?" Landon's curt voice answered.

"Did everyone get home safely?" I asked.

"If you are concerned about them, I'll send you their addresses and you can check my work," he shot back. I accepted that Landon's and my relationship was always going to be tumultuous and rife with tension. What I didn't expect was this level of hostility.

"Is that all?" he asked.

I could feel his impatience through the phone as I debated whether to ask my next question.

"Xavier?" I whispered finally.

"Is none of your concern. He has been handled in a

manner that I felt was just. Perhaps have less interest about him and more interest in keeping Damia in check, because to me, you two are forever linked. Her misdeeds are your misdeeds. Her assaults are yours. And will be handled accordingly."

Mephisto's deep, rich, ominous laughter filled the space. The phone stayed to my ear, but Mephisto's voice rose enough to be heard by Landon. "I've applied the same to you and the vampires concerning Erin. My promise still stands."

Tension filled the air and the silence from Landon was heavy. I wasn't about to continue this testosterone and threat of violence contest.

"I guess this concludes our business." Not giving him a chance to respond, I ended the call.

We continued the day by visiting all the people after Landon supplied their addresses. We received blank stares from them. They had no idea who I was nor why I'd showed up unannounced at their door. I simply provided the lie of having the wrong home. I was aware that Landon compelling them to forget the incident and us was about his and the vampires' protection, not mine or the elves'.

It had its advantages. I might be a new addition to Landon's personal non grata list, but there was protection in that status. Landon and the vampires didn't want to deal with me any more than I wanted to deal with them. Smartest thing was to stay away from situations that would be mutually assured destruction. And Mephisto had made it clear that would be the result if our paths crossed.

Forgetting the discord with Landon, Mephisto and I sat at a beautifully styled table in the cozy restaurant. The dramatic chandelier cast a warm ambient lighting. I liked that he chose a small restaurant; it felt intimate.

The soft music created a sensory experience that was inviting and refined enough to obscure any noise from the few people around us. In any event, the intense way Mephisto was looking at me made it easy to forget that anyone else was there.

I fully appreciated his departure from his casual wear to his usual style. Now he wore a midnight-black tailored suit, slate-gray shirt, and complementing patterned tie. A small candle in the middle of the table lit his high hollow cheeks, alluring features, and enchanted his dark eyes that traveled over my face to my bare shoulders, revealed by the spaghetti straps of my sage-green body-hugging satin midi dress. His eyes dropped to my legs that were hiding the revealing slit in the dress. When we'd dressed at his home, I had to remind him of our reservation.

"Do you miss it?" I asked, drawing his attention back up.

"The Veil?"

I nodded.

"I thought I would, especially with the possibility of not visiting it again. I don't. That world seemed so far away. I won't stop looking for a way to return, but not because I want to live in the Veil—I just don't like the restriction."

"It's odd not seeing the Veil," I admitted.

He nodded, took a thoughtful sip from his wine. "It makes it easy to not think about it."

He'd spent so many years searching for a way back, I wondered how he would occupy his time now. "What now, Satan?" I teased.

"I'm sure I'll find a way to fill my time," he said with a pointed look. "Besides, my love for obscure and dangerous magical objects hasn't changed. I still want them." A hungry look flitted across his expression.

"Don't make enemies of the pack," I warned. His expression was mirroring the covetous one he'd had in their vault.

"*Or* you can redirect your love of finding obscure and

dangerous magical objects, and turn it into good deeds by turning them over to Supernatural Task Force," I suggested.

He chuckled, the deep sound of his laugh reverberating through me. Taking a long draw from his glass, he dismissed the idea with a lopsided smirk.

"So, I take it you're planning to take the archives job Madison offered, since you're advocating on their behalf?"

"No." She'd offered the job months ago and I'd declined it then as well. "There's a reason the job is still available. It sounds boring as hell." I had magic now and didn't need the adrenaline as a distraction for my restricted magic. But I was still Erin, undeniably Erin, and I'd never be happy working in an office. "I'll probably return to my job, with a few changes. I can't work for you anymore. So, I might become your competition."

I was more interested in finding missing elven magical objects. I hadn't decided if I'd turn them over to the elves or keep them. Handing over powerful objects to the elves could tempt Damia into desiring more than just balance, setting the foundation for creating another Fabian.

Amused by the prospect, he leaned into the table. "Ah, will I get the Erin who fights dirty?" he asked, a dark excitement heavy in his voice.

"I fight to win. No tactics are off limits." We were both leaning into the table now. His hand found mine, lightly caressing it.

"I like seeing you like this," he said softly.

"Challenging?"

"No, smiling."

"Smiling," I whispered. "I smile often."

He leaned back in his chair, studying me with a gentle smile curving his lips. He shook his head. "Not like this. These smiles are different. Easy and unburdened. And whenever I want to see more of them, I can drive to your house." Mephisto sighed. "I don't miss the Veil." His admission appeared like a new realization. Our eyes held each other and remained locked, stirring emotions that filled me with a deep sense of contentment.

The world around us disappeared, only interrupted by the server taking our order. During dinner we discussed the closed meeting that would remove the elves' anonymity. Occasionally I searched Mephisto's face for signs of concern that they might be the next ones embroiled in a similar meeting. But there weren't any. I hoped the new places Kai had found would satisfy his need to fly. His impromptu flight at Damia's had led to reports of sightings, which led to him searching for more options to allow him to spread his wings and take to the sky.

To Madison's surprise, there hadn't been any chatter about the moment of darkness, except for complaints from the witches because the darkness had been attributed to them and weather spells. They didn't appreciate it, but they were intrigued by who could create a spell that could do that. I suspected their search for the culprit would occupy a great deal of their time.

During dessert, I looked around the restaurant, taking in the exquisite art on the walls, the linen-covered tables, and leather and wood seating. The solitary calla lily in the center of the table made me crave more days like this with Mephisto.

"What?" he asked.

"I like this," I admitted, and he seemed to understand without any further elaboration. A feeling we shared. After the bill was settled, Mephisto extended his hand to me and we left the restaurant. Neither of us in a hurry to get in the car, we walked hand in hand until we ended up at a small park where others had had the same idea to enjoy the evening.

When it became increasingly crowded, we retreated to his home, where he guided me to the room I'd dubbed the war room. Despite the name I'd given it, the room was the smallest, and oddly, felt the warmest to me. I remembered the time he said to me, "The wisest thing a person can do is know his weaknesses. The most foolish is to believe he has none. I think when it comes to you, I suffer some lapses in judgment. The others have noticed."

In some aspects, we were each other's weakness, but it cultivated our strengths.

He sat on the sofa, and when I took a seat next to him, he coaxed me over onto his lap, straddling him, a position he seemed fond of. One hand caressed my back while the other reached over to a table next to the sofa and produced a ring box.

"What's this?" I whispered.

"Open it."

When I hesitated, he said, "It's not an engagement ring."

"I wasn't worried about that," I rebutted quickly. Opening it, I saw a platinum signet ring with a raven.

"It's beautiful." I examined the intricate designed creature and the skill that went into making it seem so ethereal, powerful, and battle-weary. "Thank you."

"You're welcome. But I do have a question," he said, taking the ring from me and sliding it on my finger.

I nodded, waiting.

"Having an anniversary date seems really important to you, so can it be today?"

"I'd love that."

He kissed me and whispered against my lips, "To many more years together, my demigoddess. And for you to continue loving what we have together."

CHAPTER 27

Nine days later and I couldn't believe I was reflecting on my last interaction with Landon as I reached Dr. Sumner's office door. I wasn't expecting to see him dressed so casually in relaxed jeans, a faded black t-shirt with the Evanescence logo, and vintage square-rimmed glasses. And I definitely wasn't anticipating seeing Damia, who was relaxed back on the sofa, a cup of coffee on the table in front of her. Another was placed on a table next to where Dr. Sumner typically sat.

My eyes bounced between them. Then I gave him a look in an attempt for him to signal if he needed help or felt in danger. Since she was munching on a biscotti, it didn't seem like a hostile situation. Just a weird one. Even more bizarre were the moving boxes scattered throughout the office.

"You're moving?"

"Taking a sabbatical," he provided, with a polite smile directed at Damia who seemed very comfortable and not taking his cue to leave. She just continued drinking and eating. Based on the crumpled papers on the table, she'd had three biscotti. How long had she been here?

"Damia." Dr. Sumner's relaxed, familiar tone was unexpected. Her presence didn't seem like a professional visit. Even when he'd gathered information from her on the last visit, he'd had a more direct interaction. He stepped closer to her. "I appreciate your visit. It was unexpected, and I need to talk to Erin."

She gave me a long assessing gaze, starting at my feet and dragging up to my face where it lingered. Her expression gave nothing away.

"I don't think you should have been as feared," she provided. Without any inflection, I had absolutely no idea what she meant.

"Okay," I drawled.

She finished the last of her biscotti and then the coffee, leaving me waiting for her to elaborate. "Malific's daughter is Nolan's."

My brows drew together before giving up. The only thing she offered was assistance to help Dr. Sumner finish packing if he needed.

"I'll call you if I need the help," he told her.

With that she left.

"She is so peculiar," I acknowledged when she was out of earshot.

Unexpectantly, he considered my comment. "Perhaps. She could think the same of you," he teased, taking a sip from the coffee cup near his chair, then raising it to ask me if I wanted a glass.

"Have any tequila?"

"It's eleven in the morning. See? You're peculiar, too."

"Or, I don't have to work and I like tequila," I shot back.

He laughed and sat.

I looked around the room at the empty places on the wall where he'd removed the art. Books had been removed from the shelves and packing supplies dotted the room.

"Don't," he said.

"Don't what?" I ushered the look off my face that hinted at the guilt I was feeling. How different would his life have been if I hadn't entered it?

"That guilty look. Because of you I've acquired the most in-depth knowledge of the magical world, become friends with a person who'd go too extreme measures to ensure my safety, and received the humbling I needed."

Recoiling at the last bit, I waited for him to continue.

"Magic is fascinating but it's not for me. No part of it is. My previous knowledge was quite rudimentary, I know that now. Most humans are ignorant of it, which is why I was held in such regard. I just knew more than they did. I need a break from it all—the magic, not you. Call me whenever you want to talk."

"And you're leaving the profession?"

"No. Just taking a break. Just a few months. When I return, I'll probably teach for a while. Hopefully psychology for humans."

"And you might get people to actually take it for a grade rather than as an audit," I teased, referring to what I'd said when I learned that he taught two classes a week at the local college. The classes were full, and I suspected it was because of the instructor and not the topic.

He laughed, taking his coffee with him to return to packing.

"Do you need help?"

He shook his head. "I'll take Damia up on her offer if I need it." He laughed when he saw the disapproving sneer I was unable to school from my face. "You're still my favorite elf," he teased.

"That's not it. Do you really trust her?"

"As much as you do. You bet a lot on her being able to be reasoned with, and it worked. She trusts you, too." He shrugged. "And Nolan, but nothing she said earlier made sense as to why. She's a complex woman."

"Such a beautiful way to say she's weird as hell and possibly unstable."

"People wear fear differently," he offered.

Slipping over to the books, I looked them over, keeping my back to him. "I think she likes you," I told him.

"She does."

I looked over my shoulder, expecting an arrogant smirk, but his expression was matter of fact. He spent so much time downplaying his looks, I never considered he possessed any vanity.

"Not romantically. I liken it to a person who finds a wounded pup and nurses it back to health." He chuckled. "That's the reason she'll never be a danger to humans. I say that with a great deal of confidence."

That explained the look she held when she thought she was being attacked by humans. My visit extended longer than intended, and by the time I left, he'd accepted some help with packing. Packing his things, uneasiness gnawed at me that this wasn't a hiatus but rather a goodbye. Our conversation throughout had removed any lingering guilt, and I didn't want him out of my life forever.

He gasped in surprise at the unexpected hug I gave him when we said our goodbyes.

"Take care," I said.

He returned the hug. "You sound like you don't expect to see me again. Are you going somewhere?" His arms tightened around me.

At his light-hearted tone, I loosened my hold and stepped back to study his face.

"No, but it seems like you are."

"Not at all. I promise. I don't like that I've endured the things that I have, but it didn't make me fearful, just wiser." He took hold of my hand and gave it a reassuring squeeze. "Promise me, if you need to talk, you will call me? About anything, Erin. I will be there for you."

I made the promise, fully accepting another complex relationship that I was happy to have established.

———

Reviewing the information on supernaturals on the Supernatural Task Force website that mirrored the state's official website on the addition of elves, I saw that there wasn't fanfare, breaking news, or even social media information on it. They slipped the information in as if it was a simple update and not the recognition of a group once considered extinct.

Madison looked dejected that the information involving elves noted that our magic restriction was pure rhodium.

"I didn't give that information, Sanaa did," she said. Mephisto had a pure rhodium brace that didn't work on me, although it had on Nolan. It was good information to have. "You were never brought into it," she went on, "so you're still considered a mage without magic."

I preferred it that way. Maybe someday I'd be forced to reveal myself, or Landon would disclose his knowledge of what I am, or Mephisto and the others would be discovered. I was reveling in just being Erin.

Madison studied me for a long time, then inched closer to me on the sofa, bumping my shoulder with hers.

"I'm going to make the offer once again," Madison said, standing and gathering her things.

"The archives job?"

"Of course."

"Will you all still hire me for bounties?"

"Well, I can't if you work for us. It won't be part of your job description."

"You've answered your question."

"Consider it."

"Consider a job so boring, you're begging your sister to take it? Nah, I'll pass."

"Begging seems a little extreme," she teased.

"Nobody wants your boring job!" I playfully snapped.

"Fine," she huffed. "I'm off," she told me, heading for the door. "Kai won't go near our house without me. Man can fly and has the powers of a deity, but two middle-aged women scare him."

"Why do our moms want to see him?"

"Your mother," she corrected. Which was as good as "our" since they seemed to act as a unit.

"She saw my bookcase and can't stop talking about it and 'since he doesn't have any place to be' she was wondering if he could make her one."

My father was extraordinary with numbers and extraordinarily dangerous with tools. The pairing of a woman who loved handmade furniture with a man who had difficulty putting together furniture was one of their few mismatches. My mother's only attempt made her extremely grateful for her limbs because she'd come close to losing one. She admired it from a far, occasionally purchased custom pieces. Nothing was as beautiful as the bookcase Kai had made for Madison.

"Clayton going with you?"

She nodded. I didn't need to ask. Clayton seemed to be adapting best to the changes. It hadn't been long, but I'd expected to see some signs of longing or more effort into finding a way around the lock. It was Mephisto who admitted that they were afraid that the ways to circumvent it might lead to the Veil reopening. Clayton was more concerned about it causing problems for Madison than kindling more trouble from Damia.

Heading out the door, Madison opened it before Cory could knock. She gave him a quick hug, which wasn't too surprising, but the enthusiasm behind it was. He recognized it, too. Madison was different, more relaxed and perky.

"You look like a woman who is having great sex with a hot man." He grinned, lifting her into the hug.

"Why are you like this?" she grumbled when he placed her back on the floor.

"Like what? Acknowledging your face is glowing, you seem at ease, and you have a little something in your step."

"Or I'm enjoying my job and no longer have to worry about people slipping through the Veil and adding more chaos to my duties. And with the elves' status updated, I don't have the added responsibility of guarding that confidential information."

"Nope. I'm still going with regular sex with the hot god."

She rolled her eyes, and he threw his head back in a boisterous laugh that startled me. She'd known him too long not to know that this would be leveraged against her because it embarrassed her, and he delighted in the glow that ran up her nose and along her cheeks.

"Speaking of elves, what is that BS they're trying to pull? A website update of magic wielders. No, 'hey world, I present to you…elves!'"

"I doubt the elves would appreciate such fanfare and it's unlikely they'll be out in the city enough for them to be noticed. It will take time and comfort for them to integrate. They're still in the Havenage with the wards. People won't knowingly interact with them. This is for the best. Sanaa didn't give anyone reason to worry that elves would be a threat."

Madison gave me another hug and Cory a quick one. "I have to go," she said.

"Yeah, you do."

Shaking her head, Madison rushed out the door before Cory could embarrass her any more.

"Leave her alone!"

"I'm just teasing," he said, flopping down next to me. His lips twisted to the side, and his fingers impatiently thrummed on his thigh. He was anxious. "I still can't get over Ms. Harp's new appearance," he added.

"She's the only one who doesn't find it unsettling."

I'd visited her on the rare occasions that she was home. Asher had complained that she was more active. He no longer felt she was in danger, but he still liked someone to accompany her. "She just likes freaking people out with her eyes. I suggested contacts but she won't consider it," Asher had complained, frustrated. The cantankerous prima donna antics and noncompliance seemed to just make her more endearing to him. I supposed she provided a fun, nonthreatening challenge he enjoyed.

It was obvious Ms. Harp wasn't the source of Cory's fidgeting. He stood, roaming around my room, rearranging pillows, straightening items on the table, and refolding the throw on the chair.

I waited patiently, although the rigid silence unnerved me, and I started to think that maybe he was about to inform me that he'd had to reveal to his coven the source of the energy shift and the momentary eclipse. Although confident that they'd keep it within the coven, I wouldn't be happy that they knew. The fewer people who knew, the harder it would be to find the culprit if the information got out to the masses.

Just when I was about to prompt him to speak, Cory smiled and blurted, "Alex asked me to move in with him."

I squealed my excitement and launched from the chair to give him a big hug before I realized that he hadn't confirmed that he agreed to it.

"What did you say?"

"Yes, of course."

I let out another squeal and resumed the hug. He pulled away and took several steps back, critically assessing me from head to toe.

"Why don't you seem surprised?"

"I am surprised." I broadened my smile and gave him a little excited shoulder bop. "Hurray. You're moving in with your beau."

"Beau? What the hell is going on with that weirdness?" I was treated to more scrutiny. "You're happy but not surprised."

"Surprised and happy."

He inched closer and lowered until we were eye to eye. "You knew!" he accused.

I could feel the heat flitting over my cheek.

His eyes widened. "You did! Why didn't you tell me? I was so surprised, I stumbled and fumbled my answer."

I told him about meeting Alex and him wanting my opinion on whether Cory would feel pressured by the question and whether Cory would want to live with him.

"*The Godfather* is a classic, show it some respect."

I blinked. "That's what you got from the conversation? Not how adorable it was that he was shy? Or that he cares about you so much he didn't want you to feel pressured?"

His grin broadened and I was overjoyed for him. "Of course, but you withheld vital information. I have the right to be a little grumpy with you."

I shrugged, the smile in his voice and the excitement in his expression well worth the grumpiness. "That's understandable."

"However," he drawled, "I'm sure I can be convinced to be less grumpy." He rattled off a series of "classic" movies and TV shows with a cult following that he claimed I needed to give a chance.

Deadpanned, I asked, "How long will you stay grumpy if I decline?"

"Which one?"

"All of them. I've dealt with worse than one grumpy witch."

Tossing up his hand, he gave in to his smile. He pulled me into a hug. "Yeah, you have."

I sighed into his hug. I had dealt with a lot and survived. My thumb ran over the ring Mephisto had given me.

I'd survived it all and come out the other side with my family, friends, new and strengthened alliances, magic, and love.

EPILOGUE

After the closure of the Veil, the subsequent thirteen months had been riddled with unsuccessful attempts of finding workarounds to the closure. It had dominated our time for the first six months, dwindling to a seemingly less urgent matter. In the past two months, no one had mentioned it.

Mephisto parked the car at my parents' home. Before getting out, I looked at the notification for the receipt of the bounty the Supernatural Task Force had paid for me apprehending a rogue shifter. It wasn't just a race against stopping him from causing more violence but me getting to him before Asher and his pack did. We'd discovered him in a tunnel at the same time. He was more than willing to go with me, scuttling behind me for protection as he hid from Asher and a few members of his pack. Mated and expecting his first child had made him fiercer. My position as a friend of the pack was the only thing protecting the shifter and he knew it.

I was more cautious when dealing with vampires. I was persona non grata to them, and Landon made that clear at every turn. A tacit agreement not to kill each other was the best I could expect. Tension remained despite my having extended an olive branch and informing them that I had no plan to ever reverse vampirism. With the information I'd acquired from Damia and from Benton's research, I knew I could reverse vampirism on the newly created. Without a willing participant and Landon's help, we couldn't determine whether it would work on older vampires. I was fine not exploring it further without Landon's approval, which was probably the reason I was persona non grata rather than Landon's enemy. With all that had transpired between us, it was the best I could ask for.

Mephisto and I arrived at my parents' door, just moments before Madison and Clay. At the sight of Kai's car in the driveway, Madison greeted her mother Sophie with a brusque hug, already scanning for Kai. Clayton's greeting lasted a little longer. Mephisto gave her a wave and a nod.

She enveloped me in a big hug, releasing me with a heavy appreciative sigh. I was getting a lot of them over the past few months. Madison admitted to feeling relief and that they didn't feel the need to worry about me. My mother was right behind with greetings.

Following the pleasing scent of food, I went to the kitchen where I found Madison jabbing an accusatory finger in Kai's direction.

"Guess what I had to deal with yesterday?"

"Curl-apocalypse," he teased, tugging at one of her curls from the halo of hair she'd grown out and repeating one of her complaints she'd made as an excuse for being late for the monthly family dinners.

"No, I personally investigated a call from a well-intentioned human informing us that she spotted a partially shifted bird-shifter at two a.m. And that our information on shifters was outdated, a potential safety risk, and in need of auditing," she said.

He shrugged and smirked. "Two a.m.? She was probably sleepwalking and had no idea what she saw. Or perhaps she dreamt it. Sounds like a dream. You know, the kind that are so intense they seem real."

Her eyes narrowed on him. We'd worried about Kai initially, but he seemed to have made a sport of finding new places where he could spread his wings without incident. Sophie and my mother, who had adopted the same concerns, quickly discovered that busying him with woodwork staved off the need. My mother was more than happy to accommodate. At the moment, she was showing Clayton and Mephisto one of his completed projects: an entryway bench. Explaining why the wood was chosen, the details of the grain, and comfort level.

Ignoring Madison who was still glaring at him, Kai smiled at my mother's provided information, which I was positive was a regurgitation of information Kai had given her.

"Really?" Madison shot back, redirecting Kai's attention to her.

Kai occasionally had the impulse to take to the sky, which created a situation for Madison. It had only happened twice —well, three times in the past year.

"That's what you're going with. Sleepwalking? A dream?"

He was failing at easing the wayward smile that tugged at his lips. "What did you go with?"

A ruddy glow brushed over the bridge of her nose and cheeks. "I assured her she was mistaken and it was probably an illusion spell that witches were working on."

He snorted. "When lying is no longer an option, you can tell them it was a god who needed to spread his wings," he teased, heading out of the kitchen to the living room where Nolan and Madison's father were examining the chess board. Keegan's brow furrowed in concentration as a Cheshire smirk curled Nolan's lips. I couldn't determine if his smile was from us all gathered in the house or the fact he was about to beat Keegan at their game of choice, again.

Kai's comment got Mephisto and Clay's attention. They studied him, but whatever conversation went on between them was satisfactory enough for them to return their attention to my mother.

Madison grabbed a towel from the counter and lobbed it at Kai's back. He turned in time to catch it before it could hit him in the back of his head. He made a face and *tsked* her. I still wasn't used to how close they'd grown.

Cory had entered the house from the backyard, missing the exchange between Kai and Madison but catching her attempt to assault with a towel. I started to explain, but he shook his head.

"I'm fine with not knowing," he admitted, gathering me in a hug. Alex, who had entered behind him, carrying an empty plate, headed straight for the table of appetizers. Cory pulled from me and shook his head at his partner.

"This is a judgment-free zone," I said to him. "We come here and eat like we've been deprived of food for weeks."

"No, I'm judging," Cory shot back before opening his mouth to accept the cucumber slice Alex offered that I was a thousand percent sure wouldn't make it anywhere on his plate.

They were perfect in so many ways, but as a shifter Alex ate a lot and didn't share Cory's discipline in eating healthily. I liked it when they joined us for dinners, but Alex always served as a reminder that I no longer required the help of the pack. The last time I'd dealt with the pack was when I'd successfully helped them track down a rogue septuagenarian with feline eyes. Ms. Harp continued to be the thorn in Asher's side that he simultaneously adored and was annoyed by. Finding Ms. Harp granted me access to the pack's vault. Access that Mephisto had been denied, despite the numerous bids he made for it. My goal was to acquire elven items. Asher allowed me to have the two that I found. Nolan and I were still trying to discover their uses.

Cory joined Kai in watching Nolan and Keegan's game, his partner ring glinting in the light. Alex and Cory hadn't married. I wasn't sure why, but they seemed happy with the rings as a symbol of their commitment. I suspected this was the step before becoming his mate. Shifter and witch mating would have its challenges, but they were the perfect couple to handle it.

"Oh, Jaz is back!" my mother said, waving at Simeon as she passed the sliding door to the backyard.

Sophie peeked around her to a look at the vulpine creature.

Great, now they were naming the menagerie cycling into our backyard to interact with him.

Simeon was a guest at my parents' home so often that his interaction with the wildlife didn't seem weird to my parents. I assumed they were the same deer, rabbits, and now fox, but since I couldn't distinguish between them, Simeon could just be making new friends as a means to keep from interacting with bipedal animals.

Keegan and Nolan discontinued their game, moving the set aside to be continued later after Sophie and my mom were seated on the sofa.

Nolan sat next to me and handed me a notebook of spells I had translated into Elven, which tended to make them work better. His eyes sparkled with pride when he smiled. "No corrections."

My smile mirrored his, feeling pride in learning more about the language and elves. Nolan was a wealth of information and loved sharing it with me.

Sanaa hadn't lifted her ban on Nolan's access to the Havenage, and an invitation to live there wasn't in the future. However, the elves didn't seem to hold the same animosity toward him, and he was invited to Sanaa's inaugural celebration as she was officially given the position of the elves' leader.

Nolan had met with Sanaa on numerous occasions outside of the Havenage, during which she attempted to persuade him to share Elizabeth's spells with them. His declination led to fewer visit requests from her and one unexpected visit from Damia, who was even less persuasive. He declined her request with the excuse that it was a part of his sister he didn't want to share. His response held some truth, but his primary reason for guarding the spells was to limit the temptations of the elves becoming power-hungry.

After dinner, when everyone was together in the living room, the smile etched on my face remained while I watched Clayton gazing around at everyone, as he did so often at family gatherings. He seemed to be in a state of bewilderment as if he was thinking, *how did I get here?*

He seemed to have the most difficult time adapting to our unique family dynamics. But all doubt and confusion vanished and a smile transformed his appearance whenever his eyes landed on Madison. He looked ensnared by her but was snapped out of it with a jolt. I knew it was from one of them initiating a personal chat.

My focus shifted to Mephisto, who I thought was watching the movie, but he was ignoring the tv and the multiple conversations going on in the room and was intently watching me.

Holding my gaze, he mouthed, "I love you."

I smiled. "I love you, too."

I did. I loved him and I adored the life I'd never dreamed I would have. Bi-weekly meetings with Dr. Sumner had evolved into a meeting between friends and to catching up and not for me to unload the weight of the world or express the difficulty I was having navigating new and strange discoveries about myself. It was apparent Dr. Sumner had no intention of crossing the line into our world of magic again. He'd had his fill and settled nicely into his role as a professor.

The drive to Mephisto's home was mostly in silence. As soon as we were out of the car, he took my hand into his, leading me into the house. Benton wasn't around much. Occasionally he'd visit to provide any information he had about navigating the Veil and would ease back into his life that seemed to involve travel and finding other druids in the world. Mephisto seemed relieved that he'd never mentioned unbinding himself from them. I suspected he needed Benton in his life as much as he needed the others. Once they were unbound, Benton would age like humans and eventually no longer be in the world.

"I'll never tire of seeing you this way," he whispered once in his house.

"What way?" I asked.

"Happy."

"You've seen me happy before."

In the past months, we'd shared two wonderful vacations, countless date nights, and so many memorable moments. Mephisto seemed committed to overshadowing my past with pleasant memories.

"No. You've been content. Often your look was weighted as if you were anticipating the next disaster. But the last three months have been different, and I want it to continue."

An appreciative smile flourished over his face. He exhaled deeply. His hold on my hand tightened as he headed toward the backyard. The gentle silence of the house, the oceanic scent with hints of night blooming jasmine, and the warm amber lights reminded me of the moonlit nights on our vacation in Gray Bay beach. It was intentional. I adored the many ways Mephisto used small things to remind me of the times we shared.

The lights cast an ethereal glow over the flowers and trees. The okapi that had once called it his home had been reclaimed by Simeon, allowing more room for flowers, water fountains, and seating areas. But Mephisto directed me to an empty space where a dagger lay on the grass just a few inches from us.

He turned me to face him, a finger languidly gliding over my cheek while his thumb on our clasped hands made slow rhythmic circles over my skin. "Do you remember when you said that your life wasn't one that allowed you to think about marriage, children, or a real future?"

I nodded.

His gaze drifted to the dagger.

"What about now?" he asked.

"I think about marriage, children, and a future with you often," I admitted softly with a smile.

A dark glint flickered over his eyes, and he released my hand. Picking up the blade, he slid it over his finger, staining it before he embedded it in the ground. The Veil was suddenly revealed next to us. Through the darkness of the backdrop, I could make out its landscape with the outline of wings soaring in the sky and various houses in the background.

"You found a way to open the Veil!"

He shook his head. "No, we can see it but we can't breach the entrance."

It shimmered and vesiculated as it struggled to stay in view.

"And I don't care that we can't return to it. It serves as a reminder of what I left behind and what I have now. What I —no, what *we* have here is no comparison. I introduced you to another world, and you gave me a better one."

He reached in his pocket and revealed a round cut diamond ring. "Will you make your thoughts a reality? My demigoddess, will you be my wife?"

When he placed it on my finger, I stared at it for a long

time before lifting my head to look at the Veil, which convulsed one last time before closing.

"Yes." I examined the ring, a small smile lifting the corners of my lips.

"What?" he asked.

I tapped on the side of the ring. "Do you think we can have it fitted so I can trigger a small dagger in it? I have no plans of ever taking it off, so it might as well serve a dual purpose."

His deep rumble of laughter filled the space. A roaring sound that I loved as much as I loved him. "Undeniably Erin," he said, his lips pressed against mine.

"Always," I whispered.

MESSAGE TO THE READER

Thank you for choosing *Spellcast* from the many titles available to you. My goal is to create an engaging world, compelling characters, and an interesting experience for you. I hope I've accomplished that. Reviews are very important to authors and help other readers discover our books. Please take a moment to leave a review. I'd love to know your thoughts about the book. Whether you write a few sentences or several paragraphs, your review will be appreciated.

For notifications about new releases, *exclusive* contests and giveaways, and cover reveals, please sign up for my mailing list at McKenzieHunter.com.

www.ingramcontent.com/pod-product-compliance
Lightning Source LLC
Chambersburg PA
CBHW060704190726
48289CB00002B/526